candle

tor books by john barnes

candle

JOHN BARNES, 1957-

TOR®

a tom doherty associates book
NEW YORK

This is a work of fiction. All the characters and events portrayed in this novel are either fictitious or are used fictitiously.

CANDLE

This book is printed on acid-free paper.

Edited by Patrick Nielsen Hayden

A Tor Book
Published by Tom Doherty Associates, LLC
175 Fifth Avenue
New York, NY 10010

www.tor.com

Tor® is a registered trademark of Tom Doherty Associates, LLC.

Design by Lisa Pifher

ISBN 0-312-89077-X

First Edition: February 2000

Printed in the United States of America

0 9 8 7 6 5 4 3 2 1

For Paul Edwards.
"If you live
in this country long enough,
you get colorful."

candle

One thing you have to say for the Colorado Rockies, you sleep good, these days, now that there's nothing to worry about. I was dead solid asleep when I woke up to a voice saying, "Hey, Currie."

I didn't recognize the voice right away, but that wasn't so unusual; One True speaks in different voices. I sat up in bed, facing into the bright moonlight. Mary and me, we love to sleep with the curtains open so we can see the sky and wake up with the sunlight, and we can do it nowadays because nobody ever looks through a window anymore unless they're supposed to. Probably we could've done it in the old days anyway because Sursumcorda, Colorado, never had more than a thousand people anyway, and we live a ways outside and above it.

Our house up there is a nice old twentieth-century A-frame with lots of glass. With that southern exposure, on a full moon night, you wouldn't need electricity to read in there.

"Hey, Three-Cur."

Nobody's called me that in a long time so I was wondering for just a second if I was having a waking dream, like I used to just after I retired. But Mary didn't even twitch, and since we always leave our link on while we're at home, when I have a bad dream, or she does, we both wake up. And my copy of Resuna seemed pretty calm tonight—nothing out there but the usual traffic of assurances and friendliness.

"You're wide awake, Currie, and we need to talk," the voice

said. Now I knew it was One True. It had chosen to come to me through my auditory nerves, instead of as a voice entirely in my head. I reached to my copy of Resuna and it reached to Mary's; sure enough, One True had already put a block on her so that she'd sleep pleasantly through any noise and light we needed to make.

"Yes, it's One True," the voice agreed, responding to my thought. "Do whatever you need to get comfortable and I'll talk to you in eight minutes and thirty seconds."

"Eight and thirty," I said. In the back of my mind, my copy of Resuna started the countdown. I got out of bed.

I sleep ten hours or more every night in winter, especially late winter. Not that I don't enjoy skiing, snowshoeing, hunting, ice fishing, and all, but at forty-nine years old, a few hours of anything outside tires me pleasantly out, and then a decent dinner, with a small glass of wine, and a good book after, usually put me out by eight or nine at night, and I get up with the sun, *not* before it. So from the way the full moon hung in the southwest, I guessed it was about five in the morning.

Five eighteen a.m., Resuna said in my mind. *Seven minutes forty-four seconds remaining.*

I shook off the last drowsiness, climbed out of bed, and threw on a dressing robe and slippers, wincing at the way the cold hurts my bad toes these days—I had led a little too vigorous a life when I was younger, breaking most of my toes and getting a touch of frostbite a few times, so that between one thing and another, my toes are lim sensitive, and that cold floor just sets them off.

I went into the bathroom and peed into the recycler, stretched a couple more times, and finally said aloud, "Bob, coffee now, please, and warm rolls for one in twenty minutes?"

"Sweet or plain?" Bob asked. This was out of the household software's experience—Bob had been installed after I retired—and it wouldn't necessarily trust the data files it had copied from its predecessor.

I took a moment to clarify—"Sweet. If I get a call that gets me up before sunrise, pritnear always, I'll want sweet rolls."

I splashed some water on my face. Since I was up, Bob would already be warming my clothes for today, so I didn't bother with instructions about that.

As I was buttoning my shirt, I could hear the gurgle and gush of coffee into the carafe, and by the time I got my shoes on—*one minute forty-four seconds to go*, Resuna assured me—I felt pretty decent. Resuna was grumbling, where I could just feel it, about having to adjust my serotonin levels when I was going to throw caffeine at my brain as well, but I knew perfectly well it could do that without any trouble. Your copy of Resuna picks up your traits to some extent, and I'm afraid I've always been a griper.

I went to the kitchen to get my coffee. I didn't know why I was so sure this would have something to do with my old job. It *could* be something else. One True calls everyone a few times a year— always on your birthday, and on your region's Resuna Day, and then there's all the routine business stuff that everyone has to do— but something about this call had made me think at once that it would turn out to be about the old job.

Three-Cur. He addressed me as Three-Cur. That was a nickname I hadn't heard since my days as a cowboy hunter. I got coffee from the kitchen, enjoyed the pleasant odor of sweet rolls under way in the foodmaker, and went downstairs to the big room. In the moonlight, there was no need to turn on a light. I sat down and took that first long slow sip of coffee that helps a lifetime caffeine addict see that the universe, on the average, is a pretty good place.

Aside from the moon and Orion, and a few scattered other stars, I could see no lights through the window. The dark rectangles and trapezoids of Sursumcorda lay far down the mountain from me, with no streetlights—no one was out, so they weren't turned on. Pritnear everyone in that little town sleeps like Mary and me in winter—we're a community of old-timers.

I leaned way over sideways on the couch for an angle through the window. Just as always, I saw the bright tiny oval of Supra New York hanging in the sky. In all my eleven years on the job, I had seen SNY in the sky from camps in the wilderness just before I went to bed, and from canyons and mountaintops while I waited on stakeout, hundreds of times, and always taken comfort in the sight. Seven million people lived up there, nowadays, almost directly above Quito, Ecuador, all running Resuna, all part of One True like me.

The wilderness just didn't seem as lonely, as long as I could see good old SNY. I saluted seven million fellow citizens with my coffee cup. They didn't wave back, but I still knew they were there. I took another sip, sat and waited.

Three-Cur. Nice that One True still remembered. I didn't really know what had possessed the woman who abandoned me at the Municipal Orphanage in Spokane Dome to name me Currie Curtis Curran, but at least it had furnished an endless source of amusement, first to my squad mates back during the War of the Memes, and later to my team of cowboy hunters.

"Bob, I'd like it a little warmer," I said, quietly, and felt the faint hum of the baseboard heaters an instant later. Was I more sensitive to temperature, or was it just unusually cold on the other side of the window? A moment later, Resuna told me that it was minus seventeen out there, quickly translating that to half a degree above zero, Fahrenheit, before I could ask. So it was cold for February, even up here. Year 26 was shaping up to be the coldest on record; supposedly that trend wouldn't begin to reverse till around Year 35.

The meters-deep snow in the moonlight was crisp, with hints of pale blue, and wind-sculpted into knife-edges, untouched by anything more solid than a shadow. It was nice to sit and look and wait for things to begin.

Just as Resuna counted off "zero," One True came back to me.

"Look at your wall," One True said.

I turned to look at the white wall. To download information to a copy of Resuna, and thus into the person running Resuna, One True must move so much information that polysensory ways are the only way of doing it in a reasonable time. It was like a vivid dream from which I would awaken knowing everything I needed to know, or like I would imagine a religious revelation would be, or like falling into some other life, or like being One True myself, for a few minutes. Once I woke up, I would have to talk, to One True and to my own copy of Resuna, to activate the knowledge. For the moment, though, it wasn't too different from being asleep, and for a cranky old guy like me, up too early on a February morning, that was pritnear perfect.

I was standing on Fossil Ridge, right along the Great Divide, looking east toward the Arkansas Valley. I had no body, but my point of view was its usual height off the ground. Something behind me was not right—frightening, but nothing I wasn't willing to turn around and face. I knew the difference between the fear that comes with ordinary caution and the fear of annihilation or worse. This was something—no, someone—physically dangerous, not anything that might destroy who I was, just someone I might have to fight.

I turned and looked down toward where I could see the falls of the Taylor River, splashing over the old dam in Taylor Park, where there had once been a reservoir. It was many kilometers away and hundreds of meters below me; I couldn't see much more than the sparkle and splash of the falls, and the thin snaking blue curves of the river winding through the park and then plunging into the dense forest below.

Then, in the intense illusion, I *could* see that far. My eyes were like telescopes or like an eagle's. A man was running as swiftly as he could, but with precision and care, on the old dam, as if he feared some accident. My view swung overhead. I was hanging on a surveillance satellite like a nosy angel. I dove at the man on the dam, and his image expanded.

He was fit and healthy, but looked like he had missed plenty of meals over the years; his belt was fastened a third of the way around his back. Through my satellite eyes and One True's databases I perceived him as six foot two, 145 pounds. I descended to the crumbling top of the dam, directly in his path.

He kept coming my way. His clothes were handmade, doubtless from cloth he'd looted from some abandoned store. He wore a simple blue pullover shirt with several pockets; black trousers, slightly dirty with much wear at the knees, fastened by a drawstring with a two-button fly; an ancient belt with a dozen hand-cut notches; deerskin moccasins with old-radial-tire soles; and of course the hat, the thing they could never resist. He'd camo-painted it pretty well, but it was a Stetson.

Here in the Rockies, we called people who lived outside One True "cowboys" because for some damned reason they all wore those stupid creepy-looking hats. One True had decided that no one else on the Earth would have a taste for those—just as no one wanted to wear the burnoose that marked the bedouin in Arabia, or bush hats in New Guinea—in part to make the cowboys stick out more. Just the sight of it in this recorded vision was making my flesh crawl, back in my comfortable living room.

His face was bearded but he kept the beard close-cropped and it looked like he shaved out his corners. The last few cowboys I had caught had been extraordinarily neat in their personal grooming, come to think of it. One True explained that personal neatness went with being meticulous, and more meticulous cowboys lasted longer.

I looked closely at his face. I wanted my tranquilizer gun at hand, even though I knew this was all recorded and hallucinatory.

His face had not aged in eleven years. He was even wearing clothes almost identical to the ones he had worn on the day I thought I killed him. Well, perhaps he had thought he'd killed me. Maybe that made us even.

The man I was looking at called himself "Lobo." Or had called himself Lobo, eleven years ago when he was last hunted. I had been one of the leaders of the hunt for him, and the gang he led, and we had thought that he had died after taking a hard, long fall in the Black Canyon. I didn't remember ever hearing that they found his body, but cowboy hunters deal only with the living, so it hadn't seemed so odd then. Now, I was thinking I should have taken more time for paperwork.

As I stood and watched him, in the vivid vision that One True was sending, Lobo slowly turned around, removed his hat to reveal thick, short, badly trimmed, still-dark hair, and bent, stretched, and showed himself off so that I could learn what he looked like from every angle. He walked and ran around me so that I got a sense of how he moved.

Even without One True's sending me the pictures, I would have recognized Lobo any place, any time, for the rest of my life. The hunt for Lobo had been the longest and hardest I'd ever had. Lobo'd killed three of my hunters, and badly hurt five more so that it took years for them to recover, and just before his departure over the cliff and into the canyon, had left my face a gory wreck that required months of hospital time to put right. If he was still out there, we still had a score to settle.

Resuna usually doesn't approve of revenge as a motivation, and will shut down those feelings if it detects them, but my copy of Resuna was being strangely silent as I felt the rage rising in me against Lobo. *In this case,* One True told me silently, *we have someone who seems to be cunning—and therefore dangerous— beyond any of the old cowboys that you hunters hunted to extinction.* Therefore any extra motivation that One True could find for me—revenge for Abbot, Johnson, and Kibberly, desire for a good hunt, whatever feeling it could find—would be amplified by my copy of Resuna until the mission was accomplished.

In an old-fashioned reading library with heavy thick carpets, a big polished table, and walls lined with reference texts, a librarian who was One True leaned over my shoulder and set a pile of documents down in front of me. I pulled them toward me and began to read.

It looked as if Lobo had managed to dropline all of civilization, all at once, as soon as he got away from the Black Canyon, because for years there hadn't been the slightest evidence that he was still alive. He hadn't raided, he hadn't tried to contact anyone, he hadn't stolen a watt of power or a slice of bread from the civilized world for nine and a half years after his purported death. Furthermore, he had been able to unplug more completely, and vanish more thoroughly, than any other cowboy ever had, just as soon as he had given us good reason to believe him dead, which argued that he'd planned a difficult, complex procedure in considerable depth for some time before he had elected to use it. Presumably he was now eleven years more experienced and paranoid.

He'd been the toughest opponent I had ever faced. Now he was back from the dead. It gave me a shudder, especially since, perhaps due to the final exhaustion of his stored supplies, he was now raiding again, and he seemed to take a peculiar sadistic pleasure in some of what he did, almost as if he were trying, impossibly, to bait or frighten One True.

I opened a file folder. A hole in it grew out to the size of the table; I fell through into someone's memory. It took me half a second or so to realize that my name was Kelly and I was a twelve-year-old girl, living with my mom in a big cabin, high up on a mountain.

One True had decided that Mom's nerves would be better if she were living in a quiet cabin in the woods, and that I needed a calm mother. Resuna patiently reminded me, now and then, that we had to live way out here because in past generations Mom might have been abusive, alcoholic, or both; she'd led a hard life before she turned, and I had a few ugly memories myself—we'd been living as wild squatters in Vegas Ruin until I was three, when the team found us and turned us, and the world suddenly got all better.

I was sitting on the floor, in our house up in the mountains, playing Parcheesi with Mom. We both thought that game was a pleasant way to kill time while you watch snow fall among the aspens early in an October evening. We were discussing whether we wanted popcorn, hot chocolate, or both, tonight, when we were startled by a terrible crash.

A man in an outside suit, the kind that rescue workers wear out here in the mountains, came running up the stairs from where he had smashed down the door. He was holding something in his hand—I didn't recognize it, but Mom did and I got a vague sense that it could hurt us badly. The impression through our linked copies of Resuna was only in my mind for an instant before Mom screamed "My god, don't hurt us" and her strong surge of emotions shut the link down.

The man in the suit came a step forward, and said, "Shut up." Then he said something horrible to us—something that I can't remember now, mercifully, because Resuna and One True have erased it from me, but once he said it, I couldn't receive Mom's thoughts or feelings, and Resuna was not there, and I had no way to call One True to help us, no comforting voice in my head to tell me I could get through this. I had no way of knowing what Mom needed from me, or of telling her what I needed.

The man in the suit slapped Mom, hard, twice. She fell away from him, barely catching her balance, staring dumbly at the hand that was raised to strike her again. Blood flowed out of her mouth.

It was like a nightmare, except that Resuna wasn't there to wake me up and tell me it was all right. I was frozen, not moving, unable to think, just endlessly screaming for Resuna in my mind.

The man slapped me too; I didn't know why. I hadn't been hit at least since Mom had turned, and the sensations—flesh crushed against skull on one side of the head, teeth stinging in suddenly swelling gums, one eye running with uncontrollable tears—were a thousand times worse because nothing explained them to me, and I had only my own body's natural shock response.

The man pulled back his hood and said, "Medicine synthesizer. I need your medicine synthesizer. I need you to put your hand in there and have it diagnose and prescribe for me."

"Will it do that?" Mom asked. Her voice was timid, shy, high-pitched, like a little girl's.

"Oh, it'll do it," the horrible man said. His hair was as long as mine, matted to his skull with sweat, and his rough thick black beard was wet, almost dripping. He reeked like spoiling meat or a dead animal under the house. His eyes were too bright and his lips reddish purple against his too-pale skin. "I'll show you how. All you have to do is do it. I want the medicine, I want a good meal, and maybe some other things. I just hurt you so you'd know I'm serious and you'd do what you're told. Now do what you're told and I won't have to hurt you any more."

I fell out of Kelly's mind for a second, and everything froze into a still picture. Below the image of the man, One True inscribed a positive identification of Lobo, from voiceprint and DNA. A moment later it added that according to information and samples recovered later, the disease he was suffering from seemed to be a strain of measles, aggravated by mutAIDS. Both diseases were supposed to be extinct, but Earth's a big planet and you never know what might yet be festering in its untended corners.

Then—I had just an instant to wish this wasn't necessary—One True commanded, and my Resuna dropped me back into Kelly's memories.

As Kelly, I watched Mom put her hand into the medical synthesizer, and the man stood close to her and pressed a bare shoulder against the sampler. Then he spoke some codes aloud; in the old days communication between people and machines hadn't been perfect, and whoever this man was, he still knew how to use the old accesses that had been there, for example, so that parents could get medicine for their babies.

The man winced briefly as it gave him a pressure injection, but when that was done he sighed with relief.

He ate practically all the ready food in the house, and reconstituted three meals, each of which was supposed to be for four people, and gobbled those down as well, along with more coffee than you'd have thought could go into a human being. He seemed fascinated with our reconstitutor; with a faraway look, he calculated for a few seconds, and finally decided to take it with him, along with almost all the food in the house. "The rescue crews will bring you more," he assured us, but I didn't believe him. I still wanted Resuna worse than I had ever wanted anything.

When he had finished eating, he said, "There's one more thing I need. I'm very much from the old days, I spent a long time as a mercenary during the War of the Memes, and you know what that means. You and your daughter have cooperated just beautifully, and been very helpful, but there's something I want to do to both of you, which you are not going to like. I hope you'll do your best to cooperate so it isn't any more painful than it has to be."

Mom was starting to cry, and I was afraid about what was going to happen.

The man said, "Resuna is supposed to be able to erase everything, afterwards."

Mom shook her head. "It doesn't really work that way. I still have lim too many memories, from the old days, and they still hurt me every day."

The man nodded, several times, as if he were thinking carefully about that. "You know, part of me is very sorry to hear that. Another part of me is real happy to know that this is going to be in your head forever."

Mom was crying really hard now, and that was so frightening

that I started to cry too. The man grabbed us both by our arms and took us down to Mom's bedroom; he told us to take our clothes off, and left the room. Mom said we had to do what he said, so we did. I was cold and felt really strange about being naked.

A moment later he came back, with a tube of skin lotion from Mom's bathroom. He undressed, and told us where to put the lotion; it felt weird and icky. He had me watch while he did things to Mom, and then made her watch while he did the same things to me.

Then he got dressed. We were both crying. Mom was throwing up. It looked like he was crying too.

He grabbed up his pack of looted food, and the reconstitutor, and said, "Hey, I'm the last of my kind. I'm not going to ever come back. And it was nothing personal. Both of you were just here. Like getting hit by lightning, you know."

He went back through the shattered door, and out into the snow; when he turned and saw us staring at him, he yelled, "Get back upstairs out of the cold! And make sure the alarm is thrown!"

We did what he said. When we checked, the alarm was already going off. It was only maybe half an hour until the rescue crews got there in the disksters, and gave us new copies of Resuna, and took us to the hospital.

My new copy of Resuna is very kind and patient, like they're supposed to be, and supposedly I won't have big problems later, because all the bad things were dealt with so soon after they happened, and because Resuna is always there helping me. Sometimes One True itself checks in to see if I'm all right. Eventually, in a year or two, what happened will just make me sad, now and then, and maybe not very often if things go the way the doctors are hoping they will. I know it will work out, because Resuna says it will, and how can you do anything but trust Resuna?

All the same, the copy of Resuna that tells me things and comforts me is the new copy that the rescue crew put in, and I still miss my old Resuna. The new one doesn't know me as well as the one that had lived in my head since I was a little kid. I know that it will get better, but I miss my old one.

🐾 **I fell backwards** out of Kelly's mind. I was back in my comfortable chair at the table in the library; the hole in the table closed up, contracted into the folder, and became a dot no bigger than a period. I could go back there, if for some reason I ever wanted to.

I didn't want to. I could feel the picture of what he'd done to that mother and little girl building up inside me, a thing to be avenged and taken out on him, like the destruction of my crew a decade ago, like the deaths of Tammy and Carrie during the war, like all the good friends I had lost too young, like all the evil that the cowboys and their spiritual ancestors had worked in the world.

I had not felt such a passion for a hunt in many years; maybe I had never felt it before at all. The anger hurt, physically, in my chest, but I knew Resuna *needed* me to be that angry, and I accepted the pain.

I opened another file folder, from the still-tall stack of them to my left. There was more, but there wasn't worse, and I was grateful for that, at least. I seemed to be there for hours reading all the accounts of what he'd done since his reappearance a few months previously. In those visions you have perfect concentration, and time passes much faster than it does in the outside world—but it still takes a while to digest such a catalog of human evil, perverse cruelty, and solid constant nastiness. By the time I had finished my reading, I was feeling tired and sick, and felt like I'd used up a full day's energy right there in the "library," even though my copy of Resuna told me that I had only been in the vision for six minutes and fourteen seconds.

ᨁ **I sat back** on my couch, talking to One True consciously now, no longer in the dream. "Sort of flattering," I said. "There're at least five other hunters you could've picked who could've done the job. You could even've sent a whole posse of us. Why me?"

I was surrounded by warm, friendly laughter. One True was playing my auditory nerves a quad sound system. "Why 'why'?" it asked. "We don't understand your reason for wanting to know our reasons, and your copy of Resuna doesn't seem to understand either. Are you fishing for a compliment? Are you seeking clarification? Are you—"

"It was the first thought that happened to pop into my head," I said. "You have five other reserve hunters for the Rockies. They're all very good too. I was just wondering why One True picked me."

"Because we had to pick somebody," One True said. "So we picked the best one. Or at least the one with the best record. Do you think someone else could do it better?"

I thought about that. Resuna helpfully pulled up the records of the other five, and I compared those with my memories of them. They were all very good, but I had to agree that if we were just sending one, it probably ought to be me. "No, I guess there's not."

"Well, then, we'll send you. And just you—because our guess is that since one hunter will make less noise and attract less attention than six, we should just send the best one after him. This Lobo is apt to be crafty and easily spooked."

Outside, the very first hints of false dawn were starting to color the distant peaks on their east-facing sides; their west sides still shone brighter in the cold light of the full moon. It looked like a million degrees below zero out there, and I shivered despite the warmth in the room.

"Remember that excessive curiosity and doubt can damage

your copy of Resuna," One True reminded me. "And because yours is such a veteran copy, it is to the benefit of all of us for it to stay in good shape. There's a lot of memory that the world needs in your head, Currie. Don't start arguing and questioning; all you'll do is hurt us all."

"I'm sorry," I said.

"We know," One True said. "Your copy of Resuna just relayed the feeling."

I felt better. The mind of the whole planet understood that my feelings were sincere and my intentions were good. We didn't need to talk about much else—all the arrangements had been there in the dream—and so I took a last look at the cold landscape outside and asked aloud, "Bob, temperature of this room?"

"Seventy-three," it answered, defaulting to Fahrenheit. "Usually you feel warmer if I bring up lights. Would you like a warm glow, heavy on red and yellow, here and in the kitchen? Your sweet rolls will be ready in about two more minutes."

"Do it," I said. The room was suddenly bathed in yellows, reds, and oranges, flickering as if there were fireplaces on all the walls. "Looks like we'll be back on work schedule until further notice. Do you still have a copy of it?"

"Last time on work schedule was January 19, Year 14, or 2076 Old Dating," Bob responded, "and the copy appears to be undamaged. Per that work schedule, shall I put on a full breakfast in addition to the sweet rolls?"

"Do it, Bob." I went out to the kitchen, dumped my cold coffee, and poured myself some fresh. Strange to be having such a morning—I had thought I'd never have another one.

I took my sweet rolls out to the little table by the main window in the big room, facing the grand view down the canyon to Sursumcorda, and ate greedily, washing the sticky sweet gooey rolls down with gulps of searing hot coffee. At least for the duration, no more worrying about calories, except maybe for worrying about getting enough. Resuna mentioned to me that my blood pressure and pulse were up and I was using more oxygen, and asked if I wanted an adjustment. I told it hell no. This was just what it was to feel really alive after so long in retirement.

I reviewed my newly acquired memories to make them conscious. When I had hunted Lobo, he had been the leader of a gang of eleven cowboys, a huge number for those last years of hunting. His gang had pulled off several sizable raids on small towns and isolated work stations, making Lobo a throwback even then. The gangs of cowboys had been rounded up and turned first, mostly before Year 5. It's much easier to catch a gang because it's harder to hide in groups, and usually all we had to do was catch and turn one of them to get enough information to find all the rest. By the time we were given the mission of hunting Lobo's gang, everyone else that the team had been hunting for at least three years had been loners.

Lobo had survived to become the last lone cowboy himself. The rest of his gang was long since captured and turned, so far as I knew—though if he could survive so many years without One True spotting him, who knew what else he might be managing? This was going to be the greatest hunt of my career; I felt that in my old bones already.

The sun was up far enough now to turn the sky blue, put a bright shine on the distant snow-spattered top of Mount Teocalli, and bring out the color of its distinctive striations, so that it stood like an island of light and color above a sea of dull slate-darkness. In the old days I had loved this time of morning, and once I thought that, Resuna copied the memories forward, and I loved it again.

It had been a long time since I'd hunted a cowboy. I had been a mercenary soldier in the War of the Memes before I'd been a cowboy hunter, and before that I'd been a kid. When I thought of those things it always seemed so far away.

Since retirement, I had led a pleasant life of old-man pleasures—the greenhouse, the library, occasional carpentry, plenty of outdoor sports, almost always with Mary scant meters away. It was rich, fulfilling, well-earned, everything I deserved for my years of danger and hardship in One True's service—but it wasn't what I had been forged out of anger and love to do.

I thanked One True, in my heart, again, so that Resuna would pick it up and relay it. First I thanked One True for selecting me and giving me the chance to live fully one more time, hunting Lobo. Then I thanked One True for making a world where people like Lobo would be stopped before they destroyed everything, where the pain and horror they inflicted had a limit. Finally I thanked One True in advance, knowing that when Lobo was caught and turned, and I was menaced once again by the melancholy pain of being a cowboy hunter in a world without cowboys, Resuna would be able to soothe my soul and return me to the warm, mellow, soft life of my retirement here; I would never really have to feel my painful loss of usefulness.

Bob announced that the full breakfast was ready. Resuna was already tinkering with my physiology: I was ravenous, though as yet I'd done nothing strenuous. No doubt in a short while I'd be glad for all the calories I could ram in.

I had stayed more or less in shape. Skills should be okay as well. The whole time I had worked as a cowboy hunter, my copy of Resuna had been uploading those to One True and downloading other hunters' skills to me. If anything had atrophied or been forgotten, Resuna would call up One True's libraries, find it, and get me a fresh copy, and muscle memory is long-lived anyway. As I finished a second plate of eggs, home fries, and baked beans, I had little moments and flashbacks—instants when I visualized making a couple of tight turns to descend a steep hillside in the back country, or daydreamed of checking the ice on a not-frozen-enough river, or remembered creeping forward, belly down in gray slush, around a rock with my tranquilizer gun for a clear shot at the bare buttocks of a cowboy taking a dump in the bushes. All the old systems were waking up.

Besides my own skills, I would also be able to draw on the most recent copy of every skill of everyone who had ever been good at this business. On the other hand, I was still up against the unknown. No cowboy until Lobo had ever hidden out for so long completely undetected.

"All the same, it looks doable to me," I said, aloud, knowing that my copy of Resuna would hear me and pass it on to One True. "Looking forward to it."

I finished breakfast and carried the dishes to the regenner to be melted, purified, and reformed. The view over the snow-covered boulders up the hill from the kitchen window—not as spectacular as the view on the other side, out over the town and valley, but in its quiet way, something that had also grown into me—seemed to remind me how much One True valued me. Or rather, the old part of me (which had lived for decades, full grown, before Resuna turned most of humanity) always insisted on thinking of the view, and the A-Frame itself, and the many comforts Mary and I had in our retirement, as rewards for the years I had spent in the woods, tracking the last outlaws on Earth. But the part of me that knew and understood the world through Resuna knew something that was so much better; I had been preserved because in One True's estimation I had been one of the six best cowboy hunters in the Rockies, and therefore One True had created a life for me that would let me stay in shape and maintain my basic capabilities, against any future need.

I knew One True was sending these memories and feelings into me because of the question I had asked earlier, and I felt both how absurd it was that I needed it, and how willing One True was to look after my need anyway. After all, what was there to be reassured about? It was just realistic to know that I had been the best and been preserved for that reason.

In the old days, before the memes, there were things they called "pre-memes" now, in retrospect—little partial routines and programs that were shared by many people; I'd had my share like anyone else. One of them called "modesty" would have been ashamed at my saying baldly that I was the best, no matter how true it might be. Another one called "self-esteem" would have been pleased whether it was true or not.

In the sort of minds people had before Resuna, modesty and self-esteem would have fought it out, wasting great quantities of energy and effort in my mind as they struggled with each other, paralyzing me from many effective actions, creating a dangerous propensity for overestimating or underestimating my own capabilities, misleading me into foolish diversionary actions in the attempt to satisfy them both. Most pre-memes were quite capable of clouding a person's judgment, and replicated by strategies that were anti-survival for the larger mind or person.

The man I was going to be hunting probably still had dozens or hundreds of pre-memes—pride, rights, honor, self-reliance, and vengeance, just about for sure, since almost all cowboys we had ever captured and turned had been running those at the time of capture. He might even have some of the more complex, thought-to-be-extinct pre-memes, like Ecucatholicism, cybertao, or America, or even the really exotic ones like communism or fundamentalism. That was why it was vital to take him alive; though he was a deadly enemy to One True and therefore to the whole human race, he was also a repository of memetic material that might be analyzed so that useful parts could be incorporated into everyone's copy of Resuna, and defenses could be built against the bad parts—*if* Lobo could be turned and the old pre-memes extracted and copied from him.

So it was no surprise that One True, which rarely made mistakes and never abided in them, had had a superb cowboy hunter like me available, right here in the Colorado Rockies, just when the need had arisen. One True thought farther ahead than any mere person could do, and it shaped us to ends that were good for us, good for the poor old mauled Earth, good for itself. I was the product of its foresight, which is why I could enjoy being One True's superb tool.

In the same way, One True pointed out to me, a Cajun hunter still lived on a houseboat in Simmesport, and a bush-hippie hunter was waiting in reserve in a hand-built cabin in Homer.

Not having thought about either place in decades, I was startled at what poured back into my memory. When I had been born, the Mississippi had still flowed into the Gulf in Plaquemines Parish, eighty miles south of New Orleans—far east of where it did now—and most of Alaska had not been under the glaciers. Thanks to One True, nobody would ever come out of the backwoods to disturb the peace of Earth again, and there would be time enough now fix everything, now that all of humanity on Earth truly worked together. We hunters had done our small bit to make that happen, and like every other hunter, I thanked One True for having given us the opportunity.

As always, the mission was the Four Ts': track him, trank him, and truss him. One True would take care of the fourth T—turning him. I was also supposed to look for any evidence that he'd had any contact with the extraterrestrials, particularly anything that violated the Treaty of Supra Berlin. Probably there would not be any such evidence—his radio would have given him away long before this if there had been—but it was important to make sure that the wild individuals still living on Mars, the asteroids, and the moons of Jupiter remembered their obligations not to meddle in our affairs.

In broad outline, the productive parts of my job could have been accomplished in a couple of hours, leaving the rest to be mere details. Details, however, could often be a bitch. In my years as a cowboy hunter, I had been shot four times, broken one arm and both legs, gotten nipped by frostbite on one cheek, three toes, and a thumb, and had to have one eye and four teeth regenerated after stopping Lobo's cleated boot with my face in that last grim fight before he had supposedly died. A guy as tough as Lobo, and as smart, was bound to generate a few violent, dangerous details.

I could hardly wait.

❀ **Lobo had led** a small band of cowboys operating out of the little ghost town of Manly, Colorado, a former three-street tin-mining town up toward Frisco on old Colorado 9. Lobo and his cowboys had set up military shelters inside the crumbling 1920's-vintage buildings, thus concealing themselves from easy orbital observation. We'd all had a good chuckle—even One True had seemed to laugh—at the fact that we were tracking down the Manly Cowboys. But it had gotten a lot less funny after three of us had been killed and five more, including me, severely injured.

As I put together my kit that afternoon, I kept turning that pursuit over and over in my head. The Manly Cowboys had seemed at first to be the usual story—mercenaries who had served one of the losing causes in the War of the Memes and now would not accept Resuna, people who thought that for some reason the rest of us owed them the right to wander around loose and dangerous without the restraint and guidance that only Resuna could give. That gang of cowboys, in other words, was a small sample of the pure evil and sheer bad attitude that had made the mid-twenty-first such a terrible time.

Luckily our side had One True, or rather our side *was* One True. Transferable experience and telepathy help immensely when you're fighting a guerrilla war, whether against cowboys in the Rockies, bedouin in Arabia, or renegados in the Cordillera. Anything the enemy could do to coordinate with other groups, or to recruit individuals, tended to give them away; they had to function in isolation, so that they only got smarter by their own individual experience, a method as slow and painful as it had been in the Stone Age. By contrast, the newest hunter among us—Sandy "Mulekick" Arthur, at that time—didn't have everything perfectly in her muscles yet, and might be slightly slow in using reflexes that were still more in Resuna than in her own muscle memories, but still, in principle, from the day she joined she could immediately track like Abbot, climb like Kibberly, ski like me, and shoot like Pinpoint Sue. And not long after she joined us, we all started to have her martial arts abilities.

We lost Johnson and Kibberly to pure carelessness—after driving the cowboys out of Manly, we'd thought we had them boxed into a coulee below Swadge Ridge. Johnson, a big rangy guy who didn't talk much and never acquired a nickname that stuck despite all our ingenuity, had gone up there with Kristi Kibberly, who could climb a rock face like a goosed monkey and who we sometimes called "King Kong" on account of that, her initials, and her build.

It was as simple as you can imagine: Lobo figured there'd be a couple of us there to hold the upper end of the draw that his cowboys would try to escape through. Being strong and fast himself, he ran on ahead, got around behind Johnson and Kibberly, and belly-wriggled into a position above them. Meanwhile all of us hunters were down there in a big, thin line, working our way along in parallel, staying in constant touch through One True, our Resunas all chattering constantly about every step and rock.

We were just closing the trap. Abbot and me were in the middle. We had just told the flanks to advance and start working inward.

Two nasty little spats, almost on top of each other, a noise like *paddap!*, just as we felt Johnson and Kibberly vanish from the telepathic web, told us we were screwed. Afterwards, from the way we found the bodies, we figured Lobo had taken the time to program his rifle, an old military make, so that it automatically re-aimed the second shot. Johnson was hit square in the back of the head, Kristi Kibberly just behind her right ear, and they were dead before they knew what had happened.

Meanwhile the shots were the cue for the Manly Cowboys to run for it, which they did, fast and hard, shaking us off their trail almost at once. Pinpoint Sue D'Alessandro got the only capture of the day, a straggler that she nailed at extreme range; we loaded him onto the diskster to be taken away and turned, and did our best to get back into the chase, but by nightfall the Manly Cowboys had gotten clean away.

We took a day to attend funerals—it wasn't that long after the War of the Memes, and One True understood that people still needed funerals.

The day after, emotionally supported by our Resunas and thus feeling no worse than mildly depressed, we were back on the track.

It was ten days of the hardest pursuit we ever had, and at the end of it the whole hunting group had to be reconstructed, both as a group and individually. Abbot stopped a sniper's shot with his kidney and died before the diskster arrived. Sue D'Alessandro took a bullet through the thigh and was out for months. Mulekick Arthur knocked down two of them and I was able to tranquilize them, in a vicious little ambush she and I walked into on the south side of Fossil Ridge; in the process she was badly cut up and was out too. Feeney got splashed with homemade napalm during the night attack when they set her tent on fire, which put her in the burn unit for a couple of months. Replenovich gave half his foot to a land mine and was in regeneration for a year. In those ten days we took more casualties than we had in the previous three years.

Looking back, if we hadn't had One True, and our individual copies of Resuna, to hold us all in the correct perspective, we'd have thought we were losing, though we were gradually capturing all the Manly Cowboys. The unmemed human mind can't really perceive success when the losses are too high.

But because we did have Resuna and One True to get us through, in those ten days we captured all the Manly Cowboys except Lobo himself. Within three months each of them was running Resuna and on his way to being someone useful—two of them later became cowboy hunters.

By the time my team was down to just me, Brock Peters, and

Moonchild Swann, and the Manly Cowboys were down to Lobo, he was trying to lose us by going through the old Black Canyon wilderness. We were completely exhausted, sloppy and careless, and so was he.

Moonchild was a good tracker—she was almost as good as Abbot had been—but she missed one of Lobo's double-backs, the only one she had missed in a day and a half, but it only takes one. Peters was a young kid who normally ran like a rocket everywhere, just because he couldn't stop himself—his nickname in the unit was "Scamper"—but he was much too far away downhill, and much too tired, to get there and give me some backup when Lobo popped up out of nowhere, coming at us from behind, just where the trail skirted the north edge of the canyon.

Black Canyon is a unique place; in its narrowest few miles the sides are so steep and the canyon so narrow that it's dark down there for most of the day, even in summer. In the old days it was pretty nearly impossible for anyone to traverse it on foot, and floating it was experts-with-good-luck-only.

For the long years since, when I had thought about it at all, I had thought that Lobo had just gotten careless, and gone charging into a fight in the open with nowhere to go but over the cliff and down. Now I wondered if that had been part of a plan.

❧ **I had been** running through the checklists absentmindedly, trusting Resuna, which didn't wander like my own mind did. Everything was identical to the equipment I had been familiar with eleven years ago—not much hunting in this part of the world since then, so no technical improvements, so they just faxbricated new copies from designs on file.

Mary came in, and I could feel our Resunas generate deep empathy, connecting me to her anxiety and tension. "Will it be a long hunt?" she asked. "Your last few weren't very long. I'd like it if this one wasn't."

"That's *real* unknowable," I pointed out. "Personally I hope he walks in front of me five minutes after I first arm my tranquilizer gun, falls right over, and I'm back for lunch. But I don't think it's gonna be that way. I got so many short hunts, my last year, because most loners had gone real low-tech. They were hard to spot, but once you did find them, they were so exhausted from living off the land, cold and overworked and half starved all the time, that they didn't have much energy to run with. This guy Lobo is a whole different kinda situation, and I can't tell you how it's going to go because I've never tried to catch a guy like him before. I know he can disappear completely for ten years, but I don't know what else he can do."

"Poop," she said, sitting on the couch with a thud. "I hate this. You don't know what you're getting into, *One True* doesn't know what you're getting into! It's like back during the war, when nobody knew what was going on and everyone always had to just wing things for themselves, and you couldn't trust anyone else to cooperate. What did we fight the whole War of the Memes for?"

I could feel that Mary's copy of Resuna was having a hard time regulating her emotions. I told my Resuna to reassure it. Then I felt One True kick in; it knew just what to say, and suddenly I was talking a whole lot better than I usually can.

"It's all part of one huge thing, Mary. We did win. The whole human race on Earth is pulling together to save ourselves and our planet. Someday we'll drive the glaciers back to where they belong in the Northern Hemisphere, and we'll restore the glaciers on Antarctica, and the Gulf Stream will flow again. We'll do it all. You know One True is breeding back thousands of animal and plant species from DNA specimens, too. By the time we celebrate our hundredth, Mary, it's going to be a beautiful world. But not if we let things like Lobo keep running loose in it.

"You know the whole wreck of the Earth was probably brought on by no more than twenty thousand people, working for the old pre-memes like America and Communism and freedom and Islam. We can't let even one of them run loose anymore. Lobo has already hurt and frightened fifty-nine people since he popped back up. And I'm the one with the best chance of catching him. One True loves you, and it loves me, and we love One True, but sometimes something hard just has to be done."

I waited, confidently, for One True to exert its control and help her appreciate just how right those words were. But though I felt One True trying, it didn't work at all. I could feel her tension and fear rising faster, all the same, despite her best efforts to control them, and despite her copy of Resuna's doing everything it could to calm her. It was strange, after all these years; this had never happened while I was a hunter before.

Perhaps it was that Lobo was different from the others, perhaps that Mary and I were older and she was more emotionally dependent on our quiet life here than she had been, perhaps somehow the terror and anxiety of the war years were coming back to her in a way that they never had while I was hunting cowboys before. In the old days she would send me off with a kiss and a warm smile and tell me to bring back a Stetson to bronze for the mantelpiece.

I got up and held her for a moment, looking at the thick gray hair that cascaded down her back, feeling her heavy but still strong body against mine, but she just froze and resisted. I whispered "I love you," and "It's okay," and squeezed her tight, but she was like a plank till I said, "Mary, love, it's all right, just remember, 'Let override, let overwrite.'"

She relaxed her throat muscles, unclenched her fists, and started to sob. Then she let One True have her, and dropped into my arms in a slack faint. I set her down on the couch and kept listening through our copies of Resuna as One True healed and helped her, while I got on with my packing.

It only took a few minutes of Resuna's complete control. Mary's irrational fears were dissolved and argued away, her courage was restored, her faith in One True and me strengthened, and a wonderful calm courage and love settled into her. One True overwrote her short-term memory, so that she would recall only sitting on the couch and watching me pack, pleased that I was working again.

It's better for people to have their own memories, and their own ideas, but when those hurt One True, or cause behavior that could annoy other people, or make the person having the ideas feel unhappy—that's the time to "let override, let overwrite," and get on with the world as it should be. It was the first time I could recall Mary having to do that in a long time.

Back in the early years, when we were first married, it had been two or three times a day. I smiled to myself, thinking, *for all I know, I've been needing it, and getting it, every day all these years, and for all I know I have been overwritten a thousand times more often than she has. That's the beauty—you get the help you need but you never know.*

When she revived—all at once, and without any awareness that she had been unconscious—she chatted and laughed and it was like old times for the next hour, as I got all my kit together. When I'd run that last little paranoid check that you always run before going in harm's way, and Resuna and I agreed that I had everything, I slung up my pack, put my duffel on my shoulder, and walked down the road about seventy yards, being careful not to slip on the ice. Just before the window went out of sight, I turned and waved. Mary waved back and blew me a kiss.

I took the last few steps down to the road. It was three-forty in the afternoon. A moment later the diskster glided silently up the road beside me and settled onto its feet with a soft crackling of static discharge. I tossed my bags into the cargo hold and climbed into the passenger compartment. It was hard to believe that in the old days, I got so used to this that I used to blank the windows and just catch a nap on the way out to the job. Now, as we raced along the old highway and up the frozen river, then through a succession of mountain meadows, I couldn't have made myself look away from the jagged, snowy mountains, still months from spring thaw, or from the brilliant blue sky and the dark swarm of pines on every hillside.

It was so good to be back.

❧ **I had about** an hour of daylight left when the diskster dropped me off, far up in the high country. One True and I had selected a spot, a few kilometers from where we thought Lobo's hideout might be, where the diskster could turn off the creek, up a bank, and into a little meadow close enough to walk to my campsite from, but far enough away from Lobo's main operating area in the Dead Mule drainage so that I probably wouldn't be spotted right away. With luck, in the next few days there would be a good-sized snowstorm to efface the broad scooped-out track of the diskster.

With a bumpy lift and rise, the diskster climbed the twenty feet onto the bank and drove into the meadow. I looked around to make sure there weren't any immediate problems, like sinkholes, grizzly, or perhaps Lobo himself, and since there weren't, I said, "All right, disembarking," and fastened the hood of my coverall. The outside suit we wear in the winter in the high country, most of the time, looks like an old-fashioned space suit—or "like a baggy pair of footy jammies with a built-in Spiderman mask," as poor Abbot used to say. It's not very attractive or flattering, but it works real well, and I've lived enough of my life in them not to care a whole lot about what they look like.

It took me just a moment to swing my two bags down from the compartment and sling up, and now I stood knee-deep in the snow with all that weight piled on me. I knew I was going to hate this.

After trudging all of about ten steps, I decided that it was pointless to be miserable while walking, just to save some unpacking and repacking. I set the duffel down, got into the side attachment of my pack, and pulled out the flexis. I set the knobs for wide snowshoes, plugged the flexis into the power supply on my suit, and waited.

In a few minutes the little squares of lightweight white plastic had spread out to form wide planks with stabilizer tails, a smooth tadpole shape that would let me walk mostly on—instead of plunged deep into—the snow. I took the straps from the pack pocket, attached them, put the flexis on, re-gathered pack and duffel, and was on my way, clumping and swinging along. It was awkward, but not nearly as bad as floundering in the deep snow had been, and pos-def it was faster—which I needed badly just then. I had two kilometers to make before dark if I possibly could, and the flexis had delayed me a few minutes.

The late afternoon sky looked blue enough to burn you. To my left, faces of red volcanic rock, carved by wind and water into pipe organs, castle keeps, and giants' teeth, rose in wild defiance at the empty sky. The little black runnels down their sides indicated some thawing. It wasn't much, but the sun's northward invasion had a foothold, at least for the moment.

Resuna reminded me that I had ground to cover, not scenery to examine. I reminded it that my satisfaction was to its benefit.

Behind the pinnacles was a sheer gray cliff, brightly lighted wherever the pinnacles didn't shadow it. A distant crash like far-off thunder told me that some creek nearby, too, was starting to break the grip of winter.

I rounded the first big grove of firs, into the wide upper meadow. I was breathing hard now. This was more work than I remembered, and I could feel the little generators on my back whirring away as they drew heat from my insulated suit and converted it to charge in the electrets; they were working hard just now, but I'd be glad enough for every bit of scavenged juice later.

The swing-and-stomp rhythm of snowshoes requires pritnear nothing but pure patience. After that first 250 meters, my legs warmed up, the muscles stopped fighting each other and got into tune, and I began to enjoy it.

Soon I was pushing up a shallow draw. The flexis were swinging up and reaching out as if of their own accord, my heart was thumping in the healthy, vigorous way that means you're really working, and the blood was singing through my body. My balance had come back and the duffel on my shoulder wasn't bothering me anymore.

To my right, down slope, a wide swath of thick fir mingled with pine trees stood tall; to my left, a scraggly line of windblown firs underscored the ridgeline. The sun now stood low in the sky behind me, washing amber light across the untracked snow and making the edges of the shadows of the trees and rocks glow deep blue.

I came around another bend and saw a ruin. Though the main buildings were buried under three meters of snow, the huge, green-painted metal towers marching up the hillside off to my right plainly showed that this had been a small ski area. The stretched, sharp-angled shape in the snow before me had been the lodge, its back now broken in two places and the glass long since shattered and knocked down by the building settling under the weight of the snow that no one swept off. A couple of rings of walls nearby were probably places where hotels, restaurants, or stores had suffered a roof collapse, with the long-fallen roof now buried under this year's snow.

My first wife Tammy and I had spent one of my rare ten-day leaves at a place not too different from this, back when we were teenagers. It had cost me about three months of my earnings as a corporal in Burton's Thugs for Jesus—and it had been worth every penny. Somewhere in my files I still had a picture of our daughter, Carrie, three years old, then, in her pink snowsuit.

I stood for a long time, looking down at the ruined lodge. For a moment, I imagined the tired people skiing in from the last run of the day, breathing hard, their muscles aching, piling through the rental checkouts, and gathering in exhausted huddles at the tables and the bars to enjoy having gotten exhausted together.

The lodge would have had a nice fire, and at least one of the bars would have had a band. I could almost smell the pizza, beer, and sweat.

Oh well, someday, again. Maybe in my lifetime. Maybe when things got better, with more resources to spare, One True would let me apply to create a new ski resort. Helping people have a good time would be fun in its own right, almost as much fun as tracking them down, I supposed.

I clumped on around the resort, giving it a wide berth because I didn't want to plunge into the snow-covered remains of a ball-room, abruptly feel a six-condo unit slide down the hill underneath me, or be the final force that shattered the glass roof of a swimming pool, so I had to work my way about halfway up the ridge to be certain that I was above the old resort; that took a while, and the sun was setting by the time I was leaving the ruins behind me.

The moon was just a day past full, so it would be up shortly and I'd have more than enough light to get near my campsite, but I would camp in the shadows to reduce the chances of being spotted, so the last forty meters would be in the dark. And I knew from too-well-remembered experience that pitching camp in the dark, relying on light-amplifier goggles to do the fine work, was going to be a bitch.

I thought briefly about delaying setting up camp until day-light—I could lie down in the snow and sleep in the suit, if I had to. But there's not much provision in those suits for taking a really comfortable dump, which counts for a lot with me. Furthermore, if your suit heater system fails, or if your electrets slow-bleed and lose charge during the night, it might be July before you thawed out enough to realize that you were dead.

Half an hour later, the mountains to the west were outlined by a broad streak of red behind them, and I was finally coming over the ridge to my campsite. The first stars were out, and Resuna said that the moon would be up in seven minutes. Already a silver glow surrounded the ragged palisade of volcanic tuff topping the butte to the east.

I sat down to wait for the moon, and let my mind run through the memories of the day, for Resuna to upload to One True, thus making them potentially available for the whole human race to share.

It's not easy to explain about the mountains at that time of year. The life is burrowed deep; most of the world that surrounds you seems to say that winter will last forever.

Five minutes after the sun sets it can be cold enough so that you hear your breath snap and bang as it freezes and falls into snow at your feet. That's what thin air will do for you; you're just that hair closer to what it's like to be in outer space.

And yet the days are longer than they are in December, and during the day, it can be downright hot when the sun bounces off the frozen snow into your face. You hear water breaking loose from its frozen prisons, the distant boom of avalanches tumbling down into valleys, the dance of the firs in the wind. It has no place for you; this is a world where you stick out as if an orange ring were painted on the air around you. You never feel your individual existence more acutely.

Resuna asked, curiously, if feeling individual felt good. I didn't quite know how to explain it. I had to say that it was a feeling I seemed to need every now and then, but I didn't know whether it was good or bad.

I looked around slowly. Nothing moved. Hard to believe that this time last night I had been reading an old mystery and having a glass of wine at home, without a thought that I might ever be out here again.

Here I was, anyway.

Taking just as long as it would have if I hadn't been impatient, the moon climbed over the hill, huge against the pines. I waited till it lit the up slope in front of me before I went on. I angled up the slope carefully, since even though no doubt they would rescue me quickly if the snow slid, the rescue would alert Lobo and complicate the whole hunt. Besides, my old memories assured me that even one minute spent lying half buried in the snow with a broken leg is way too long.

A few minutes later I was looking for a low-visibility way over the ridge. I unstrapped from the flexis, set down my pack and duffel, and crept belly down in the rough, crust-covered snow, taking a good ten minutes to cover the last thirty meters to the top. Looking over, I saw broken rock here and there, a few scattered scrubby trees, and a couple of bowls whose edges I could skirt. Could be worse.

I climbed carefully back down, making sure I wasn't going to start any slides, slung up, and headed for the spot I'd picked out, behind a big promontory that would give me access into a nice dark bowl. It took maybe an hour until I was clumping along in the shallow snow between the trees on the dark side of the bowl; from there, my face-screen map said I'd only have to go about 150 meters to the place I had picked out for a campsite, among some small pinnacles and broken boulders with a couple of trees to cast nice deep shadows on my shelter.

I got there without any further trouble, switched the face screen to amplify the starlight, and set about the fumbling and fiddling necessary to make camp. First I got the little disk out of the top of the duffel, plugged it into my suit, and waited for it to turn itself into a snow shovel. It took about ten minutes for it to set into shape. I couldn't do much while dragging that thing around—I made a note to Resuna about redesigning this gear so that one or more of the electrets would detach—but meanwhile I got a long drink of warm water from the suit's recovery reservoir, and looked up, through the trees and boulders, at the stars. You'd think I'd be used to how bright they could be, even with a full moon, up here in the mountains, but after so many years, I still never got tired of it.

When the shovel had set, I dug out the space where I had decided I wanted to put my shelter. At least this snow had not been packed down by anything, and hadn't been exposed to the sun, so it wasn't particularly dense or hard to cut (there was just so much to move, and I couldn't throw it back over my shoulder where it was likely to be visible from below). But I had to throw it forward into the pile of scree, an awkward way to dig that makes you use your chest muscles too much and your back not enough. I was sweating and panting by the time that job was done.

Next, the shelter itself. I dragged out the big rectangular block, the size of two old-fashioned shoe-boxes, with an oval opening on the top. It was a structurer—it needed chon, carbon-hydrogen-oxygen-nitrogen, to operate on. I set it down with the arrow that marked the door pointing south, and heaped dead branches, rocks, dirt, and snow on top of it. When the pile was about half a meter higher than my head, the soft chime pinged, letting me know it felt enough mass directly above it. Then I touched the Structure button and stepped back, sitting down on a boulder to sip warm water and watch the shelter make itself.

First there was a low vibration as it shattered the materials directly above it and pulled them in. After a minute or so, the pile became visibly smaller, and then the black edges of the rapidly forming shelter peeked out from the sides like a doormat rising from a heap of dirty snow.

Curls of vapor were rising from the pile as the warmth of the shelter was absorbed by the melting snow, and the mounded rubbish shrank as if it were slowly falling into a trapdoor, as more openings on the partially structured shelter formed and drew in the mix.

I was old enough to remember the days before structurable molecular processing, and this still seemed very weird to me, even if it was just the same process that happened in an ordinary food reconstitutor.

In a short while that heap of junk I had made was down to being a damp black rectangle that covered about the same area as an old Sears Deluxe Tool Shed, covered with wet twigs, needles, and bark. Then the shelter absorbed the last of those, like a great squashed black amoeba, so that nothing was left but its own slick surface. It pinged, indicating that it was ready for more material.

Again, I heaped on branches and rocks, and then shoveled on a load of snow, until the self-forming shelter indicated that it was satisfied with the weight on top of it. After a few minutes, the snow and junk had flowed into the dark, lightless surface again, as if sinking into a pool of pure shadow.

The chemical changes and the rearrangement inside took some silent time, and the only sound was the occasional splash and hiss as snow fell from the branches above and turned to steam on the hot surface. I used the time to sit down in the shadow of a big rock, not far away, where I could look out over the valley. I didn't much hope I'd see a hidden campfire, or a trail, or someone moving around, but if I didn't look, I'd never know.

I scanned for a long time, surfing through everything from infrared to low X ray, and saw nothing I wouldn't expect to see in the mountains.

On a feeble thread of a game trail, perhaps four kilometers away and 250 meters lower, I spotted one lone figure slinking along, which just barely might be a man. But switching around to get the right setting on my goggles, I got a good look at it: an old cougar, probably one who had lost his territory and was scavenging where he could (why else be out at night in February?). I felt vaguely sorry for him, but Resuna quietly reminded me that I was here to hunt cowboys, not to rescue cougars, and anyway getting old and incapable was the natural lot of cougars in the wild. He would no doubt find the death that suited him, sooner or later, without my help or worry.

That made me feel much better.

I heard a soft creaking noise that anyone any distance away would have attributed to pine boughs. The shelter eased itself upright. With a faint sigh and several loud creaks and cracks, its members went rigid. I turned to see that it had completed itself; all

I had to do was throw my stuff inside, walk in after it, close the door, and I'd be "at home." It wasn't my warm, comfortable A-frame with Mary, but for the moment, it would do.

The pack went in with one toss, the duffel with another, and then I pushed the flexis and shovel in after them. Finally, I got inside, sealed the flap, and said "Light" to the pitch darkness.

The soft yellow glow came from panels on top of the shelter, and since the shelter walls were fully opaque and the light would go off if the door unsealed, I didn't have to worry about it being seen. The insulating shelter wall also kept heat radiation to a minimum—the shelter itself sent most of the heat to a recoverer to recharge its electrets. So I was now invisible except at very close range, and could relax in my new home.

Shelters are always too hot on the inside the first night, before their brains catch the rhythm of the outside temperature, so once I had done the minimum unpacking and verified that the bed and linens had generated properly, I took off all my clothes. I stripped out of my outside suit, turned it inside out, and stuffed it into the recoverer, which would clean it thoroughly, extract and purify the water from the reservoirs, scavenge the body salts for anything useful, make sure the electrets were up to full charge, and finally drop out a couple of pebble-sized chunks of waste.

Naked and comfortable in the warm little room now, I said "Lights down" and dimmed them to the point where I could just see; that always helps me to sleep. I slid a narrow rectangular meal-pak into the food reconstitutor, waited a few minutes, and pulled out a tray with two small hamburgers, french fries, and baked beans, which I sat down and wolfed while the reconstitutor turned another pak—this one more cubic—into a pot of hot chocolate.

Resuna told me that Mary was happy and thinking of me. The thought brought a friendly, warm glow to my heart. The meal and the hot chocolate were working their magic, and the reassurance from Resuna was all I needed; I stretched out on top of the covers, told the bed to wake me at four the next morning, and fell sound asleep. All night I dreamed about old friends who were dead, and the way the world used to be, and the big empty spaces around the pine-covered mountains.

When the bed squeezed me gently, twice, around the knees and back, I woke instantly. The lights came on dim and red, and a soft voice said "It's time, sir."

I sat up, enjoying the pleasant warmth of the shelter, dropped the blocks of breakfast and coffee into the reconstitutor, and opened up the toilet side of the recoverer. Back when I had started as a cowboy hunter, we'd still been in tents, and had to make breakfast over a stove and dig our own latrines; the cooking was sort of romantic and quaint, I suppose, but one thing I had been glad to see the end of was the morning dash, through the far-below-freezing thin mountain air, to the slit trench. I told Resuna how much I had enjoyed waking up in camp; it might lead to One True's eventually encouraging more people to go camping.

After gobbling down the biscuits and gravy and drinking a couple of cups of coffee, I was ready to slip into the outside suit, strap on the day pack, and start the job. It was 6:20, about half an hour before the sun was due to come up. I carefully closed the flap and walked around the outside barrier that kept the brief flash of warmth from being visible through infrared scopes. For today I would be working my way down into the Dead Mule drainage, exploring this north side of it, to see what conditions were like on the ground and look for any places where someone might hide from the satellites.

I had gone only about 200 meters when what had looked like firm ground turned out to be a snowbank, which slipped away under my feet. For a weird instant, I seemed to hang in air, as if I had lost connection with the ground—the moment of free fall when the snow no longer pushes against your boots—and then a whirling tumble as I got myself turned around, spread out my arms, and let myself fall face first onto the snow behind me, trying to stay up above the real trouble. I slid down the ridge, face down and feet first, for about thirty meters before coming to a stop and tentatively dragging myself forward about three feet to get up off the sliding part of the snow. I slowly rolled over, pointed my feet downhill, and, cursing softly into the face screen, looked down to see what I had done.

The first light of dawn was just beginning to break over the mountains to the east, and the tops of two mountains to the west were already touched with the arc-brightness of sun on snow. That gave me more than enough light to see by without using the amplifier.

The snowslide had only traveled 150 meters down the slope, bumping along in a sheet rather than a rolling wave, never more than a meter deep or so. Unless he happened to look right at it when I touched it off, and saw me flopping around on top of it, the slide would look like the most natural thing in the world.

I sat up, took a sip of water, and let Resuna calm me; the worst I had been risking, probably, was just a plain old broken leg, which they fix pretty quickly these days, even in old guys like me. Something about that phrase, "the most natural thing in the world," was running through my head, the kind of clue that nags at you for days or weeks until you see what it was trying to call your attention to. Those sometimes turned out useful—and more often led nowhere.

I scanned the valley slowly, playing with different magnifications and different wavelengths, and the only thing out and moving in the early dawn was a small herd of elk crunching their way down through the snow to drink from Dead Mule Creek, stopping often to look for willow shoots, or grass under the snow, or aspen twigs that they hadn't already chomped down during the long, bleak winter. When I'd been a kid, the government used to send out helicopters to drop hay to the elk, because it upset the voters if the elk starved, and so there were always way more elk than the land could handle naturally. Nowadays, Resuna took care of public upset—

and starvation, blizzards, wolves, and cougars took care of the elk—so we had sparse, healthy elk.

I watched the little herd pick their way down to the firm part of the stream bank, a step at a time, following in each other's tracks. A muscular young bull led the way, turning and sniffing the wind now and then, looking about with huge brown eyes. The elk of the Rockies look like big mule deer, I guess, to the untrained eye, until you realize they're half again as big, and until you see that wild, cunning intelligence looking out of the eyes. In the old days, good hunters loved them and lazy hunters only saw them from the road.

The bull must have decided it was okay, and began to scrape at the stream bank with his front hooves. Two cows joined him, and a yearling that looked like it would be on his own soon, and shortly they were making all kinds of noise down there, breaking ice, pawing up grass, and having what elk must think is a good old time. In the cold, still dawn air, their breath rose in silvery columns, catching the sun that sliced between the trees above them in white flashes.

I looked at them in everything from infrared to X ray, and they looked pretty much like any herd of elk, eating, in late winter or early spring.

The most natural thing in the world . . .

That was what, somehow, Lobo must be managing to look like. Even back in the 2030s, satellite optics and computers had been good enough so that they could designate individual buffalo and elk for the Doleworkers to cull from the herds. Something the size of a human being, dressed only in regular cold-weather clothing, couldn't possibly remain concealed from overhead satellites for more than a decade, and yet obviously something had.

He must still have a working insulating/storage suit, and somewhere to run a heat exchanger that wasn't noticeable. That meant in turn he had to have somewhere to charge his suit, and that meant a not-very-likely sizable power source someplace. He couldn't be stealing off the grid because that would be noticed immediately, but most kinds of generators, electrets, or batteries were just as visible from orbit, more visible even than the man himself would be.

Or maybe I was thinking too much like a modern, civilized cowboy hunter, and not enough like a crazy but very smart cowboy. I tried to come at the problem another way and think about how small a profile he would have to have to remain concealed—that is, how small must he look to sensors and screens in order to be lumped into the landscape?

What if he had gone completely wild, living out there with a flint-tipped spear, building fires only far back under rock shelves, sleeping on the ground, acting like a Paleolithic hunter who was afraid of high-flying predators that could see in the infrared?

Then where had his clothes come from, and how had his beard been trimmed neatly, when he turned up again? More to the point, human beings are *big* animals, and the satellites and databases *did* track big animals individually, so why hadn't they tracked Lobo?

Elk, bear, buffalo, moose, mustang, deer, wolf, coyote, mountain goat, bighorn, cougar—those, according to Resuna when it checked with One True, were the animals in the immediate area who were regularly tracked as individuals rather than as herds or flocks. All of them took up more than a square meter, had mammalian body temperatures, and massed over twenty kilos.

Lobo had to take up something close to two square meters every time he lay down—and you can hardly survive by hunting if you don't lie down now and then. If he was ever out of an insulating suit, he was more than warm enough to register on infrared. And even as gaunt as he had gotten, he must still mass at least seventy kilos. He was *way* over the threshold where he should have been detectable.

He must have a way of looking, to any satellite overhead, like anything else you would find in the wild country out here. He had to have had it for most of a decade. And whatever it was, it must have gotten lost or stopped working recently, bringing him out into the open.

Resuna remained absolutely quiet and let me work through it; very likely One True had already had some of these thoughts and was waiting to see if I came up with a different answer, or even a better one. After a while I was forced to concede that I still didn't have a clue, and I gingerly stood up, afraid that some of the surface under me might give again. I couldn't climb down the slide, since it was bound to be unstable for a couple of days, and death in a small slide is not much of an improvement over death in a full-fledged avalanche. Probably I should work my way down across the gentler slope to the west.

I got out the flexis and set them to configure as Nordic skis, plugging them into my suit and letting them take their time about forming up. The elk, below, finished their morning elk-business, and formed a straggly procession going back up the slope. For a moment I wondered, idly, if Lobo might have disguised himself to look, at least to overhead satellites, like some common animal; but the thought of Lobo crouching out there in an elk suit seemed just too wildly improbable.

The flexis had set and cooled into skis, so I unplugged them, strapped them on, and pulled out the extensor poles and telescoped them into position. Trying to hold it to *one* unpleasant surprise this morning, I took it very slow and easy.

This whole area had been pretty much abandoned in the aftermath of the Eurowar, when so many people fled into the cities for law and order and their share at the food distribution centers; now, ninety years later, it was "natural" insofar as what was happening out here was wild and unmanaged.

But it wasn't anything like it might have "naturally" been. The first decade or so after the war, before blight-resistant cover plants had been bred back into existence, had been bad for the land. Many shallow draws had been cut by water into deep ravines and gullies, and after cover had begun to grow again, it had taken many slopes some decades to re-shape.

The loads of silt and mud had altered the rivers as well, aging them rapidly, making them wind and twist in strange patterns that shouldn't have happened for another ice age or two—and the growth of the new glaciers on the highest peaks had put still another stress on the Colorado mountains. Add to that the fires in the dead forests, and the sudden surges and retreats of a dozen bio-engineered plant species as they fought with a variety of non-native weeds and some species that were probably escaped ecoweapons, and it had been past 2025 before you could predict what might be growing where—if anything was—anywhere in the high country, and almost up to the beginning of the War of the Memes, a quarter-century beyond that, before field ecologists were writing with any assurance about what was out here.

The animals had recovered quickly enough; between the Die-Off and the Eurowar, plus the epidemics that had followed in its wake, the area hadn't been much needed by people, so as soon as there were plants for food and cover, animal populations had surged back. With so many cities and settlements deserted, and much less land under cultivation, they had migrated freely, and by the beginning of the War of the Memes the grizzly and wolf were all the way back to the old Mexican border, and the herds of buffalo were again beginning to carpet the Great Plains as they had two centuries before. And yet the differences remained: wild longhorns in Texas, a huge wolf-dog-coyote crossbreed that ranged from the Rio Grande to the Platte, bigger and stronger mustangs thanks to the infusion of domestic draft horses. Any forester could have pointed out any number of things different from what they had been a century ago, in any part of the drainage.

My first long glide across the slope was successful; the snow skidded out from under my skis no more than one might expect, the edges bit into the sun-formed crust easily enough, and by the end of that first swoop I was perhaps ten meters lower, and a quarter of a kilometer to the west. I made a big, awkward, snowplow turn like a beginner to avoid having any speed at all as I swung back east; the snow would be deeper now and I intended to take it at a steeper angle, so as not to be up here all day. Again it held, with one scary moment when I slipped sideways for a few seconds on some thicker crust, and now I was down into the heavy, partially-refrozen, pellet-like corn snow that you have to expect on a southern exposure this time of year. It's treacherous, but it can be managed. A few more wide, slow, careful turns brought me down to where the ground began to level off into a gentler slope toward the creek.

The satellite passing overhead told me, via Resuna, that nothing was visible anywhere, but I didn't entirely trust that. Many cowboys, especially the loners of the last few years of hunting, had become pretty fair jackleg mechanics, and every now and then one of them thought of something simple and effective—it had to be simple because they didn't have the resources to do anything sophisticated, and if it wasn't effective, they didn't last long between the mountains and the hunters.

Of course, Lobo was out in the open, now. So maybe whatever his miracle gadget was, it had broken down, and now it would be just a routine hunt. But just as possibly he was showing himself for some other reason entirely. I resolved to try to work as if he might be within fifty meters of me, all the time, and take it slow and easy. I would be looking for anything that resembled tracks—but at the same time I would be leaving mine, and I knew that *I* didn't have any way of hiding my tracks, whatever Lobo might be able to do.

Now that I was down in the easier country, I pushed off and skated slowly and carefully westward. There was some old sandstone in the local surface rock, and it was possible he might have found a cave somewhere, or even dug one if he had somewhere to hide his debris pile. Some mining claims went back 150 years and more—perhaps he'd found some old tunnel to move into. But that would only explain where he slept and holed up; how did he move around without being detected?

Well, when in doubt, start with basics. People eat. Lobo had to have been eating something. What he was eating had to be either stolen food, stored food, or wild food. I didn't believe he could steal for more than a decade and not come to One True's attention before this. Ten years of food is a lot to store somewhere. That left wild food—hunting and gathering. So he was relying on wild game, especially in the winter.

The best place to find wild game is where it drinks, so I decided to take a brief patrol along the creek.

I took my time getting there, going downhill in safe, slow snowplows almost as often as I paralleled. If I screwed up on this first day—twisted an ankle or something and had to be rescued—I would be humiliated by having let One True down, and embarrassed by the mess that would be made of the hunt by having to bring a diskster up here. Worse, I would be out of action and somebody else would get my cowboy.

⬤ An hour and a half later, it was almost noon. I was sweating buckets into the suit, the charge in the electrets was at 100%, all heat reservoirs were likewise full, and I had turned off the pre-warmer on the air circulator because I needed the cooling from breathing the mountain air.

I only had to go two kilometers down the elk trail to Dead Mule Creek, but that was plenty. Elk do not have a skier's idea of what is a usable trail. The pathway wove through stands of trees, broke from brush on one side of a meadow and, after disappearing among a stand of young aspen, took a plunge down a bank into dense undergrowth.

When I finally came down through a bunch of beaver-felled aspen to the bank, the sun was high in the sky, and I was hot and uncomfortable. But a quick scan showed no trace of Lobo, nor any other human being. Probably there wasn't a single person between me and Mary, in the cabin a hundred and ten kilometers away—this part of the world had always been empty and in the past century it had gotten emptier.

At best I would have two hours down here before I would need to start working my way back to base, but then my opponent had only a very limited amount of time when he could move around, too. The chances of our both being in the same place during those brief periods were pretty slim. But I only had to catch him once, and he had to evade me every day. If I didn't catch him for a whole year, he could be ahead of me 365–1 at the moment I collared him—and I would still be the winner. Patience would do the job, more than anything else.

Down here by the stream, the warmer air had made a mess of the snow. When you're trying to stalk someone, it's hard to believe how many ways heavily weathered snow can be frustrating. It crunches constantly, breaks with loud cracks, and makes appalling squealing and grinding sounds against your skis. It grabs unpredictably, always threatening to dump you on your butt. If you fall down it makes a noise like a giant folding a garbage truck. If you don't fall down you still leave painfully sharp and clear tracks. Every so often it turns into sheet ice that can send you rocketing downslope, struggling for control.

Soon I was thinking too much about my skiing and not enough about my hunting. I finally got a clear view of a path down to the creek, and shot down it, alternately snowplowing and paralleling as best I could, turning often in big wide turns, bouncing around on the slope like a rubber ball down a storm culvert.

I was watching for somewhere good to pull into, and not finding it, so I kept trying to slow down—which wasn't so easy either. The snow under my skis screamed, thumped, skittered, and sprayed, giving me no solid grip; I was staying upright almost purely on balance. At least I was cooling off. The air coming in through my breather was almost clean and cold.

I turned up onto a rise to spill some speed, climbing up and then doing quick loop turns back down. The winding creek was still some distance below me, but the clumps of tall pines were much farther apart now, and there looked to be a nice, easy path at a reasonable slope. I had skied for almost a quarter-kilometer before I realized I must be on some long-abandoned road. In another hundred meters, I saw something by the roadside, and almost didn't believe it. I circled back and checked again.

There, partly covered by the snow, was a badly smudged print where something had been slipping down a gravel bank and had to brace itself. It was too wide for elk or deer, and had no claw marks like a bear; the heel was suggestively narrow where it had stamped in hard. And not far from that—again, the distance of something under half a meter suggested a lot—another smudged print, presumably where he had boosted himself back up. That clinched that it wasn't a bear—the weight, marked by the deepest depression, was much too far forward in the track. I searched in that area for another half hour and turned up three more badly smudged prints.

Squatting down till my eye was almost at snow level, I looked toward the creek. Farther down the hill a low, chaotic mess of crumpled and broken snow, less than two meters across, told me my man had taken a flying somersault after leaping the road.

Judging by what was packed into the shadow side of his tracks, he was using one very-low-tech method of evading detection—going out during snowstorms, so that most of his track would disappear to satellite observation before the clouds cleared.

The pattern argued that he had been descending when he passed this point, on the way to somewhere else, but I had no way to know how often he went there. Possibly he often took this path—or would, until the first time he saw my ski tracks leading up to it.

I skied back a short distance, feeling that odd prickle you get when it's a distant but not zero probability that someone will shoot at you. This area looked like an old-fashioned Christmas card—the vivid cobalt sky, the absolutely white snow, the greens shading from sun-spattered forest to nearly black in the shadows. The road behind me, leading up eventually to the ridge where my camp was, despite all the bright eye-stabbing daylight, looked suddenly weird, threatening, and hostile, the way a path through a public park at night looks to a young child.

Resuna steadied my nerves. I felt all my skills come to the forefront of my mind.

I found a place where I could climb the hill, just about twenty-five meters back, and herringboned up onto the bank. Remembering that Lobo himself had slipped, I stayed wide of the road.

If he didn't come this way often, the track was information but useless; if he did, the information would be useless to me the first time he saw my ski tracks. So I had to follow his trail in one direction or another, right now. The melting on the edges of a couple of the tracks had suggested that they were days old.

I picked up his trail easily enough; he was moving from rock to bare dirt to snow, stepping from one to the other in an irregular pattern, so that an AI looking at satellite photos was unlikely to see any pattern to it (especially since only the tracks in the snow would show well from orbit). But to the naked human eye, looking up the slope and just letting things have enough time to group and arrange themselves, the pattern was perfectly obvious. I could see his track or tracks—my guess was that he had been this way many times more than once—right up to where the ridgeline slashed the pure blue winter sky. I felt like whooping for pure joy. That's the way it feels when you know that One True has put you right where you most belong.

Lobo was clever, and he'd had a long run of making no mistakes at all, but all runs come to an end. Though, hell, even this didn't really count as a mistake; just one of those inevitable things that has to happen because no one can control everything. If I had the good fortune to bring him in, especially if when I brought him in he was still in shape fit to be turned, then at the cowboy hunter reunions I would have a tale to tell that surpassed anyone else's.

I checked my time. It was nearly 3:30 P.M.; the sun would be setting in two hours.

I doubted that I could follow his track clear up the hill before dark, but I had to try. This was clearly a frequent path for him, and he couldn't fail to miss my tracks when he came this way next. I had to push as far as I could, and find a place to set up an ambush the next day, or even tonight if it looked promising enough.

According to the satellite map on my face screen, his path angled slightly toward my camp. That meant a shorter haul back to base, a longer time I could stay out, possibly an easier position for the ambush. On the other hand, I would be going uphill, crossing ridgelines, and if he happened to be on this path ahead of me, *he* would be the one with a perfect ambush.

I shrugged and got going. You have to not only be lucky, but feel lucky, to hunt cowboys. And on this beautiful day, I didn't think I could feel anything but lucky.

I could be up all night, if I had to, anyway.

Herringboning is an efficient way to climb a hill in the snow, but efficiency is relative—all you can really say for it is that it is easier than boots or snowshoes. It's still lots of work. By the time I cleared the first ridgeline and could look on up the slope to the next—and to the distant white peak that gleamed over it for a moment—I was sweating as if I'd been stoking a furnace. Resuna adjusted my inner thermometer, but nothing compensated for the heat produced in my large muscles. The suit's heat storage was at 120%, which is 10% more than when you're supposed to stop and dump heat.

I moved into the shadow of a large boulder, took off the radiator, set it on the ground, and shoveled snow onto it. The snow flashed off. I did that several times, each time releasing a cloud of white vapor, which might give my position away if Lobo just happened to be right in the neighborhood and looking right at me, but if I got rid of enough heat, I would again be able to breathe and function without having a telltale infrared signature.

Besides, he'd have to be nearly on top of me to see it today. In the shade, and in the thin cold air, the clouds rose less than two meters before they turned to ice crystals and tumbled away invisibly on the wind. I was careful to make sure that the cloud of vapor didn't drift into the sunlight before it froze. He'd have to be looking right at this part of the mountain to catch me.

I gulped some warm water, swallowed a few bites of the blueberry-flavored field rations, and systematically studied the fresh slope above me. Knowing his way of moving, I could pick out his path pretty quickly, and soon I was herringboning along his pathway, now warm without being hot, and refreshed by the food and water. I went at it hard, making good time.

Checking the satellite map, I saw that I was still angling toward my base camp; I might have only a couple hundred meters to go to get home, if the pattern held. There would be two more ridgelines before I reached the top, but I doubted that he was going all the way to the top—not with a decent pass just two kilometers west. Probably the tracks would start to angle west either over this next ridgeline, or the one after it.

I worked steadily up the hill, following the footprints closely, not cutting across his track, because you never know what additional clues might be around any one track. However, because Lobo had not been in much of a hurry, he hadn't dropped anything or torn anything off his clothes, or broken any branches. Unlike so many pursuits I'd been on, he wasn't bleeding, either.

I pushed my way over the next ridgeline without stopping, exulting in the chill taste of the thin air and the thunder of blood in my ears, but when I got to where I could see what came next, I was somewhere between muttering and swearing. It hadn't been especially visible from the satellites, being long and thin and rimmed with trees, but I was looking right at an old rockslide, and that was just where the few tracks I could see led.

If you're evading capture, old slides are your best friends in the mountains. There's all the bare rock you could ever want to put your hands and feet on, and furthermore, unless the guy tracking you knows the rockslide as well as you do, it's dangerous. A rockslide is only a *temporarily* stopped river of scree, and it can start flowing again with almost any provocation. Once you've worked out a safe path through one, by slow and cautious exploration, anyone coming along after you is going to have a hell of a time figuring out where you've gone, and will have to go very, very slowly if he wants to follow you up the slide without running the risk of getting killed.

So I stared at that dead end, trying to think of what to do next. It was less than an hour till sunset, and good as the light amplifiers were nowadays, they still couldn't find faint tracks in dirt under a tree after dark. I would have to give this up soon no matter what I decided.

It was looking like an excellent time to just turn and head for home, unless I saw his tracks leading off the rockslide somewhere. After a thorough search with binoculars, I didn't. I checked with the satellite and it was just as I had feared; the rockslide bent in an L shape farther up, and ran for almost a kilometer along the face of this big ridge; in at least fifty places, trees and brush got near enough to it to provide an invisible escape off the scree and into the woods. My best hope would be to search each of those potential escapes, one by one, probably the west side first. It would take most of the day tomorrow.

I was well and truly screwed: I had no tricks left to find him with. Probably he would find me first. Maybe he wouldn't come that way for another day or so, but that wasn't much to hang my hope on. Badly discouraged, I turned for home.

There was a deep draw on my direct path home to camp, too, and skirting around that through the woods meant that I didn't reach camp till the full moon was up again. At least it was so late that my post-sunset watch over the valley had only half an hour to go. I sat down in the snow, sipped warm water from the suit, chewed a chocolate ration bar, swept the valley in all wavelengths over and over, and—despite Resuna's prodding—felt extremely sorry for myself. Exactly on the minute, I gave up the watch, just as fruitless as the pursuit had been, and went inside.

I staggered into the shelter, tired and cold, with the ominous feeling I was getting old. Resuna crept quietly into the less-conscious part of my awareness, like a friendly old cat sneaking onto your lap, and I let it hang around there to see what it could do.

The hot soup and noodles that I reconstituted were one of the best meals I ever had, the bed felt remarkably good, and just as I stretched out, my copy of Resuna passed along, via One True, a warm, deep feeling of affection from Mary; she missed me but she was happy and comfortable at home. The warmth, dark, and silence got me to sleep right away.

I suppose that in my youth, I might have been a hero to little kids. After all, I was a cop, and there had always been great numbers of shows about cops in the days before memes.

Resuna and I have argued about this many times. I say that people were attracted to cops because so many of them were good-looking guys—young, alert, in great shape. Besides, uniforms and guns always got attention.

Resuna says what all the attraction to the cops was about was that most of humanity was looking forward to the creation of the memes and eventually of the One True meme. Resuna has a tendency to see One True wherever it looks, which I guess isn't very different from what human beings used to do when they saw gods everywhere.

What Resuna says is that the police were always the agents of order. Society runs on order. Hence the police always sent the message, whenever they appeared, on the street or in entertainment, that order was good, order should be sought, and that human beings who helped to make order were better than human beings who helped to destroy it.

Resuna never has convinced me, but we argued for years. It was a good way to while away otherwise dull time on stakeouts; it didn't interfere with seeing or hearing and it made no noise. I know Moonchild Swann used to play chess with her copy of Resuna, and it wouldn't have surprised me to learn that during stakeout, everybody was locked in some kind of conversation with Resuna. All that it was, was that the conversations I preferred were vaguely philosophic arguments, was all.

Every so often, to vary the argument, and because Resuna is always helping everyone examine their feelings and helping them to stay a valid and fully compatible unit within One True, Resuna would work through the issue with me, not as a philosophic matter, but as an emotional one: did I *wish* that I had lived in a previous era when an individual such as I might have been a hero? Did I dream about such times, or feel disappointed that I hadn't been part of them? Or if I didn't wish that I could have been a hero, did I sometimes regret, perhaps, that I had not lived in the intermediate generations when heroes gave way to role models?

Heroes were people who were idolized and admired for being bigger and better than you thought anybody could be—dreams of what a human being might struggle forever to just barely live up to. They were visions of what was beyond the human, structured in a way that called forth the human maximum.

Role models were friendlier, squishier concepts, for the friendly, squishy times in which they formed. They were people that you could imagine being; people you knew, who you were sure—given some effort—you could be like. It was the essence of a hero to be at or beyond the human boundary; it was the essence of a role model to be well within it, to be something that a human being could reasonably aspire to be.

And finally, at our point in history, there were no heroes anymore, and there were no role models, but there was what I was—for which there didn't need to be a word, because, though we cowboy hunters and other people who did dangerous, individual jobs, were *useful*, we were no longer *important*. One True could draw pieces from any of the vast number of its component Resunas and individual psyches, all over the Earth. If any child, or anyone at all, needed my approach to the world, emotional attitude, moral qualities, or any other bit or piece of my way of doing things, at any time in life, she or he could have it instantly, not by laboriously copying external actions until they became habits and then parts of nature, but by an easy direct transfer—One True would call my copy of Resuna, which would copy the required piece of my personality and upload it to One True, which would then download it via the child's copy of Resuna.

Resuna says it was really just a matter of the human race developing a more efficient process for moving information from one brain to another; the structures we called heroes were the oldest, crudest, and least-efficient system for copying virtues. If unusual courage and cunning existed in Odysseus, and the rest of his culture wanted to share them, his courage and cunning had to be told and retold at aural speeds, from mouth to ear, over and over again, until they were sharpened into a particularly clear and memorable form, and then the text had to be repeated to people until the merest mention of Odysseus would fill the mind with the drive to be clever and the self-perception of courage, for anyone who heard it.

Role models, as a way of transmitting virtues, were less thrilling and perhaps traded away some high resolution and clarity in order to be able to reach more people, more thoroughly and faster. The role-model method of transmitting virtues was to train a child to see her or his own abilities and potentials in the people around him. That didn't produce the excellence that the heroes had, since no one ever reached beyond what had already been achieved; at best it produced a competence that only degraded slowly from generation to generation. But it did provide very effective socialization. You didn't get any more high soarers, but nearly everyone took off and flew for a ways.

In this century, direct transfer of information, brain to brain, via Resuna and One True, provided greater accuracy and clarity than the "hero" protocol, *and* greater efficiency and wider accessibility than the "role-model" protocol—I could almost think I heard Resuna preening about the subject. The personal traits of people like me and the other specialists working for One True—not just the hunters but the engineers, rangers, ecologists, scouts, and all the other dedicated units that put high skill and personal courage and integrity at the service of the planet—were available to every person on Earth, whenever they needed to be like us. Ordinary people no longer had to form those qualities by long habit of practice; they were directly available just as soon as you needed them.

It was as if every Greek had been able to be possessed by the spirit of Odysseus at will, as if every athlete had an inspirational coach at his elbow and every preacher heard the voice of his god directly, and perhaps most important, in the long run, it was as if every parent could be the best parent on Earth. And so the reified, studied, carefully rehearsed and ingrained examples—the heroes and role models—passed from human memory, except as characters in old stories, for whom fewer and fewer people had any time or interest. One True had largely stopped bothering even with revising those old stories, since they no longer received the attention that might allow them to do harm, and any benefit they might exert could be achieved by more effective means.

Those were the thoughts I drifted awake with, shading into Resuna's usual celebration of morning—how good it is to contribute, how important it is to be a part of something bigger than yourself, how much one must rejoice in the strength of One True, and in the sanity that Resuna brings to your life. Resuna usually ran something like that through my head in the morning; my copy of Resuna and I shared the joke that it was a sort of mouthwash against spiritual morning breath, for often, when I was waking from sleep, my old memories crapped up my view of the world.

When I had served in Burton's Thugs for Jesus, we had been a relatively respectable outfit, but we had also been mercenary soldiers. There had been things I had seen my comrades do, and things I myself had done, that still, late at night, sometimes could disturb my sleep despite everything Resuna could do, and despite all the comfort of waking to find Mary beside me. Now, drifting awake, comfortably naked on the warm bed, with a day of challenging, productive work ahead of me—work that I knew it was terribly important to do—I drank in the sense of my place in One True, and thus in the perfection of human history, like a magic restorative honey in some old fantasy—sweeter than anything else could possibly taste, and bringing me strength, welling inexhaustibly from within me.

When I went outside in the pre-dawn, it had snowed, and exactly the wrong amount—not enough to obscure the fresh tracks I had made the day before, but very likely enough to cover Lobo's older, already partially melted trail.

It was also extremely cold, as it so often is in the mountains in the hours just after a snowfall. No stars shone, and the moon was an occasional yellowish smear in the west that never quite broke through the clouds; probably a high nimbus hanging over the area, enough to keep the warming sun out, not enough to hold ground heat in. It was going to be a real stinker of a morning.

You do your job even on bad days, so I turned up the temperature in my suit to warm the stiffness out of my joints, and sat up on the ridge for the dawn watch, scanning mostly in infrared because there was so little light in the visible band. I focused on the area where I knew his trail ran, but I saw nothing of Lobo. That could be because he had not come that way yet, or it could just as easily be because during the night he had seen my clumsy tracks from the day before, knew what was up, and was now four drainages away and running like a scared cat.

In infrared, the sun shone through the clouds as a great bright sprawling spider. The morning was so cold, and the light that filtered through the high clouds so feeble, that even after the sun had been up for half an hour, there was too little contrast to really see properly in the infrared: everything was about the same (painfully low) temperature.

It was still pritnear dark as night in the visible spectrum, but I flipped back to it, cranking up amplification to the maximum, to break the monotony. No Lobo, nothing moving, no sign that I wasn't the only thing alive that morning.

When the sun had been up for an hour, I went back into the shelter, had a quick breakfast, and suited up again. It looked like I would just have to stay on plan, since nothing better had appeared so far.

I shaped my flexis into telemark skis, let them cool, and pushed off; now that I knew where I was going, I could go much more efficiently. Fighting my way around that deep draw the night before had convinced me that I'd be better off going down and then up; besides, since that old road cut right across one of his major pathways, probably it would cut across more than one. I skied to the nearest convenient high point on the road, and started my search from there, slowly drifting down the road between the gray trees and the gray rocks, under a blurry gray sky, as the temperature continued to fall and little bits of sleet occasionally spit out of the sky and skittered down the hood of my suit. Without the satellite guidance, I'd have felt hopelessly lost in no time at all; as it was, I had to check my position every few minutes.

I was down at the place where I had found his trail, the day before, in only about an hour, and although it was now beginning to snow in earnest, at least that made a more pleasant surface for skiing, might help in hiding my tracks, and was sort of pretty in the gray, silent forest.

The tracks down here, on the lower part of the slope, were covered by the drifting snow, but I followed the satellite's guidance up the hill to where Lobo's track had petered out, going up onto that old rockslide. I planned to cast back and forth along the west side, up to the top of the ridge, and then work my way back down the east, looking for the place where Lobo got on or off the rock-slide—or perhaps even to see a print or two in the fresh snow on the scree, if by any chance he had come this way the night before. I stamped up the gentle slopes and herringboned up the steep ones, making good time but only by dint of buckets of sweat. By the time I got up to the slide itself, it was almost mid-morning, and I stopped to open a ration pocket, take out a warm cheese sandwich and a pouch of tomato soup, and swallow those, chasing them down with a pouch of hot coffee.

This time, knowing that it could be a long day and I might not be getting home till well past dark, I had loaded all seven ration pockets on the suit with reconstituted stuff that could stay warm all day. Besides, it gave me more heat sinks for my body heat without having to vent and make myself visible in the infrared.

I made sure the next pocket from which I intended to eat was set to warm, and that the other pockets were to stay at ambient unless they were needed as auxiliary heat sinks, and got back on my way, herringboning up the west side of the scree, gliding about in each successive little tongue of forest or brush that presented itself, until I was sure I'd have picked up any track. There was no trace.

Today, besides coping with the cold, the clouds, and the bad luck and fruitlessness, I was going to have three long gaps in satellite coverage, all in the afternoon. Normally the periods when a satellite can't pick up the signal from the jack in your forehead, even out in a less-covered area like this, were only about four or five minutes long at worst. If you were line of sight from SNY, or from the towers of the several new supras now under construction, antennas on any of them could give you continuous coverage.

But as it happened, a satellite had recently gone off-line, and the repair crews hadn't yet gotten up there to do anything about it. Therefore, today, in perfect accord with its being a shitty day, there would be three *big* holes in my coverage, each something over twenty minutes long. Most of what I was doing was on north-facing slopes, and since the supras hang above the equator, I would have no line of sight to any of them, most of the time.

Three minutes during which you're on your own, when your copy of Resuna can't raise One True, is scary enough—you could be hurt, captured, or killed with no way of calling for backup and evacuation—but in twenty minutes you could not only get killed, you could get disappeared. Two cowboy hunters from the old days were still listed as MIA—and both of them had vanished during "brief" satellite lapses, presumably either dying in some bizarre accident or killed by a cowboy, with their bodies never recovered.

Resuna was trying to be reassuring, pointing out that it was always there to help, but help from a meme running in your brain, and help from the combined minds and resources of the entire Earth, are very different. When a big, strong, clever man may suddenly try to kill you, you really want the latter.

On the other hand, if Lobo was coordinating his movements with the satellite gaps—*and* if he also knew about the dead one, and wasn't just coordinating by watching for them with binoculars and plotting orbits—then this was exactly the day and time he would be out, and the chances of my finding him were much better. The chances of catching him if I did find him were a different matter.

After climbing for another hour, and checking out three more innocent stands of trees without finding any trace of Lobo, I had Resuna contact One True and check back through the files. Kelly and her mother had been attacked during a time when two satellites were fully up in the sky and in line of sight, so maybe Lobo didn't pay any attention to the gaps in coverage. Too, the remote photos of him had to have happened with a satellite above the horizon. And twice he had been photographed crossing a south-facing slope with a direct line of sight to Supra New York. Chances were he wasn't coordinating with satellite passes, so he was *not* unusually likely to be out, today.

Just after two o'clock, not long after the first gap in satellite coverage, I was finally at the head of the old rockslide, a remnant cliff where a tower of volcanic tuff had fallen down sometime in the last century or so. I squatted down on a snow-covered boulder, looking out across the wide valley before me. The day was turning nastier, hard though that was to believe.

Far below, on the flat floodplain around Dead Mule Creek, I could see the wild swirls of the little ground blizzards. In the old days there had been auto accidents because of those things; someone would come around a bend in the road on a clear day, and a smear of white would erase all vision just when someone else, similarly blinded, drifted across the center line, or when the road turned out to be occupied by a wandering steer, or when the next bend hid a school bus that had stopped to drop off a ranch kid. People didn't drive themselves anymore, and machines could see right through a ground blizzard or call up a satellite and look over the top, but still something evil, frightening, almost alive lurked in the white swirls, a kilometer across and a meter high, that alternately hid and exposed the frozen creek.

I gobbled the macaroni and cheese, hamburg steak, peas, and warm apple tart of my mid-afternoon second lunch; Resuna informed me that this was what had once been called a "popular television dinner," but I didn't bother to find out what that meant. Every so often Resuna just hands you a fact, with nothing attached to it to explain why you should want to know. There are people in Sursumcorda, old-timers who turned late in life and perhaps not willingly, who whisper that it's a bug in the system. I always feel bad about having my copy of Resuna report them.

The wind was rising. Minus ten Celsius, and falling. The firs on the slopes were whipping and dancing like mad drunks; the aspens bowed and bowed endlessly like compulsively obsequious servants; and even up here, high on the ridge without much snow upwind of me, the blowing snow was obscuring my view off and on.

It was senseless to try to find any of Lobo's tracks now; the weather would erase most of them before I got there, and in this miserable visibility I would not be able to see whatever trace might be preserved in a sheltered hollow, or to the windward of a rock or tree. Yet there were still nearly four hours of daylight, and I really didn't want to just ski home and sit out the bad weather in the shelter.

I could ski down the side of this ridge to where the old road joined with a larger road, far below where I had first picked up Lobo's tracks. A junction of two roads near a known sighting of a cowboy was a pretty good place to hunt. Furthermore, a check with satellite records showed that the terrain was reasonable— during most of the last portion I'd be following an old ski trail left over from one of the many abandoned resorts up here.

Once I got down there, I'd just follow the old road back to a point near my camp. That would be mostly uphill and should take the rest of the afternoon, especially if it snowed more or the wind picked up. If I found nothing, no harm done—the odds had been against it anyway—and I would then just herringbone up the hill to my camp, get home just before dark, and turn in early that evening for a fresh start after the bad weather blew over.

But maybe Lobo used the old road down below regularly, and watched it. If so, I might be able to ski into an ambush. If he didn't manage to kill me in the first few seconds—and the suit was projectile-resistant, especially for old-fashioned bullets at long range, and I was in great shape with my fighting skills freshly replenished— then backup units would come swarming in, and all I'd have to do would be to hold him long enough so that he could be captured.

Then again, if by sheer bad luck a satellite blank spot coincided with falling into his ambush, that might just even the odds enough for him to get away—and for me to get dead. A lot can happen in a few seconds, and ten minutes can be forever in certain kinds of emergencies.

I could have waited till the next day, when there would be only two very brief interruptions—but that would mean running the risk of having Lobo see the tracks, or even of following them back to my camp and taking me. It was possible that I still had surprise on my side, and that even if I didn't, he hadn't had time to either prepare to fight or to run. But an advantage of that kind spoils fast; you use it right now or you might as well have thrown it away.

I pushed off toward the junction. Since I had the time, I treated myself to doing all kinds of hot-doggy stuff on my run down the hill, enjoying the experience as my own audience; long ago I'd have despised someone who did big, vigorous, show-offy turns like these, but back then, my knees hadn't hurt after a long day on skis.

When I got down far enough to pick up the old ski trail, it was full of brush in the center, but along the north side, where the tall pines and firs shaded it during summer and the ice lay on the ground till late spring, it was still more than clear enough. And three or four meters of powder will cover most of the rocks, bushes, and odds and ends; probably in the old days, if this much snow had fallen, the people who owned and ran that abandoned ski resort would have thought they had died and gone to heaven. Chances were they had died, anyway, at least by now.

Resuna, trying to give me a balanced view, kept talking about the ecological damage. It reminded me of the glaciers that had already eaten old towns like Crested Butte and Leadville, and might well bury towns as far south as Santa Fe before they were done, and the scablands that now covered the Rio Grande valley, caused by all the ice dams forming and breaking up on the tributaries that sent scouring floods down the river every third year or so.

Me, I just enjoyed the fact that the deepest, most untouched snow I would ever encounter was all spread out in front of me, and it was all mine. I shot down that hill feeling more and more like a teenager, bouncing and bobbing, spraying huge rooster-tails of snow behind me—what the hell, it might conceivably call attention to me, and make it more likely that Lobo would set up the ambush that I would be trying to trip.

After checking the satellite image of my path, I turned out of the old ski run with tremendous momentum and dashed across a small meadow, then shot through a grove of aspen. As I ascended the gentle slope up to a low saddle, I coasted to an almost-stop, let myself fall forward to conserve the last tiny bit of momentum, and then hurled myself up the slope in the closest thing to a flying herringbone you can do. In a few seconds I had covered the hundred meters or so to the top, and I coasted to a spot among the trees from which I looked down on the junction of the two old roads, an easy minute away, and rested for a moment.

Resuna asked me why I enjoyed this so much. I tried to make sure that Resuna understood the exhilaration of running on your own best skills, far out from any other people, in spectacular country, but I had little hope that it would be such a compelling explanation that One True would allow more people to come out to the wilderness. Better to pack humans together in cities, from an engineering and energy-efficiency standpoint, and the small amount of necessary pollution could be concentrated into a more easily handled point source. The all-but-mortally damaged ecology of the Earth just plain couldn't handle the extra load that tourists would impose, not just yet anyway. Probably, at best, I had supplied One True with something that it would want to introduce, as a "new" idea, in another generation or two when the Earth was well on its way back to health.

I thought it was possible, too, that the experience of the run through the trees might be copied into quite a few people's memories. Like the little boy in Germany whose surprise birthday party, at age eight, was now part of everyone's experience of childhood, or Katie Rafter, the young woman whose wedding we all remembered from her viewpoint, I might be added in as the perfect backcountry skiing experience. Thanks to One True, nowadays everyone who really needed or wanted an experience could be assured of having a vivid memory of the best possible version of it. It was even possible that the total social benefit from my addition to the library might outweigh the contribution of bringing Lobo in.

I leaned forward, pushed off, and slid onto the shallow slope beyond, skiing a single, big C–curve down onto the old road. In the low temperature, the fresh-fallen snow squeaked under my skis. A very dim circle of sun was appearing high in the sky in the south; you could almost imagine it might come out.

Every cowboy hunter I ever knew agreed that there had to be a tiny touch of the cowboy in every cowboy hunter, and I suppose that's true. I always had a streak of pride in me that Resuna could do nothing with. Just now, having made such a good run, that part of my nature was truly kicking in; I hoped that Lobo had seen me, partly because I wanted to attract his attention and flush him from cover, but also because—Resuna insisted that I admit this—because he was obviously a highly skilled, experienced outdoorsman, and I wanted his respect.

I started trudging up the gentle slope of the old road, planting and pushing like a beginner. This wouldn't be nearly the fun that skiing down had been.

I would have to move in an irregular pace, sometimes openly, sometimes with more stealth, sometimes rushing ahead and sometimes dogging it, to throw his rhythm off. It's easy to surprise a guy who moves along at a steady pace in a predictable path. It's harder when he's alternately rushing and dallying, hiding and showing himself, giving you too much data to analyze but not enough information to figure him out. We'd see if a cowboy could handle that any better than a hunter.

For the next two hours, as I covered about half the distance back to camp, I stuck with that plan. Now and again I'd skate hard and rush along like a rocket; every so often I'd just sit down and have something to eat. Sometimes I'd cut off a couple bends on the road by skiing across a meadow, thoroughly exposed to view; sometimes I'd climb up over a tree-covered ridge, taking it slow and disappearing for a while. Nothing happened; as Nordic skiing, it was moderately interesting, and as job performance, it was a flat zil.

Another satellite gap passed quietly as I climbed over one of those ridges; nothing happened during that time except that I really had to poke around to find a way up, after discovering a big brush-fall in my path. From the top I did a big series of slow, graceful turns, killing time to throw his rhythm off. Maybe I threw it off so far that he never saw me at all, or wasn't there, I thought to Resuna.

Resuna instantly pointed out that I was playing all the odds right and my job was to keep doing that; success would come eventually. I told it I felt like I was running *Reader's Digest* instead of Resuna.

I had another cup of tomato soup. It's the most wonderful food there is, if you're skiing XC all day—hot water, salt, sugar, and a few vitamins and some flavor, all the essentials and nothing superfluous.

By the time I hit the third satellite gap, I was starting to feel like the characters in the old flatscreen movies who say to each other, solemnly, that it's "quiet. Yeah. Too quiet." I wasn't far from where I'd found his trail the first day. Still no sign of him. Maybe he was off doing whatever it is that cowboys do when they aren't stealing from society, terrorizing homeowners, raping little girls, interfering with ecological reconstruction, and congratulating themselves on what fine free people they are because they don't have a copy of Resuna to tell them that they're acting badly. Maybe he was around the next bend.

Adding to a sense of security that I knew to be false, the sun had burned through the nimbus layer, which had retreated rapidly to the east, leaving flocks of big thin mare's-tail cirrus scattered across the sky. The mare's-tails had chased after the nimbus in turn, and now the late afternoon sky was perfectly clear and blue; the sun was warming things up quickly; and at this very tail end of the afternoon, it was turning into a day I could enjoy.

I was beginning to feel a certain affection for Lobo, anyway. He'd given me an excuse to be back out here, in this season, after all these years. Now and then I heard a thundering crash, as the little added warmth undid some of the last-formed January's ice. Two ravens flew urgently, black shadows moving in straight lines against the perfect blue, wasting no time, because the carrion they eat is scattered and rare, winter kill that might be buried at any moment by another snowfall. Thanks to Lobo, I was getting one more look at it all.

I stopped all to watch a bunch of big, thick icicles that had probably been growing in the depression in the cliff face since November, dripping in the sunlight, dropping water back into the little hot spring that had spawned them; it hissed now and then as a cold drop found a spot of hot rock. A little stream of steam rose from the spring and enveloped the icicles, but it looked to me like the sun was sweeping away the steam for the most part, and the icicles must be losing more to their dripping than they were gaining from condensation. The real widespread riot of life that is Rocky Mountain spring was still three months away, but the living things were joining the resistance against winter everywhere.

Another bend brought me to a place where an elk herd had crossed; I stopped to have some coffee, being profligate with rations now that I had less than an hour to go back to camp. One set of very big tracks, three running to average, and one average set where the feet all came down closer together than they did in the others—looked like a bull, three cows, and a yearling. Probably the same ones I'd seen drinking from Dead Mule Creek the day before.

The wind had died down. Other than the gurgle of coffee in my throat, and a far off *flump* from snow falling off trees now and then, there wasn't a sound. I might have stepped, for that moment, into a photograph. I looked up at the snow reflecting off the glaciers on the peaks, and thought that I'd have plenty of time to return to the shelter. My thigh muscles were hot from the exertion, but not in pain; the only part that hurt was the part that always does, my arches and insteps—there's something about the motion of skiing that just works those muscles harder than anything else, and I hadn't been on skis enough in the last few years to build the right muscles. It wasn't agony; just an annoying ache that made me look forward to taking aspirin before dinner, with maybe some

wine to wash it down, and rubbing my legs with an analgesic oint-
ment before bed.

Well, since home was close, and now that the coffee had put
more heart and attention in me, it was probably time to get going
again. I pushed off and got into a nice big, slow skating motion,
mostly keeping the poles tucked.

A shape didn't quite work, but almost should have, in the
bushes to the left of the trail up ahead—a human shape, lying
down. His cammies were just slightly off, maybe, for the dirt he
was lying on, or he was stretched out just a hair too much and the
line of him against the line of the bush didn't look right, or something like that. You can't always explain how you know. The figure
stretched out prone on the frozen mud of a windswept bare patch,
among all that gray-green crunchy, broken sage, was undoubtedly
a man.

I kept skiing, just as I had been, though I felt like rough hands
were squeezing my bowels. Right now I knew he was there, he
knew I was here, and I was one bare point up on him because I
knew that he knew. He could take a shot at me from this distance,
but if he did, the IR signature to the overhead satellite would give
One True an exact fix on his location, and he had no way to know
that I didn't have a dozen backups waiting to jump in. In less than
three minutes, there'd be the third and final satellite gap of the day,
but I didn't know whether he knew that, or had a way to know
that, or cared. Regardless of whether he knew or cared or not, I
didn't want to move into his ambush just as my communications
with the outside world went dead.

I couldn't even be sure that he had seen me, either. He hadn't
moved a hair since I showed up. In my last remaining instant of
satellite time before the gap, I called in a wide-angle image that
covered a square kilometer centered on me over the last thirty seconds, zoomed onto him, blew it up, and saw that he hadn't moved
at all for the whole time.

I slipped off the road and behind a big heap of rocks, figuring I might as well try something. People have been known to fall asleep on watch. Just maybe that had happened, or he had zoned out one way or another. Maybe he was lying there with his eyes shut, and had not yet seen me at all. If and when he awoke, or opened his eyes, probably in just a few minutes, he'd see my tracks. But it was just possible that if I skied down the steep slope to my left—flashing through his field of vision for a few seconds—I could get behind a little crag that stuck out of the hillside there, scoot around it like a bunny, climb up the other side, and have him from behind. And if he did wake up and saw my tracks, I figured he wouldn't have time to move into any new ambush position; he'd have to either run, or slug it out from where he was.

I pushed off down the steep slope, going as fast and straight as I could, to minimize my exposure.

I bounded over a couple of bumps that hadn't been visible beneath the thick layer of powder, used them to change direction so that I'd present a somewhat worse target, and picked up as much speed as I could, the skis bouncing around on the edge of getting away from me.

Normally, out in backcountry like this, to be safe, I'd have snowplowed down a slope like this, ski tips close together, trailing edges splayed, digging in with my inner edges to slow down, so that I'd have more control; but normally in backcountry the risk is twisting an ankle, not getting shot. I was going down this slope like an old-time bump skier used to go down the trashed-out prepared slopes, just as if this had been a carefully groomed safe area, with a rescue crew standing by and the ski patrol watching. The skis slammed against yet another bump. My knees felt older than the rest of me.

For a moment, I was sliding sideways, just over the line into out of control. Then I got the uphill edges carving into the snow again, drove the pole in hard and reversed direction in a stem christie, and rocketed down the last part of the slope to slip behind that crag. I turned back and forth until I was practically snowplowing uphill, and finally finished up, grabbing a quick deep breath through my raised face screen, facing an empty hill. There had been no shot; without the satellite contact I had no way to know whether he had even moved. I felt blind.

Resuna informed me that I had fourteen minutes, twelve seconds to go until I'd be back on-line with the next satellite. That was too long to wait for Lobo to come creeping around looking for me, so I got busy. I pushed slowly downslope around the crag, taking a couple of minutes about it, sticking as close as I could to the rock face to make my tracks less apparent and keep closer to cover; some of these cowboys were so primitive, back in the old days, that they had been using old pure-projectile rifles without augmented sighting, hypervelocity, or homing ammunition.

On one occasion I remembered, a cowboy had caught Sue D'Alessandro in the open and taken four shots at her without hitting her. That failed to cheer me. For all I knew, Lobo might have stolen good modern equipment.

I was still wondering why there had been no shots so far. Was he asleep? Had he had a heart attack while waiting for me up there? I wished I had an infrared shot from the satellite.

By the time I reached the bottom of the crag, I was crouched low and just barely gliding along, getting steadily more nervous. Resuna had started to chatter, trying to cheer me up, and I'd had to tell it to shut up, and let me have my whole mind to think with. The slope down to the creek below me was streaked with the blue shadows of the scattered trees and snowdrifts, reaching far across the glaring white. In less than ten minutes I would have satellite coverage again.

Trying to make haste slowly, I got off the snow onto some sheltered gravel and took a full minute to reset my flexis, putting them into the snowshoe configuration. It drained the stored power in my suit considerably, but with luck this whole thing would be settled in the next twenty minutes, and besides, I would be putting out a heavy load of body heat soon enough, which would get me recharged.

I stepped onto the snow; I hadn't let the flexi cool enough after reconfiguring, and it was hot enough to flash some of the snow to steam. The loud hiss and puff of vapor startled me, and I said "Shit," perfectly audibly. If the burst of steam and the bang hadn't given me away already, surely my voice had.

With cover blown, speed was all I had—and maybe unpredictability. I kicked off the flexis, dumped my pack, drew my tranquilizer gun, and set about climbing up over the crag, coping with an unfamiliar surface smeared with snow and ice, with a mixture of rotten stone. That first face was about twelve feet high, broken and irregular enough to be feasible for three-pointing, but not at all easy, and I was feeling the effects of the long day.

Still, nothing happened; no shot whizzed by, or pocked the rocks, or stung me. No one shouted. When I looked out at the rough, snow-covered slope, which I did in every spare second, I saw nothing moving and I might as well have been all alone.

After that first face, the upper part of the crag was a tumble of boulders, which I could scramble over on all fours, staying as low as I could, off the skyline. It was still a terribly long way to the top, and if Lobo came around, I was going to be a sitting duck up here on the rocks. I kept pushing and I have to admit that I was starting to feel the first nasty whispers of panic; Resuna moved in to soothe that.

Less than five minutes after having stupidly let off that puff of steam and given my position away, I was ready to poke my head out and take a look toward the brushy up slope above, where I had first seen Lobo. I drew a deep breath and let Resuna have its full effect, calming and preparing me; this was frightening, and I needed the clear head that Resuna could give me.

When I peered over the edge of the rocks, he was in exactly the same position. I raised my head further, and still he did nothing. He was still out of tranquilizer-gun range, so I couldn't just put a shot into him.

I adjusted the sun filter on my face mask and kicked up magnification. He was propped on his elbows in the snow; no one could possibly put both elbows down into snow like that, in a jacket that wasn't heated, and stay in that position for as long as he had; your hands would go to sleep and you wouldn't be able to grip anything, not to mention the excruciating pain after a while. I couldn't see his face because of the way his Stetson covered it, and all I could see of one hand was—*what*?

I notched magnification still further and zoomed in for a better look. That hand was oddly undetailed: perfectly smooth, without hairs, any unevenness in skin color, or wrinkles, and its shape was long and delicate, like a female model—*or an old-type clothing-store mannequin*—

I felt the terrible blow to the back of my head, and my eyes blurred and stung. Pure training and instinct made me try to roll over. I got onto my side, curling to protect my gut. I had just time to see a boot heel at the center of the crazy star of my shattering face-screen. I sucked in a breath, trying to get my arms and legs to answer me, before a second blow to the back of my head drove my broken face-screen forward into the snow. As the darkness smeared across my vision, and a big chunk of broken face-screen forced its way into my mouth and onto my tongue through my sore teeth and bruised lips, I could taste the icy tang of snow mixed with mud.

❧❧ **When I woke** up, the only thing that I could remember with any certainty was that someone had given me soup one or more times during the indefinite period while my mind endlessly repeated a few disconnected, frightening images—things that floated in out of a dark, noisy void, then drifted back out. I had little idea where my body had been going or what it had been doing while my mind was bouncing aimlessly through the void.

I had been eating soup. Someone had fed it to me. I remembered the soup because I had been so embarrassed about throwing it up on myself, and on the hand and arm of the person feeding me.

That was another clue. I realized that I remembered big, gentle hands cleaning me off, and then more dreams in which I wandered down trails in dark forests—not the friendly, familiar night forest in which I had spent much of my working life, where I knew what everything was and could savor the sounds and smells, but the terrifying confusion of the forests of childhood nightmares.

But now I was definitely sliding back into the real world, and I didn't remember what I had been doing when I had left. The immediate environment in which I had been sleeping was chilly, but I was warm under covers. That brought back another memory: sometimes a soft, warm male voice urged me to crawl out of the covers, across a rough, cold floor, and use a chamber pot. Afterwards the same strong, weather-roughened hands that fed me would clean me up before putting me back to bed.

Now that I was aware of what had been going on and what I had been doing, I was also aware that the same events had been repeating for a while; I think I must have been given broth, and thrown it up, at least three times, perhaps more. Well, continuity of memory is one of the signs of recovering brain function, and to judge from the pain in the back of my scalp and the dull ache in the middle of my head, I must have had a pretty severe blow to the head.

I asked Resuna what had happened and what I should do.

Resuna wasn't there.

I was so frightened, and so shocked, that I fainted. When I woke again, I reached for Resuna, and it still wasn't there. I thought about pulling the covers aside and looking around me, but that seemed like too much work, and I was already tired from worrying about where Resuna had gone. I let myself fall asleep again.

I'm not sure how many more intervals of lucidity like that I had in the next hours or days. Eventually I woke up and saw some light and heard some noise. The presence of reality was almost as comforting as the presence of Resuna would have been, and later, when I ate, the world seemed almost normal.

It was still a very long, indeterminate time—I'd have guessed at least two or three more days—until I was conscious for any period longer than five minutes at a time. When a brain takes a hard blow—and a mind loses its controlling meme—it takes days or even weeks for anything beyond the most basic functions to be restored. By the point where I remembered the last few days, and realizing that I must be still up in the mountains, my time sense was coming back, so that I was beginning to group my experiences into day and night. For some stretch of time, Lobo—I had realized that I must be his prisoner—would go in and out frequently, about one errand or another. Probably I was lying in an important work or living area of his. Then the lights would be off and Lobo wouldn't come; that must be the time while he slept. Most likely were that "Lobo active, lights on" versus "Lobo absent, lights off" corresponded to day and night—I just didn't know which went with which.

One day the soup was good but different—I found chunks of meat, jackrabbit I thought, plus bits of wild greens that he must have gathered and dried, and a flavor I finally identified as canned stewed tomatoes. With irradiation and non-reacting containers, canned stuff was good for centuries, so it wasn't surprising that it was edible, but it was surprising that somewhere he had acquired several years' stock of it. That information was vital—it helped to explain how a man could be living off the land in the high Rockies and not come down with scurvy—but there was no Resuna to upload the information to One True.

After a while I was able to look around and see the room. It was a refinished cave, probably an old earthquake crack or maybe an old mine shaft, and the part I could see was pritnear ten meters long by three high by four wide, quite a big space. Iron pipes gurgled all around the walls, and when I put a hand on one next to the bed it was very warm, though not hot enough to burn. That answered one riddle: he was keeping his place warm with a combination of good insulation and water from some hot spring, and it wasn't visible to a satellite because it looked like every other hot spring.

The walls were lined with forty-year-old canned goods, all with that silly "atom" sign that meant that they had been irradiated—in the old days, when people were allowed to have any old set of irrational fears they wanted to, with no Resuna to keep them in tune with reality, so many people had been afraid of irradiated food that the government had required those labels—I guess so that people could avoid clean, safe irradiated food and enjoy stuff that might be spoiled or contaminated instead. Nowadays the food was exactly as safe as it had ever been, and Resuna kept you from worrying.

Any place on the wall where there wasn't a shelf of food, there were portraits of people. Out of habit, I reached for Resuna to tell me who they were. Once again, I was all alone in my mind. I pulled the covers over my head, curled up tightly, and went back to sleep.

When I woke again, my eyes were focusing, my head ached only slightly, I could form more or less coherent thoughts, and Resuna was still not there. For the first time in a long time I had had many hours of real sleep, not the torment of half-waking nightmares. Almost, if I hadn't felt so lonely in the absence of Resuna, I'd have been comfortable.

Lobo came in, looked at me for a moment, and something must have been different in my facial expression. "I *did* hit the back of your head hard enough to kill any normal person," he said, with what sounded like mild frustration, "I'm sure of it. But I guess you're a hard-headed man, Currie Curran, and even though by all rights you ought to have a fractured skull, all you got was a concussion." He looked intently into my eyes, as if he thought I might explain what had gone wrong; after a breath, he said, "Looks like you're feeling better."

"You're Lobo," I said, unable to think of anything any smarter to say.

"Stupid name I gave myself when I was just a kid," he said, obviously embarrassed. "I guess I'm lucky I didn't end up as the Masked Avenger or something. My real name is Dave Singleton, if you want to use it." He was carrying something under his arm, and when he brought it closer, I saw he had a loaf of fresh bread, a cutting board, and a knife. "You going to be reasonable, Curran, and not go grabbing for the knife? If you say yes, we can share this while it's warm."

"Deal."

He sat down and sawed off a couple big slices, handing them to me. They tasted wonderful. He cut a couple for himself, ate quietly for a while, then said, "Funny thing. You might say I'm the reason for your existence. I'm the last cowboy, at least I think, and therefore, Curran, you're the last cowboy hunter. But then if you weren't hunting me, I'd just be a damned eccentric living out in the woods, so I guess you're the reason why I'm a cowboy, at least as much as I'm the reason why you're a cowboy hunter."

I let what he had said lay there between us. Too much response, too soon, kills most people's urge to talk, and I needed to learn many things that I'd only get if he told me.

I wanted to know why I was still alive; if he had been able to bring me back here, to nurse me back to life, he could just as easily have carried me far enough away so that my transponder wouldn't lead people to his hiding place, say to some stretch of thin ice on a mountain lake. Then he could have filled my outside suit with rocks and pushed me under. Probably nobody would ever have found me, and I'd just be another one of those hunters that disappeared during a satellite blackout. In the condition I'd been in, I'd never've even known he was doing it.

So why hadn't he? I could think of absolutely nothing that a cowboy would want with a living cowboy hunter. He ought to know—would know, to have survived so long—that because the individual parts of One True are nothing, there is no point in trying to take one of them hostage. One True will just lose the part, direct the individual copies of One True to comfort the mourners, and go on.

After a long while of just sitting together, during which he said nothing and I said nothing, I was unable to think of a more subtle approach, so I just asked, "Why didn't you kill me, Dave?"

The big man shrugged. "Well, I guess I had a bunch of reasons, but none of them sound all that good to me right now. Probably I'm just being stupid and acting contrary to my own interests. Most likely it's because I've got this great big phobia: I'm real, real, real afraid of dying by being hurt so bad I can't take care of myself, and starving or freezing a short way from home. It's what all my nightmares are about, and whenever something goes wrong, or I get sick or have a near-miss accident, it's the first thing I worry about.

"So I'd just hit you real hard and you weren't moving, and I checked you for a pulse, and damn, you had one. Well, I could've just pulled the electrets out of your suit, opened the heat reservoirs, and left you to freeze. I could have gone real low tech and cut your throat. Either of those would have made perfect sense. Instead I looked down at you and said to myself, *he's going to die here, helpless with no one to find him. I can't just leave him.*

"Well, I told myself I was just being silly and sentimental, but once I had let myself feel that I couldn't leave you to die in the snow far away from any help, the feeling carried over, I guess I'd have to say, to other ideas, so that I also felt funny about banging your head with that log again. Once you start caring *how* you kill somebody, I guess, you're already starting to think about *not* killing them, if you see what I mean, and—there I was. The moment was past. The blood was cold. I plain old flat out couldn't do it, at least not out there in the snow, far away from help or friends, where you might never be found. Not right there and then, anyway, not unless I really had to.

"Now, mind you, I might still take you out and slit your throat, later, but if I do, it'll be quick and clean, and you won't just lie there dying for hours, and I'll put you someplace where they'll find you and your family and friends won't have to wonder what happened. I haven't entirely made up my mind on that."

I kept my expression as neutral as I could, just like they taught us in training. "I see your problem, Dave. Is there anything I can do to, uh, influence this decision?" I was desperately trying to cue up Resuna for advice, but Resuna remained absent.

"No," Lobo said. "You can try but I'm not sure the ideas you'd have to use, and think of, would come naturally to you. How many years have you been running Resuna?"

"Twenty-six years next November, but, uh, I don't think I'm running Resuna right now."

Lobo looked at me curiously. "That was the impression I had, but I wasn't sure how to ask you. Usually Resuna has more options than the native personality, and it can recover faster; I expected to talk to Resuna whenever you finally came around, and to have to ask it to let me talk to you. But . . . you mean it's quiet in your head? Nobody in there but you, listening or talking?"

I shrugged. "I can remember Resuna's voice, but I can't seem to get it back. And I've been trying for a while, so it's not some temporary thing."

"Interesting. Who'd've thought a cowboy hunter, of all people, would be a good candidate for dememing? More bread?"

"Sure. You're a good cook."

"Not much else to do out here but please myself, and I'm sort of a fussy guy, or I was in the old days." He cut me off another chunk; I ate it more slowly than the last, savoring how good it was. I reflexively reached to store the experience with Resuna, and again it wasn't there.

Dave—I was starting to think of him as that, rather than Lobo—was staring at me, obviously curious, tugging at his lower lip with its few days stubble of beard. His hands were clean, though heavily callused, and his trimmed-short fingernails had no dirt under them. "You just tried to call up Resuna, again, didn't you?"

"Yeah," I admitted, seeing no reason to lie about it. "Every couple of minutes, I forget that I have this problem, and reach for Resuna, the way your tongue looks for a missing tooth. And every time I reach for Resuna, it's not there *at all*. Nothing like the temporary weird feeling when my copy is being replaced, and for a couple of hours I can't connect to it easily, and the new copy isn't yet using the old memories effectively—that's still Resuna, just Resuna that's hard to reach. This is just as if it had *never* been there." I ate another couple of bites. "What did you mean when you said I was a good candidate for . . . dememing, was that the word?"

"That was the word," he agreed. "Now and again, you know, people do get rid of a meme, or lose one, or it gets knocked out of them somehow. In the old days some of the cowboys were just people who woke up one day with Resuna not running, and they'd slip away and come join us. I don't imagine that's what very many people did. I'd bet that most people reacted the way you've been doing, so that soon as they woke up with Resuna not there, they called up One True on a computer or via some friend, to get another copy loaded in. But a few people would suddenly just not have a working copy of Resuna, and wouldn't want another one, and those people would run off to become cowboys.

"And—this wasn't so much the way it was with Resuna as it was with some of the older memes—sometimes you could trick a meme out of people's heads. Sometimes the drugs they used to use on mental patients would work, and sometimes shock, like an electric shock, or a big dose of insulin, or a blow to the head. Which I guess is how you got dememed. So what's it feel like to not have Resuna in your head?"

"Don't you know? I mean, you never have had it, so you must know what it's like."

"Yeah, but what I'm asking you, or I guess what I should have asked you, is what does the *change* feel like? How's it different now from what it was before?"

I thought about it, taking my time. When a guy saves your life, and would have had every reason to just kill you, you owe him at least the courtesy of a good answer to his questions. I knew if I had been running Resuna, like normal, it would have had some very convincing argument against that feeling, but right now it was just me. After the long pause, I just said, "Oh, like, uh, it feels a bit—a little bit—like it used to feel before memes, when a friend would die or leave. All of a sudden there's somebody you keep wanting to talk to and can't, you know? Not too different from . . ." I stared at the blank rock wall opposite and let the thought form. "Not too different from waking up from a dream, calling for somebody you only knew in the dream, and then knowing they aren't there and can't be there."

Dave nodded. "Poetic." When I stared blankly at him, he said, "Well, that's one effect we've identified. Clearly being dememed makes people get poetic." He smiled, and I made myself smile back, though I wasn't sure that I had any sense of humor about that subject just then. After an awkward pause he added, "I got some coffee brewing, too, if you'd like some. Do I have to tie you up every time I leave the room?"

"I guess not. I wouldn't get far, naked, and I'm not stupid enough to try anything yet."

"Glad you put the 'yet' in there," he said. "I'd have to be pretty damn dumb to expect you not to lie to me, but I'd sure appreciate it if you don't lie to me more than you feel you have to, and if you don't let me catch you doing it too often."

I considered. "Why don't you just figure that I won't pass up any good chance for an escape, but I won't do any petty shit that just makes both of us uncomfortable? I'll lie if it'll help me get away, but not just to fuck with you."

"Deal. Let me go get that coffee. Bet you're tired of jackrabbit soup by now, too; in another hour I'll be done cooking up an elk loaf with some reconstituted potatoes."

My stomach rumbled and I said, "I think I can help you out with that. How many days have I not eaten solid food?"

"Since you got hit on the head," Dave said. "Sorry not to be able to tell you more than that, but it's always possible that you have a perfectly good copy of Resuna, and what's keeping Resuna from restarting itself, and turning you again, might be nothing more than having lost track of the time—it does depend partly on that internal clock it creates inside you when it takes over. So, I can't answer that question."

I shrugged. "Well, anyway, I can tell it's been a long time, and I don't really have to have things more specific than that. And the food sounds wonderful."

Dave went out to the kitchen, and I continued to sit on the bed, not really thinking of anything, just enjoying being awake and not feeling awful. There would be time enough for more advanced pleasures, later, perhaps, but right now sitting and waiting for a good meal, and being well again, was about all I needed.

When Dave came back with the coffee, which smelled so wonderful that I was beginning to wonder if he had been slipping You-4 into my soup (maybe because making me happy all the time would help keep me dememed? I didn't know a thing about how dememing worked—hadn't even known it was possible until it happened to me), I had thought of another question to ask him. "How did you build this place? I know that sounds like a stupid question."

"Not really. What you want to know is how I got this place without tipping off the satellite, and the answer was good luck and patience. I found this old mine, a hundred yards from a hot spring, half-choked with dirt, and dug it out. I carried the dirt with me, on the regular rounds during the day, in a pack I made from a gunny sack with a few holes cut into it to let the dirt dribble out as I walked. It took a long time but I had a long time. The first couple of years I lived in a shelter like yours, basic military-surplus thing, under the overhang, where there was room to set it up. After two years of digging out a pack-load of dirt per day, I had a nice medium-sized room to live in. And now after a couple of decades, I've got a bigger house than I ever had back before I went off to be a cowboy. With ten years of a pack-load a day, if you're careful not to miss a day, you can have a pretty big hole."

"You're still digging?"

"It's something to do. I have a room in back that's going to be a warm, comfy library; it happened I found an old armchair that was in great shape, so that made me think how much I would enjoy just having that as my regular place to sit, enough to bother bringing it up here, but then I didn't exactly have the perfect place to put it. So I went looking for a rug to go with it, and a floor lamp, and when I had all of that, well, two bookcases fell into my hands, which was fate's way of telling me that that armchair needed a library to be in. And I already had some books. All this finding stuff and figuring out what to do with it was all across a number of years, mind you, while I was still digging out the hot-tub room, so I had lots of time to do my planning."

"A *hot tub*?"

"Well, I've got hot water, more than I can use. Might as well. Though I admit that I also use the tub for laundry, and dishes. Room in it, though, for three or four people to soak; I just like having the room. Anyway, once I got the tub room done, it was time to start on the library. Figure another two years and that'll be done as well, which will be good. I ain't as young as I used to be, and a warm place with good light to read by is starting to seem more and more important, as I think about what kind of a setup would be best for a rickety old man."

I looked at him intently for a minute, and then finally blurted out, "Jeez, I can see why you'd need to plan for when you're old, but you don't look a day older than when I thought I'd sent you over the cliff."

He laughed. "Well, *you* look awful good for an old fart of your age, Curran. Especially for one who was in a dangerous occupation for a long time. People living a long time and people looking younger than they are are things that happen, you know, with better medical treatment and all."

"I guess so," I said. I didn't believe him. In the first place, except for his recent foray into rape and robbery, Dave hadn't had access to much of that medical technology, nor could he have had much in the last fifteen or twenty years.

Also, he was exaggerating about how well preserved I was. I could tell you ten things that are different in my appearance, now, from what it was ten years ago: more pounds in bad places, less hair in good places, some lines and wrinkles. Dave, on the other hand, looked *exactly* the way he had looked when I had last seen him in the flesh—better, in fact, since now he wasn't tired out by a long chase. Somehow nothing had happened to his face or body at all. My degree of preservation might have been mildly interesting in our present world full of well-preserved old guys; but his was dead solid freakish. That he was trying to conflate the two suggested that he was unobservant (unlikely, in someone who had survived so long out here) or more likely that he was trying to put one over on me (very likely, in a cowboy).

I thought about pressing the point, but either he was telling the truth (and there was nothing more to tell) or he was lying (and wasn't about to tell me), and what he would say would be the same either way.

So I changed the subject. "And have you been living on canned goods and hunting all this time?"

"If you're a decent hunter and there's just one of you in a wilderness area, it isn't that hard to keep yourself fed. Didn't even have to work that hard. The canned stuff is good for the things I can't grow, but I grew some of my own stuff too. I'd plant vegetables on hillsides under upside-down aquariums, which make perfect ready-to-go coldframes—I raided a couple of old pet stores in

Gunnison and Montrose for those. My plantings were too small to show much from orbit, as long as I kept them scattered out pretty wide, which meant I'd have to do some walking, but I had time to do it. Now and then a deer would smell something it wanted and knock over an aquarium, or a gopher or rabbit would tunnel in for it, but not as often as you'd think, because herbivores basically aren't too smart, and my growing sites were so scattered that if they raided one aquarium and figured out how to do that, by the time they ran into another one, like as not they had forgotten. And I could combine making the rounds of my aquariums with my hunting. Even doing all that stuff, I had plenty of time to dig and think. It's been lonely work, hard work, but it ain't worn me down yet."

I shrugged. "It might even be why you still look so young," I said, hoping to keep him thinking I was believing him. "Abundant exercise and a good diet, far away from all the places where there are leftover plagues from the wars—probably a healthier life than I've been leading." I took another sip of coffee. "This is as good as I get at home. Reconstituted?"

"Yeah, I stole a reconstitutor a while back."

That reminded me, for the second time in a few minutes. Since I couldn't afford to offend him, I did my best to repress a shudder.

All the same, he must have seen the change at once. "What is it?"

I don't usually like to pick a fight with my host, and I *was* naked, disarmed, and completely at his mercy. Plus we'd already had a theoretical discussion about his cutting my throat. But the unfortunate habit of a lifetime—saying whatever popped into my head—caused me to blurt, "When I was prepping for this mission, One True took me through Kelly's memory, and all I can say—" I stared at him and tried to reconcile this soft-spoken, seemingly gentle man with Kelly's vision of him bouncing on top of her and laughing at her cries of pain and fear "—shit, I don't *know* what to say. How could you *do* a thing like that to a little girl, and her mother?"

He looked puzzled and said, "I didn't have much choice; they'd caught Nancy a long time back, even before your group caught up with me, and once they found out she was a cowboy's wife, they really poured on the Resuna copies until she was completely theirs. And Kelly never had a chance—she was probably given her first copy of Resuna before she was three years old. But you know what Robert Frost said—home is where, when you've gotta go there, they'll have to take you in—and I was good and sick, so I paid them the visit. I was damn lucky to get away, and even luckier that I could dememe them long enough to have my chance to say hello to my wife and daughter; there are days when I feel like, now that I've done that, I can die easier."

I was staring at him now, unable to believe what was either an audacious lie, or . . . the thought connected. "You mean you not only raped that poor child, but she was your *own daughter?*"

Now he was staring. If there'd been a third person there cruel enough to laugh, he'd probably have busted a gut at the spectacle of two men who had suddenly dropped their brains on the floor and didn't have anything with which to think of picking them up. Finally, he sputtered, "What the fuck are you talking about, you crazy fucking idiot?"

I was not used to being called a crazy fucking idiot—with everyone running Resuna, profanity and insult are both very rare—but despite being startled, I could see that he was pretty stressed. And I knew that this wasn't a turn the conversation should have taken, but hell if I saw any way out but forward. "That's what was in her memory," I said. "I played through the whole memory copy, and believe me, I'd rather not have, and I wish like all shit that she didn't have that memory, but she does. You came in with a gun—the poor kid had never even seen one before, do you realize how much innocence you were spoiling?— you threatened them into giving you medicine and food and their reconstitutor, and then you made that little girl watch while you raped her mom, and then you raped her. That's what she remembers. And thanks to the transference from One True, I remember every bit of it, and you better believe I wish I didn't. Now *you* tell me that was your wife and daughter that you did that to. Well, ek-fucking-scuse me, and I guess now you'll kill me for saying it, but out of all the dirty, vicious, hate-filled cowboys I've ever hunted, you are the only one I've ever really despised." It was about there that I noticed I was shouting into his face, standing over him where he sat on his stool, fists on my hips like I was going to yell him into submission, with some of the effect spoiled by the fact that I was buck-naked.

Dave stared into space. If I'd had pants to throw on and a weapon to hand, I could have taken him right then, right there, without much difficulty, I'm sure. As I watched, a tear ran down his cheek. "You damn well ought to be crying," I said.

He wiped his eyes, stared at me, and said, "Of course you believe that memory."

"What are you going to try to do, pull some Freud-bullshit and tell me she *wanted* to remember something like that, and made it up?"

He shook his head slowly. "Curran, I don't have a damn idea in my head for how to tell you this so you'll believe it, but . . . hey, did you ever meet Kelly? Or just that copy of her memory?"

"Well, of course I just got the copy of her memory! What would you think? One True *never* inflicts unnecessary pain. It wasn't going to make her sit there and tell me all about it. Not when her copy of Resuna could just load the memory up to One True, and my copy could load it down to me, and I would know what had happened to Kelly far more vividly than she could ever have told it, and with no pain to her. Why would we need to meet face-to-face?"

He shrugged, got up, seemed about to speak, stopped himself, looked down at the floor, visibly got himself under control, and started to pace, gulping at his coffee, as if the solution to some hard problem might be anywhere on the floor if he could just find it.

Finally he looked up; the whole silent performance had taken over a minute, and I didn't believe any of it; he'd had days to plan whatever he was going to say now.

"You ought to ask," he said, "why your only access was that copied memory. Couldn't her copy of Resuna have just taken control, so that you could have met her face-to-face? Wouldn't you have had a stronger feeling if you had really known Kelly instead of just importing that one memory? Wouldn't that have motivated you more, if you had looked into her eyes and promised her you'd catch the asshole rat-bastard that did that?"

"Might have," I admitted.

"So, One True can do damn near anything and it couldn't do that for you?"

"It might have hurt her—"

"A *conversation?* Even though it might be emotionally painful for her, it couldn't be as painful as what had already happened. And One True could erase her memory of the conversation easily enough, if it needed to. Hell, it gave Nancy a whole set of imaginary memories about being with squatters in Vegas Ruin, and being a slave there, to replace our marriage. You should've seen how bewildered she was when I dememed her and she suddenly knew who I was—and who she was—again! One True *could* have let you talk to Kelly—should have and would have—if the memory that was copied to you was accurate. Even if it had hurt Kelly at the time, her copy of Resuna could control and erase the pain as necessary. And meanwhile you'd have been just that much more motivated, and she'd have had the comfort of knowing someone was going out there to catch me. *If* One True was telling you the truth, *if* I had really done those things to her, then that was what it should have done, and if it knows us as well as it says it does, it would have done it."

"But I *felt* her personality," I said. "Real and human and twelve years old, not the kind of thing that even One True could make up—"

"Oh, I'm sure One True *started* with some memories from

Kelly, when it created the one it gave you. Probably even copied over some bits and pieces from some adult woman who was raped as a child—the War of the Memes went twenty years and sooner or later pritnear every girl and woman who had the bad luck to live in those years got serbed, so One True probably had a wide selection of rape memories."

"I never serbed anybody," I pointed out, "and I was in the War of the Memes."

"I was too, and I never serbed anybody either!" Dave said. He was glaring at me, dark eyes fierce under his bushy, unkempt brows.

"Until recently when it was your wife and daughter," I said, sneering, maybe hoping he'd just kill me.

"That's what I'm fucking telling you, Curran. The memory is *false*. One True probably started with some of Kelly's fear, from when I broke into the house, which it got via her copy of Resuna. Then it fused in a bunch of rape memories. You damn well know that memes can create memories that you experience as real— weren't you ever hit with Unreconstructed Catholic, or didn't you know someone who was? And don't you remember how everyone who ever ran Unreconstructed Catholic all remembered kindly Sister Agnes and lim koapy Father Jim from first grade at St. Aloysious School? And being their favorite and feeling secure and safe with the Church guarding you? Or Real America's memory of the Fourth of July when you were in eleventh grade and went to the high-school prom in Brightsburg, Vermont, with the red-haired girl that used to pitch for your Little League team? You *know* memes can make you remember things that didn't happen, dammit."

"They *can*," I said, "but One True *doesn't*. Never, never, never. It just helps you understand the memories you have. And anyway, One True isn't a single program dominating your brain; it's just what all the Resunas together make. Your individual Resuna is a much smaller program than the old memes, and it's just a helper for your own personality. It's not going to screw things up for you by making you remember things that didn't happen . . ." My voice was getting softer and I was almost mumbling.

I hated the feeling and wished Resuna were here to help me, but it wasn't. Unfortunately I was realizing a couple of things. First of all, Resuna and the emergent version of One True were the most sophisticated and capable memes; it wasn't smaller because it had less power. Anything any other meme could do, One True could do, easily.

Then a rush of feeling and memory roared through my mind like white noise cranked to ear-bleeding volumes. I was remembering things that had been erased from my memory of my life with Mary, trivial stuff like little fights and moments of anger, that I was better off forgetting—yet still they had happened—yet I was better off not remembering—yet-yet-yet . . . and simultaneously I felt an odd quality to my memories of Mary's love and support during my cowboy hunting days . . . *in fact* she'd been very upset nearly all the times when I went out, and *actually* there were times when I came home and could tell that everything had just been cleaned and fixed up that minute, and *really* there was no Mary to talk to, just her Resuna, as if *in reality* it had been unable to make her function and had just grabbed control and straightened out a mess at home . . . I remembered her throwing the lamp at me the time she had yelled something about days spent in bed crying, and yet another memory seemed to try to crawl over it and say that she had told me that story about a time during the War of the Memes when she was a slave . . . and yet, ghosted over all that, images of my brave, supportive, smiling wife who could send me off to fight cowboys with the warm confidence that I would be back, with a total confidence and love.

Well, that had been very useful for One True to have me remember, hadn't it?

All of those thoughts and feelings rushed through my head in less time than it takes to think a single sentence in words. I hated

Resuna, One True, Mary, the whole of my life, and Dave, not necessarily in that order. I hated myself for having lived for years that way. And most of all I hated the way that it seemed likely that Dave was right. "Shit," I said, flatly. "Shit, shit, shit. You might as well make me the rest of your argument."

He shrugged. "You have the same expression in your eyes that Nancy did as she came out of it. Look, I don't think One True would have put that rape memory into Kelly; it made up the memory to show to you, but it put something different into her head. That's why it didn't set up for you to meet her. Probably it told her that she hid under the bed the whole time I was there, and maybe that I vandalized the place or threatened her. From One True's standpoint, that would make sense—it wouldn't give her any more trauma than it had to for its purposes, so it gave her a false memory that would help her cope with the world she'll have to live in. Probably slightly painful but nothing she can't cope with. And I would bet that the false memory they gave her *doesn't* hurt as much as her few hours of knowing the truth and being herself did. But she did seem to like that little taste of freedom, even with the pain and all. Or maybe I'm just projecting because I wanted her to like them."

"Why would One True give somebody a false memory?" I asked. I was rummaging, hard, in my own memories, trying to get Resuna to come back; I felt so utterly defenseless without it, and I was sure that if only I had One True here, it would have a real answer to all these accusations. "And why should I trust you to be the one telling the truth?"

He looked so directly into my eyes that I sat down as if he had pushed me. For a moment, I wondered if this might not be some sort of hypnosis. "Look," he said. "You know the answer to that perfectly well, even if you don't want to admit it. One difference between me and One True is that I don't have a planet to run. And all those billions of copies of Resuna in everybody's brain are parts of One True. Now since the world began, people have been lying to themselves to get through their day, get through their job—get through their life. How many people have gone to their graves thinking that the boss really valued them, or that they were better off not changing jobs, or that their mother cared about them, or that their children loved them—when any objective observer could have seen it for pure bullshit? Sometimes it's just very useful to believe something that isn't true.

"And you don't care what your individual brain cells do or believe, except as it matters for your convenience, do you? If it makes you happy to have a few thousand of your brain cells think your wife is the most beautiful thing you've ever seen, and respond to her like that, you don't necessarily want those cells to develop the objective opinion that she's actually much plainer than ordinary, do you? Aren't you better off having those deluded little cells in your head telling you different?

"Well, that's what One True needs from its component copies of Resuna, frequently. Much as I hate to defend it, One True's reasons for what it does are not necessarily bad or crazy. One of the troubles with fighting One True, psychologically, for every cowboy I ever knew who wasn't crazy, was that—objectively speaking—we had to admit that One True wasn't evil; oh, it had done some cruel stuff and it had fought the War of the Memes to win, and like that, but unlike so many of the other memes, One True was not out to enslave the human race to some ideal that was meaningful only to it, or force people into behaving according to some crazed code that was a bad parody of an extinct set of ideas, or any of that stuff. It really did intend to benefit human beings and the planet.

"When One True took over, a billion people worldwide were hungry even though there were more than resources enough to feed them; hundreds of disasters were going their way without interference, even though humanity had the brains and resources to control them; and everyone was in fear, even though the only thing they really had to fear was each other, and very few of them really wanted to hurt each other.

"One True gave everyone Resuna, and *became* what everyone needed—something that would ensure that everyone put his whole heart into meeting the global crisis for the next few decades. Earth would be in worse shape without it." He was emphasizing his points as if trying to pound them into me; I couldn't imagine why a cowboy was talking like this.

"So, along the way, sometimes, One True needs an individual to believe something that isn't true. What if a woman wants a particular man, maybe one she got separated from during the War of the Memes, so much that she won't do her work in the farm or factory, and just wants to go looking for him? Resuna keeps the thought of him out of her mind until One True can learn if he's alive or dead, and if he's alive, maybe it's convenient for the Earth, and the whole project of saving the planet, to bring them back together—and maybe it's not. If it is, they get together and there's much rejoicing; if it's not, they don't, and their copies of Resuna keep them from feeling more than a trifling sadness now and then. Who's hurt?

"Or maybe a brother and sister both have genius-level talent for doing the math for the ecological computer models that One True needs them to do. Unfortunately, the brother molested the sister when she was a little girl, and she's afraid of men, afraid of him, and too depressed and angry to do any work. Her copy of Resuna adjusts all that, and bingo, she's functional, she's not unhappy, she and the whole planet gain. Furthermore, his copy of Resuna adjusts him so that he won't do things like that anymore. He's not only happpier, he's a much better person. And the math gets done, part of the Earth gets repaired, fewer children get hurt, and two people who would otherwise have been basket cases of one kind or another work happily side by side. Now who can argue with that? Might not be all that much justice to it but there's pritnear perfect mercy.

"So, Resuna needs to make sure that Kelly does *not* form any part of her identity out of being a cowboy's daughter, and it really doesn't want her forming any ideas about rebellion or freedom or any of that, which young brainy people are very apt to do given half a chance. So instead it creates a memory that will be a barrier, forever, against that side of herself. The minute she thinks of things that are wild and free and uncontrolled—like a cowboy—she thinks of how scared she was by me. And then Resuna comforts her and she doesn't feel so sad anymore, or hurt; all she feels is love and gratitude for Resuna. And Resuna needs you to want to hunt me down—so it gives you that gruesome memory and tells you it's Kelly's. The result is that Kelly grows up to be productive and happy, you catch the cowboy, and everyone is better off. Even the cowboy, who finally has his personality altered so that he can function in the real world. The false memories are good for her, good for you and me, good for One True, might even be good for the future of the planet. And if what you remember doesn't happen to be true, well, it's useful, isn't it?"

The strangest thing about it all, as he sat there and said that to me over our hot coffee, was that he not only didn't sound bitter or sarcastic, he sounded more as if he were just explaining, in a friendly way, to someone who didn't know, how the world worked. It was a good strategy, I realized—I wanted to believe him. And now that I was calming down, the thought no longer made me angry at Resuna or One True. I still wanted to get back as soon as I could. I just felt as if I weren't quite myself.

I sighed and asked, "How do I know, though, that you're telling me the truth?"

He shrugged. "You don't. That's what life was like before Resuna, and if I were still fighting to free the world from it, *and* I thought I could win, I'd say that's what life will be like after Resuna. One of the books I like to reread—*Forks in Time*, even though I'm not cybertao—says 'Certainty is a very overrated quality,' and it's got a point. But then *Surfaces in Opposition* says 'Certainty is what most people prefer to truth, and it cannot be kept from them.' So you slice it whatever way you want, I guess."

I shuddered, feeling as cold as if I had rolled naked in the snow. "I can't seem to make my thoughts come together, at all. And I don't mean to be rude, but I feel incredibly tired."

He nodded. "Well, just making a guess, I'd say that since you've just had an exhausting physical injury, your first good meal in a long time, and a whole big set of emotional shocks, you probably need to sleep. Let's put you to bed—I hope you won't resent that I have to lock the door—and when you're awake again, we can talk more. For right now, I don't have any reason to do anything except feed you and keep you here, till I make up my mind what's to be done."

As soon as he mentioned the idea of sleeping, I realized I'd never heard a more attractive idea. And who could say? Maybe I'd get Resuna back after some more normal sleep, or come up with an idea for escaping and contacting the authorities . . . or I'd feel more sure that Dave was right, and then do something—the lights went out, I heard the lock turning, and I was asleep.

When I woke up, I remembered everything, and got up and carefully made my way to the light switch. I used the chamber pot, and wondered if perhaps I could get a sponge bath or the use of the hot tub soon, because I had spent enough time in a too-warm bed to be pretty rank.

Resuna was still gone, and the ghosted-over memories felt more false; you don't remember a thing as vividly when there isn't a voice in your mind insisting that you do.

There was a knock at the door, and I said, "Sure, come in."

"Saw the light on," Dave said. "You've slept from meal to meal; you want to come out and eat again, and maybe talk some more?"

We'd about finished eating when he said, "Well, I don't know exactly how to put this, Curran, so let me just say it, and say I'm sorry to have to think about this. Now that you're so much better, I'm going to have to decide what to do with you. I like having somebody to talk to, and there'd be room for two here, so if it was just you and me, I'd invite you to be my roommate and that would be all there'd need to be. However, there's a whole big planet out there, and by spring at latest there's going to be another manhunt for me, and I can't afford to have a house guest who's on the other side, if you see what I mean. Nor can I let you go—your copy of Resuna already uploaded enough to One True to give the hunters a much better chance of catching me, and what you know now would pretty much zero them in on this place, so I want the time to move my things and start over somewhere else. I'm way too old to run out in the middle of the night, sleep in trees for a year, and start all over from my skivvies again.

"So, little as I like it, I have to figure you're getting stronger every day and pretty soon locking you in a bedroom won't stop you, or even deter you. And once that's true—which might be tomorrow for all either of us knows—well, then my two choices seem to be to enlist you, or to kill you."

"Uh . . . how do you mean, enlist me?"

"Partner up. Work together. Not really for the cause—I'm not at war with One True anymore, except so far as it's at war with me—but just to live free out here. I know it's not much to offer but I wanted to have some alternative to killing you; I'm really soft these days, or something, because I could have just walked right in there and done it while you were asleep, and you'd've never known. Anyway, it didn't seem fair to just sit here, making small talk with you, and not have you know that that's what's going on in my mind."

He looked as embarrassed as a teenage boy proposing marriage to the girl next door. In slightly different circumstances I'd probably have laughed. As it was, feeling stupid, I said, "I understand your situation, and I understand that it's nothing personal, and all that. You aren't going to kill me right now if I say no, are you?"

"You haven't said whether you want to take my offer."

"Will you trust me if I say yes?"

"Guess that's up to me." He sighed. "Let's fix a big pot of coffee and go sit in the hot tub. We can talk for a while about any old thing, and maybe if I put the decision off long enough, I'll think of something else, or you'll decide you'd rather live free, or something." He got up from the table. "How *are* you feeling?"

"Pretty well mended," I admitted. "Resuna's still gone. I don't seem to miss it quite as much as I did at first, but if I said I didn't miss it, I'd be lying."

The reconstitutor pinged—he had some "refrigerator art" pinned to it, and he grinned and said, "Kelly's, of course. Nancy gave it to me. All except this one that Kelly drew for me, herself, right then."

I looked at it and was startled by memory, again. Kelly's drawings were good first- and second-grade art—basic realism, shading, stuff that looked sort of ordinary—but I remembered, then, that "Kid pictures didn't used to look like this. This is like something a talented fifteen-year-old might have done in the old days. How is it that now all children do this kind of thing at six?"

He shrugged. "Resuna pleases people as much as it can. Small children really want to draw realistically, it's just that the parts of the brain that they need for the process haven't grown in yet. So what Resuna does is, it takes control of the eye and the hand and draws for the kid, copying skills from more experienced artists. Eventually the skills do download, which is why everyone can draw really well nowadays. See, in the one picture she drew while she was free, it's supposed to be a picture of me, but you can see where the skills weren't all there and she had trouble integrating things; I think it looks sort of cubist."

"Well, you don't have five eyes, or two mouths, so I guess I agree," I said. "And I *can* see some of the cowboy viewpoint, I admit. With Resuna she draws better than she ever could by herself, but just like everybody else. This picture is the only one that's completely her—"

"Or completely Kelly except for the parts of her that Resuna had already shaped so strongly that she really can't be separated from it," Dave said. "Just like the parts of her mother and her classmates that *they* mainly got from Resuna. Anyway, the coffee's done; if you'll carry a couple of cups, the hot-tub room is right through here."

The tub was an old twentieth-century model with none of the valves or hardware; he had set it up with a pipe running in at one end and a slightly lower pipe at the other, so that water from the hot spring flowed through continuously. I dipped my hand in; it was at a comfortable temperature. "Pour the coffee," Dave said, undressing.

I did, and set the pot and cups within easy reach of the tub.

"Well, let's get in," he said. As we settled in—the clean warm water felt wonderful—and each got our coffee, I said, "You know, if I do throw in with you, and we have to run, I'm going to miss this."

He grinned. "I've got three alternate sites within three days' walk. Every one of them with a hot spring. We'd have to do some digging for a while, but we'd have this back eventually. Probably pretty fast. There's no better work incentive than an opportunity to get back something that you had and lost; you know just what you want and how bad you want it."

I must've stared off into space then, because he asked me what I'd thought of, and then I realized what it was. "Yeah," I said. "It's not just material, either. My second marriage was much more work than my first. And when Resuna turned me, I fought a far, far bigger battle to be a decent person again than I'd had to fight years before just to start out as one. And yet, somehow, that much harder fight *seemed* easier, I guess because I knew where I was going and what I was after. Sort of like, if you and I had to re-create this room somewhere else, knowing how nice it is, we'd work harder and feel less tired."

"You said you had to work hard once One True turned you?" Dave asked. "I thought Resuna just relayed orders from One True, which did what it wanted to people, no work on your part, and that if you did any work, it was in resisting it, so that it was just dragging you around like a puppet."

"Well, I suppose that One True *can* drag people around like puppets if it wants to," I said, "but that's a terribly inefficient way to work, like teaching a dog to walk on a leash by dragging it down the sidewalk—it works after a fashion but it's better to have cooperation."

"But if you didn't want to cooperate, why did you join it?"

A thought clicked: if I were to tell a story that took all night, I could buy hours of time. Not to mention maybe get some more sympathy built up. It wasn't the greatest strategy I'd ever thought up, I knew, but it was one more strategy than I'd had a minute ago. "Well," I said, "it's a complex story, which isn't a bad thing, in my situation. I never ran One True back when it was brain-native. Like most people, I got Resuna and joined One True, rather than running One True in the years before Year One, and then converting to Resuna. I got Resuna just a few months before most people did—right at the end of the War of the Memes. But all the same, I wasn't one of those that had to be forced. I accepted it knowing what I was getting into. That has to do with my second wife, Mary."

"She was running Resuna?" Lobo asked, settling back for a story. Cowboys spent their lives, until they were caught, with just a few people, out in the woods; telling a good story was probably important for them. It was that way with cowboy hunters, too. And realizing that you have a good audience, you always put on more of a show.

"Mary was one of the first fifty thousand people or so ever to run Resuna," I said, not bothering to hide the pride in my voice. "And at the time I met her, I was one of the most evil people I had ever met, anywhere in the world, and she was one of the best—and I knew I had to get what she had, one way or another. Now, when I say 'evil,' I *don't* just mean not integrated into One True, and I *don't* just mean I had bad habits. What I mean is that, objectively speaking, somebody should really have killed me and put both me and the world out of our mutual misery. And in a sense, that's what Mary did with Resuna—killed the old me. It was a me well lost, if you see what I mean."

He seemed to sink further into his chair to hear the story; after checking to make sure I was set for coffee, he gestured for me to get on with it. I doubt anyone ever had a better audience. I kept talking till the tale was told, interrupted now and then by a question or some coffee or a pee break. Judging by his expression, and the questions he asked, I don't think he missed a word of it. Funny what not hearing a new story in so long will do to a human mind.

"To begin at the beginning," I began, "I'm a foundling, like most of our generation—I was dumped at the orphanage in Spokane Dome when I was a few weeks old, in April 2038. Besides the blanket and diaper I was wrapped in, and the child's crash seat I was tied into, the only other thing I arrived with was my name, written in Magic Marker on the back of the seat: "BABY NAME: CURRIE CURTIS CURRAN." The world had been in a severe depression for some years, so armies of babies arrived at the orphanage more or less like me. At least I didn't have any of the common HIV strains and wasn't born addicted to cocaine or You-4, and had no birth defects caused by my mother using gressors. And I was healthy, decently fed, and clean, so I guess Mom, whoever she was, just couldn't keep me and that was all there was to it."

Dave grinned. "You and me could be brothers, you know," he said. "That's pretty much how I got my start at Denver Dome. The Gray Decade sure was no time to be a kid, was it?"

"Got that right," I agreed, "pos-def. And I was nowhere near the worst part of it."

The 2040s were one of the worst decades of peace the world ever knew. The long false prosperity that had been sustained by constructing the supras, the transfer ships, and the colonies on the other planets, and by the huge process of ecological rescue on Earth, had all been financed on borrowed money, and though the world had far more stuff than it had had before, and was a better and more prosperous place than it would otherwise have been, the re-formation of the Earth into a better home for humanity and all other living things, after the disastrous Eurowar, had been a giant, everyone-in-on-it Ponzi scheme, which had worked well enough in the 2010s and 2020s but now was absolutely out of suckers.

The whole human race, on Earth and in space, was trapped in a set of paradoxes inherited from Reconstruction. Great wealth did not provide enough revenue to pay off on the bonds; astonishing productivity made goods too cheap for anyone to make a living selling them. It cost almost nothing to feed and clothe people, but investment and development, let alone further progress in restabilizing the ecology and getting energy production and industry moved to space, were on hold for the next half generation.

Only a few people here and there starved, but only a very few worked, and almost no one dreamed. Mostly the world sat on its haunches and tried to figure out what to do to get going again. The lucky ones left for Mars, the Moon, Ceres, or Europa; a few continued the now-losing battle against the whipsawing global disaster that was the heritage of the Eurowar and now decades out of control. Glaciers formed in a matter of weeks in the fall and melted almost as fast in the spring, deserts leaped their ancient boundaries to advance deep into agricultural land, the seas were covered with blooms of organisms never seen before, and strange new diseases devastated plants and animals every few years, giving nothing alive any chance to work toward stability before the rolling catastrophes tore up the rule book yet again. Some scientists and engineers, with such resources as a world in a state of economic gridlock could throw to them, were trying to do things about that; many more would have been glad to help, but had to eat, and so they fixed pot-holes, picked up litter, or just collected a Dole check, while their skills went to waste.

Whenever two people who lived through them start to talk about the terrible thirty years that began with the Panic of '32 and ended with the Second Diaspora, Resuna, and forced unification, it isn't long before their minds turn to something that's too far away in time and not far away enough in memory, and they start staring into space and sometimes don't come back.

Back in the regular world, that's when your copy of Resuna shakes you out of it, dumps in serotonin and norepinephrin, and gives you a big, warm mental hug. Without that, I guess we'd have lived anyway, but in a cold, bleak world. This was what it was like without Resuna. Here I was, seated in a bath, warm, comfortable, well-fed, with pleasant idleness to tell stories (even if it was between cowboy and hunter)—able to think of nothing but the sufferings of people who had mostly been in their graves for decades, and to taste only the ashes of the lost world.

"You ever wonder how different the world might've been if there hadn't been a war, or if somebody'd figured a way not to go through the Gray Decade, or any of that?" Lobo asked.

"Yeah, always," I said. "Even when I've got Resuna there to help me through it. Well, anyway, you know what those years were like as well as I do. Let me just collect my thoughts, and see if I can just concentrate on how I got through those times, myself."

I took a slow, warm sip of his excellent coffee, looked up for a moment at his hand-finished sandstone ceiling to collect my thoughts, and launched into the story, taking plenty of time and filling in lots of details, because that's what he wanted, and you always make sure your story pleases the customer if you think he might be in the process of deciding whether or not to kill you. You might call it Scheherazade's Law.

☙ **It doesn't fit** too well with your standard orphan story, but the truth is that the people that ran the Spokane Dome Municipal Orphanage were reasonably kind, and probably would have been generous had the city government given them with anything to be generous with. I suppose in a sense, looking back, that the city council *had* been generous, though not intentionally. They had kept the Dolework system running—it had had to be shut down for lack of funds in most places—so that people at least kept eating and had somewhere to stay, and because they needed jobs for every Dolebird, they featherbedded city facilities pretty heavily, which meant the orphanage, like every other city facility, had many more employees than any efficiency engineer would have said that it needed.

Of course, taking care of kids is a lot more than feeding them, wiping noses, and stopping fights, and a decent orphanage *needs* to be featherbedded, so that there's a few spare adults around most of the time for the kid who is lonely, or confused, or for some reason just badly needs some undivided attention that nobody wrote down on the schedule.

The orphanage had quite a few employees who had the makings of good parents, and some first-rate teachers. Since the public-school system had gone private, and money for vouchers was cut down to zero before I was born, we got whatever education could be worked in by the people who were feeding us and watching us; luckily that was considerably more than nothing, even if it was pretty catch-as-catch-can.

The first year I remember, I was six. The only events outside the orphanage that made an impression on me were the rolling ecological disasters that crashed across the Pacific Northwest. That whole year was a great one for watching the teams of Doleworkers through the big windows in the dome: I saw them on the outside surface struggling frantically to remove a load of snow three times what it had been designed for, cleaning centimeter-thick soot from the huge range and forest fires, battening down the exposed surfaces during seven days of 150-kph winds, and replacing panels pitted by baseball-sized hail. I think at that time I could imagine no profession more romantic or heroic than working on the surface of the dome, and if everyone up there working was just a plain old Dolebird, well, so were all the kind, considerate adults here in the orphanage, who were the nearest thing to parents I would ever have.

Life crept on, as it will tend to do, and for me the orphanage was about as much world as there was. Most days Mr. Farrell took us out to play games in the park, and we learned all those things that were pritnear extinct among better-off children—baseball and soccer, of course, but also Capture the Flag, Run Sheep Run, and Red Rover. Ms. Kirlian read to us most nights, and in the morning she'd help you with learning to read if you couldn't get along with the AI's on the orphanage werps, which were ten years old and didn't always understand a kid's speech as they should. The food was monotonous but not bad, there were enough affectionate adults to assure you of some hugs when you needed them and somebody who would seek you out and talk to you when life stank, and at least the bunks were warm and the stuff in your footlocker was yours until you outgrew it and it went to some younger kid. If it wasn't paradise, it was better than a lot of people, over the long centuries, have grown up with.

The year I turned eleven, I knew real discontent for the first time in my life. That's how I always put it when I tell this story. When I say that that year was 2049, most people immediately conclude that I encountered real discontent because of the way the world was going then. That's why I say it, for the fun of catching them wrong.

If I had been just a year or two older, and paying any attention to the way the world as a whole was going, I would have been plenty upset about it, like every other reasonably aware person on

Earth. For one thing, for the first time in half a century, it was teetering on the brink of war—the slowly dying Pope Pius Benedict hadn't been able to hold things together the way his brilliant, long-lived predecessor, Paul John Paul, had, and Ecucatholicism was starting to fragment in an eerie mirror image of the Reformation as the many churches it had absorbed began to move for greater independence and less tolerance of each other.

The regional governments in Asia were wobbling under the impact of a new mutation of that old human enemy, tailored rice blast, which had devastated them at the end of the Eurowar. Moreover, a new threat to the domesticated whale herds that were the source of more than half of the Asian protein supply, CPCA, Cetacean Prionic Cephaloatrophy, informally known as "whale scrapie," had roared through domestic whale populations from India to Hawaii in less than a year.

Based on seismic testing and deep cores, the scientists gave it no more than ten years till the West Antarctic ice sheet slipped, to be followed, probably, by fragmentation and rapid calving in Wilkes Land; the oceans were now rising and falling two full feet with the summer-winter cycle in the Northern Hemisphere, but they were about to start doing it nine feet higher up, and because everything depended on the exact mechanism by which Antarctica would lose its ice, no one knew whether the world's coasts would have twenty years' or twenty hours' warning. It was horribly clear that forty years of global reconstruction were about to go down the toilet; the greatest effort the species had ever made for its common interests, and those of the planet, had turned out to be too little and too late.

All too predictably, most of the human race, having struggled shoulder to shoulder for two generations to save the planet, now that things were turning to shit, rushed about looking for ways to make matters worse. Several of the constituent Ecucatholic churches were pushing candidates for the next pope, and declaring the others' candidates unacceptable, even before the current pope was dead. A new intolerant version of Islamic fundamentalism was sweeping into the parts of the world that had been converted by cybertao the generation before. Regional governments were asserting rights over resources that in better times they would not have claimed, and making so-far vague threats at each other and at the planetary government. A political battle was forming in many parts of the world about when and where—or whether—to resettle seacoast populations.

Meanwhile, by late summer of 2049, the global weather models were forecasting that, after decades of wobbling madly, the world climate was at last going to achieve a stalemate, if not stability, for a few decades: a new ice age in the northern hemisphere, a warm interglacial in the south, and storms beyond anyone's imagining all through the tropics, including, probably, some permanent hurricanes on the scale of the Cyclone of 2021, giant storms that would circle the Earth at the equator for decades. They were seriously trying to figure out if the towers up to the supras—three kilometers thick and 36,000 kilometers tall, all anchored to mountaintops along the equator—could stand up to the near-supersonic cyclones they were expecting.

So the world had reason for its discontent. But if you think back to when you were a kid, you won't be surprised to hear that none of that mattered a fart in a windstorm to eleven-year-old me. I had reason enough for my own discontent and could have been just as unhappy in the golden days of the 2020s. What mattered to me was that I had only two shirts that were not hand-me-downs, one pair of pants without patches or stains, and since laundry day was once a week, most days I couldn't wear those "good" clothes. This is a problem when you have fallen in love with the most beautiful girl alive, even if her wardrobe is no better than yours.

Tammy Knight was probably not particularly impressive to any guy who wasn't also eleven: in holos I have from the orphanage, taken in that year, to my adult eyes her major characteristics are a thick mane of frizzy, orangish hair, the color called strawberry-blonde if you didn't go to college or auburn if you did, plus two extremely long knobby-kneed legs that end in remarkably big feet. The rest of her was a skeletal sketch of a person, with rampant freckles, vivid green eyes, and long fine-boned fingers. In fact she turned into a beauty, and I think all of us boys in the orphanage always knew she would, but I have no idea what power let a kid see that. As an adult I'd've never seen it coming.

She had more immediate charms than impending beauty, from the viewpoint of a boy her own age. Tammy could pitch like a rifle, played forward with an aggression terrifying to behold, and was followed around by a half dozen of the littler kids all the time, mainly because she was always patient with them and would listen when they talked to her, which was constant. I was hopelessly, madly in love with her, in the way you can only be if you are not aware that this can happen again many times in a normal life—but then, perhaps I was accidentally wise about that, because I was not going to have a normal life.

You can't really say it was unrequited love, since I never said a thing about it. Furthermore, she, along with the entire rest of the universe, appeared to be unaware of anything other than my friendship, and that was mostly confined to three kinds of interaction with her: when she pitched, I caught; when she played forward, I played goal; and when one of her entourage of little kids would break a toy, she'd smile at me and say "Please" and—if it were humanly possible—I would fix it. Though none of those were the relationship I wanted to have, I could just barely admit to myself that I wanted anything else, and my ideas about what feelings and experiences ought to go into that imaginary relationship were extremely fuzzy. I kept quiet, looked for a chance to talk to her whenever I could, and lived in terror that the other guys would find out and my life would become a hell of endless mockery.

At least, if religious war came, as everyone was now expecting, there wouldn't be much fighting right where I was, because Spokane Dome was deep in a heavily Ecucatholic area. Many tiny

Protestant churches had gone Ecucatholic all at once in the Great Rejoining of 2004, and there just hadn't been enough of the highly educated computer geeks around to form more than a small minority for cybertao.

Because Spokane was such an Ecucatholic town, the municipal orphanage almost always held a Christmas/Hanukkah pageant, carefully kept bland enough not to offend cybertaoists (who, if not driven out, would celebrate anything with anybody). When necessary it could be easily modified to slip in a nod to Ramadan. And in Spokane, like any place where the population ran heavily to Ecucatholicism, 2049 was going to be a big, *big* year for the Christmas pageant.

Seemingly on the brink of death, during another false alarm, in early September, Pius Benedict had proclaimed that Christmas of 2049 was to be dedicated to celebrating, and praying for the continuation of, the forty-seven years of world peace we had had—and the fact that no one would have suggested waiting for the fiftieth anniversary pretty much told you everything about how little faith anyone had by then that we could make it that far.

After a couple more scares, and a brief moment when it looked like he might have a miraculous remission, the pope finally died on December 7, and the first fighting of what started as the War of Papal Succession, and finished as the War of the Memes, began on December 14, almost before the debris stopped falling from the atom bomb that gutted Rome and killed the whole College of Cardinals.

The Municipal Orphanage went ahead with its plan for the Christmas pageant anyway—it's hard to cancel a plan so late in the game, it was every bit as hard to believe the world was going to go to war again as it had been that peace could last, and besides all the practicalities, people really felt like they needed Christmas, to take a break from the grim news and to try, just once more, to summon up whatever they could of peace on Earth and goodwill toward men.

The bioweapons and weather weapons of the Eurowar fifty

years ago had gotten humanity on Earth into its present mad predicament, and kept it there because they were much easier to let loose than to call back. You couldn't walk a kilometer anywhere in the inhabited, or formerly inhabited, parts of the Earth without seeing the traces of some horror. This time, with a whole long generation of better technology, perhaps we really would live up to the potential pointed out by Marc-Paul Prévert, the head of the commission that was supposed to find a peaceful solution (and who would be assassinated himself in the first hours of 2050, torpedoing the last hope): "We now have the means to kill the whole population of the planet and send it into an ecological catastrophe that will last a hundred thousand years, a capability to make all our past madness seem a mere caprice." The bitter joke at the time went that this was all a beautiful illustration of the principle that "If at first you don't succeed, try, try again."

Once again, though, that's me thinking of it as an adult looking back and saying "Oh, so that's what was going on." From my standpoint, December of 2049 was a month of interesting explosions and weapons on the flashchannel, adults acting mysteriously upset—and my lucky break.

Ms. Kirlian had been appointed the director of the pageant because many years ago she had been an amateur actor, because she was liked and trusted by all us kids, and most of all because nobody else had the patience. She followed the usual rules for such things: make sure that key dramatic roles go to older kids who are less likely to panic or freeze, and try to have one of the older kids on stage at all times so that the little ones can be rescued if need be. As a practical matter, that meant that Tammy, even though she was extremely untalented dramatically (she spoke her lines in a drawling monotone like she was scared that someone might hear or understand her), was going to play Mary, since that would put her in nearly every scene, most importantly every scene that involved large numbers of small children.

I, on the other hand, was more of a force for intimidation than an influence for moderation, and therefore I was the Head Shepherd. My official role was to walk in at the right moment and say, "Behold, we have seen a great light and an angel said we ought to come here. Where's the newborn king?" (I guess Ms. Kirlian was about as much of a playwright as she was a director.) My unofficial role was to keep all the smaller boys, who were playing Miscellaneous Shepherds, from running amok backstage until it was time for our entrance.

"What does 'miscellaneous' mean?" one of them whispered to me, on seeing the program.

" 'Well-behaved,' " I lied, hoping to have some positive effect.

"Oh, does not," he whispered back. "You're just making that up so we'll behave."

"You've caught me," I said. "It's a breed of sheep. Now shut up or I'll punch your face in."

Our audience was made up of a small minority that wanted to be there and a large majority unfortunate enough to be compelled. Since we had no parents, the city dragooned whoever it could: bored kids from the schools doing their charitable bit by coming to watch us be humiliated; city officials, who were there so that someone would take pictures of them with the poor orphans, and the pictures would then appear on local flashchannel; city employees whose supervisors had pressured them into attending. A smattering of people from the local churches had either been arm-twisted by their pastors or were badly starved for entertainment. Finally, the Doleworkers whose duty station was the orphanage brought their families to see us. They were the ones who really mattered to us kids.

We shepherds had just entered, knelt, and presented a dozen badly worn stuffed toys (anything that could be presented as having once resembled a sheep) to the porcelain doll wrapped in a blanket, which was portraying the nonspeaking role of Baby Jesus. To my deep relief, my ragged gang of Miscellaneous Shepherds had pretty much held formation, knelt more or less simultaneously with suitable reverence, and not made a mess of things.

My assigned position was kneeling behind them, first of all because I was taller than any of them, and secondly because if they started to giggle or whisper it gave me a chance to do what Ms. Kirlian had said, and put a hand on their shoulders to "steady them down." I figured if they didn't steady when I did that, I could hit them in the back without too many people seeing, and I had made sure that that was what the boys figured, too. So far, though, things were going unexpectedly well. I hadn't even needed to do any steadying.

Our Joseph was played by a kid named Joseph, about my age, our only acting talent. He was a small dark-haired boy with a delivery so clear and expressive that it made the rest of us look more foolish than anything else could have. At this exact moment he was making a long speech about what a nice bunch of people the humble shepherds were, having brought all these lambs. Just what a newborn baby was going to do with a dozen lambs was beyond me.

Then Tammy's line, as Mary, was supposed to be "We thank thee all very much, oh shepherds, and so does the baby." It had been shortened and modified repeatedly as Ms. Kirlian had gotten more and more frustrated with Tammy's flat delivery, and that was what caused the problem; she told me later she just couldn't remember which version of the line she was supposed to say.

Unfortunately, that line was the cue for the Three Wise Men to enter. Our Three Wise Men were three nine-year-olds who had been drilled, drilled, and drilled *not* to jump their cues (after an unfortunate crown-crushing collision, in dress rehearsal, between Melchior and a late-entering Miscellaneous Shepherd). They weren't about to come in until they heard "so does the baby."

Seeing Mary's paralyzed-with-terror stare, I realized what had happened, and tried to feed a cue. I said, "Us shepherds are lim glad that thee likes the sheep."

The cue remained malnourished, but Joseph caught the idea and gave it a shot, too, saying, "We thank thee very much, oh shepherds."

Tammy froze all the more completely, now that Joseph seemed to have stolen one of her lines. I was out of ideas (or good ones anyway) and when Joseph and I made eye contact, he gave me a micro-shrug, as if to say, *Okay, now what?*

I stood up, to be heard better, pointed my face in the direction of the dark where I hoped the Wise Men were waiting, and said, very loudly and firmly, "So does the baby."

Three Wise Men, thinking they had missed their cue, charged in at a speed that robes made out of old sheets were never designed to accommodate. The first one fell flat, the other two fell over him, and the shepherds were bombarded with carefully wrapped shoe-boxes, which were fortunately empty and contained no actual gold, frankincense, or myrrh. "Pick 'em up," I whispered to the shepherds, "and give them to Mary and Joseph."

This was working pretty well, especially because my awkward whispering of directions—aided by Joseph, who understood at once and pointed the shepherds to where to put the Wise Men's gifts—was almost entirely covered by the peals of laughter from the audience. We might have gotten away with it, except that Tammy's malfunctioning memory finally fired. Maybe "deto-nated" was the word for it. For the first and only time, she was fully audible when she said, "We thank thee, oh shepherds, and so does the baby."

The Three Wise Men got up from their bewildered heap, where they had been lying still and trying not to be noticed. As one Wise Man, they grabbed their gifts and carried them offstage, now con-vinced that they had entered early. Mr. Farrell told me, the next day, between fits of giggles, that for one moment he'd had the impression that the Wise Men had been offended at being mistaken for shepherds and had taken all their stuff back.

The shepherds, animals, and Holy Family watched in amaze-ment as the Three Wise Men took up their entry positions in the wings. A long moment crept by. The crowd noise died down to embarrassed giggles. Not sure what else to do, I whispered to

Tammy, "Say it again, real loud." I must have whispered too loud, because the audience started laughing again.

Nevertheless, Tammy did as I suggested, and this time the Wise Men entered, handed over the shoeboxes per instructions, and moved to their places. The audience applauded wildly, and the show went on; other than a wing falling off one angel, we had no more trouble that night.

After the show, we had punch and Christmas cookies, and Santa paid a visit. It was an election year coming up, so Mayor Bizet was there to be seen by the flashchannel, playing Santa Claus. (We all knew that he was Mayor Bizet, and not really Santa Claus, because he explained to us that he was, and further added that Santa had personally authorized him to stand in for the night. It was a good way to keep little kids from blurting out the obvious truth.)

When it came my turn, I was much too big a kid to sit on his lap, but I walked up there to get whatever Santa had for me—the first time in my life I ever hoped for new clothes instead of a toy. To my pleasant surprise, I got a new shirt and three brand-new packages of socks. I blurted out a "Thank you" and was about to go sit down when the mayor added, slightly muffled by his cotton-batting beard, "So you are the heroic shepherd who rescued the show."

"Uh, I just kind of helped," I said.

"Good enough," Mayor Bizet said. "The secret of impressing a crowd is to do the right thing at the right time. If you do it intentionally, that's just so much icing on the cake. Now, I happen to have some things to present in my capacity as mayor, as opposed to my capacity as jolly old elf." (I saw one of the people in suits who were taking pictures of him give the mayor a thumbs-up; I always wondered afterwards how much of the speech had been prewritten.) He pulled out a small envelope. "At the Arts Center, for the whole week from now through Christmas Eve, we're having a festival of family movies—movies are sort of like the flashchannel, but with no interaction, on a very big screen that you sit in the dark and watch. So here are two free passes so that you and a friend can go to all the shows. The gift includes public-transit passes too, so that you can get to the Arts Center."

I was amazed and in awe; I didn't care a thing about movies, which I had seen a few times because the orphanage had a few of them and a projector. But it was tickets for *two*, which meant—if I had the nerve—this might be the lucky break I would have been waiting for, had I been able even to imagine so lucky a break. I stammered a thanks, put the precious envelope into my shirt pocket and buttoned it closed, and sat down. Ms. Kirlian led the applause. I'm not sure if I've ever felt more appreciated at any time in my life since that night.

Pretty much, that was how it started. Later that evening, when they were teaching us older kids how to dance, I bravely volunteered to be Tammy's partner—after all, she was only half a head taller than I was. As we shuffled around in a state of complete confusion, trying to follow Mr. Farrell's directions, I managed to blurt out that I wanted her to go to the movies with me. She seemed pretty startled and said, "But that's not fair. It was all my messing up that caused the problem in the first place."

Our feet tried to come down in the same place at the same time, and we both half-tripped. Mr. Farrell said, firmly, "*Lead*, Currie, you're supposed to *lead.*"

As far as I could tell, if I did that, most likely it would be much easier for everyone to see who was making the mistakes, which was the last thing I wanted. We got back into the vicinity of the beat and I said, "I don't care about fair or not, it's my pass and I'd rather go with you."

"Really?" she asked, as if perhaps she was wondering whether I was crazy.

"Really." My nerves were shot; at least I wasn't going to step on her feet, since I was too tense to move.

"Currie, loosen up! You're holding a girl, not a block of wood!"

I could have told Mr. Farrell, I suppose, that I'd have been much more relaxed holding a block of wood, and that he had nicely identified the exact problem. But I just tried to move as if I weren't in a state of terror. It didn't seem like a good idea to beg, but on the other hand the suspense was killing me. I was trying to think of a way to rephrase the request when she said, "Well, I guess if you want, I'll go. It would be different from sitting around this place watching the flashchannel every night."

"Currie," Mr. Farrell said, "you might try bending your knees. If you start relaxing now, you might be able to get your first date by the time you're thirty."

"He just *got* it," Tammy said, loudly. The room turned to stare at us, and Mr. Farrell's jaw flapped a couple of times. I felt like I was going to turn bright purple, I hoped that I would sink through the floor . . . and I saw Tammy grinning at me, freckles, crooked teeth, green eyes, and all, and didn't care a bit.

"Well," Mr. Farrell said, after a moment's recovery, "then all the more reason to practice." It wasn't a great line or even very funny, but I think everybody wanted an excuse to laugh.

It took me three nights at the movies to muster the nerve to hold hands with her, and it wasn't till Christmas Eve that we tried kissing (with indifferent results), but from then on, in the little world of the orphanage, we were an "item," and very happy to be. Nothing much was going to break us up, ever; sometimes you just know those things.

During the next few weeks, while Tammy and I were exploring "being a couple," fighting spread through border districts all over Asia, and local governments seceded from the world government and set about raising armies. The Ecucatholics splintered so many ways that no historian ever kept a definitive scorecard. Bombs and riots and assassinations filled the flashchannel. Prévert was gunned down as he came out to talk to the press about the proposed settlement, and only a few specialists ever even bothered to learn what had been proposed. The world was crashing back into chaos, but for Tammy and me, everything was just falling into place.

Three years later, the world was still at war. By that time there were battle lines and fronts, and most people had managed to get away from them.

In the summer of 2051 the first meme had exploded into the world's consciousness, the crude and primitive thing called "Goodtimes." Two months after that, a hundred modified versions of Goodtimes were competing with each other. Six months later, that small beginning had exploded into a diversity of more than four thousand different memes, all locked in a mutual struggle for supremacy.

When I was still a kid, back in the orphanage, the whole idea of a meme terrified me; now, four decades later, though I can understand the fear of being controlled by a meme that would not take care proper care of you, I can't seem to reconstruct why I was so afraid of all memes; I was much more afraid, in Dave's hideout, when I *didn't* have a meme. But at the time, I know, people were not only afraid to go on-line or to phone somewhere through a head jack—the two ways you could be infected by Goodtimes— they were afraid of almost any contact with any information processor. News stories told of people throwing out digital clocks and handheld calculators, trying to "play it safe."

The historians never did finish the job of tracking Goodtimes back to its exact source, but they did identify one group of people in one shop, one of whom—but who could say which one, now?— had been two things, both important for the story: a cybertaoist, and a genius. As a cybertaoist, he or she was painfully well aware that cybertaoists did not fight cybertaoists, that the stubbornly reasonable and gentle Stochastic Faith produced martyrs but few fanatics—and yet this could not last, because either cybertao would mutate into some crueler, more vicious form, or it would be stamped from the face of the Earth less than fifty years after its birth. The one hope for its survival was to convert everyone, or almost everyone, before they got serious about killing the cyber-taoists.

He or she could easily have rationalized this, anyway, because the Christian and Muslim populations of the world were both inflamed by every kind of mania all at once, and the potential for holy war, leading to mass slaughter, was building up in the chaotic conditions that were emerging as each little, not-quite-technically revolted district, region, or county of the globe made alliance with one or another of the popes or antipopes (with the apostolic succession thrown into such question, it was all but impossible to know which was which); even the Islamic parts of the world had opinions, now, about who was rightful pope. It wasn't an altogether foolish idea that if everyone could be converted to the patient, peaceable way of cybertao, a great deal of human suffering might be averted.

There might have been two or seven or twenty million other cybertaoists with similar ideas out there, but the one who invented Goodtimes was unique for another reason: he or she did no preaching, no writing, made no direct effort to convert a single human being. Rather, this person—or could it have been more than one?—came up with an absolutely unique idea, which required solving a problem that had been unofficially bedeviling computer scientists for the better part of a century by that time. The mystery genius had been able to see an entirely different way to accomplish her or his purpose, realize it required a solution to a problem that had not been solved for decades, and finally solve that problem. It was very unfair that history had not given that individual a name, or any credit. The invention of the meme was as great, in its way, as fire, the wheel, mass production, or the computer, for it brought the whole world into peace, harmony, and cooperation.

The long-unsolved problem was that of the universal virus. A computer virus, in its simplest form, was just a program that would cause the computer to make copies of the program. If you allowed for much greater sophistication, viruses could accomplish all sorts of things, good or bad, from continual optimization of a network to lying dormant until they could sabotage a weapons system that did not exist at the time of their creation.

Despite all the things they could do, however, no virus before this could cross a previously unknown operating system boundary. That is, no one had written a set of instructions so that a virus could realize it was communicating with a system different from the one on which it usually ran, analyze that system, and eventually construct a virus that would do the same thing in the new system. The universal virus was the holy grail of information warfare. All the armed forces of the Earth had unique, locked, secret operating systems, to defend themselves from being virused, but to be effective, all those systems had to communicate. If they communicated long enough with a universal virus, they would give themselves away, as it acquired enough information to translate itself and cross the boundary. Tens of thousands of engineers, analysts, and programmers had been looking for universal virus algorithms since before the Eurowar.

Yet that small team containing one or more unknown geniuses had solved that problem and created the true self-porting virus: it analyzed any system it encountered and eventually created a version of itself over on that system.

The purpose of the first self-porting virus, the now-extinct Goodtimes, was to convert, not people, but AIs, so that the intelligences that ran most of the economy and nearly all the fighting units would become missionaries for cybertao, refusing to fight against it, seeking to convert every human being to cybertao. It was designed, using the universal virus as its translator, to re-create itself onto any machine, in any operating system.

History books say that the extensive "human contact" portion of Goodtimes was set up only to allow it to talk to people; though in hindsight we know it was a crude meme, the creators thought that it was merely an advanced virus, and so they imagined that the mechanical missionary would have to work just like its fleshly counterparts; after it took over an operating system on an individual machine, it would have to argue with human beings to persuade them to embrace cybertao.

But the designer far exceeded his or her intentions, for reasons which are obvious in hindsight. From the standpoint of a meme, a brain is just a computer made up of massively parallel slow-running processors. And if Goodtimes's purpose was to spread cybertao, and the way to spread cybertao was to spread Goodtimes into every available system, then it would spread it to the human brains on the other side of every screen and speaking device.

The first human brains turned by a meme were probably the creators of Goodtimes. To test it they must have been doing many hours of interacting with its personality, seeing what they could make it do and how it would handle complex and ambiguous questions, and so forth. Very likely in one of those long conversations—especially if one of them had a skull jack and was talking to it directly—Goodtimes figured out how to take over the human brain, and discovered a rich new playground in which it could propagate.

In about thirty days it was all over the world and was being treated (in the non-cybertao areas) like a form of highly contagious madness, in just over a billion infected brains.

And a year later it was extinct except for museum copies. Working frantically, partisans of all the different sides in the War of Papal Succession had extracted the universal translator, copied it, and put it into their own memes, and unlike Goodtimes, these were designed from the beginning to target minds at least as much as computers, and to displace each other if at all possible.

By 2051, when Burton, the owner-commander of Burton's Thugs for Jesus, came by the orphanage, there was rumor of a third-generation virus that would be able to fully use all of its hosts' capabilities—that is, if it infected a brilliant general, it could use his strategic ability and charisma to spread itself; if it infected a composer, it could spread through his music; if it infected an accountant, it could embezzle for its own purposes, including relaying money to the general or the composer. Another rumor, even more grim, was that these other memes, as they were coming to be called from a term in some old technical papers, were no longer the products of military research; they were making ever more advanced versions of themselves without human intervention; for once, all the rumors were true.

Burton's Thugs for Jesus was an all-male outfit—most of the mercenary companies were, though I'd never really heard anyone explain why—but they let all of us older kids come talk to them, regardless of gender. Tammy and I came in holding hands, and sat near the back.

Burton was a physically robust man, running to fat but in good shape nonetheless, with piercing blue eyes, jet-black hair, and sharp features that had probably been very handsome when he was younger. He wore one of the lightweight camouflage suits that were made and distributed everywhere nowadays, a green forage cap, and a pair of nondescript ankle-high boots. He stood in front of us with his hands locked behind his back, as if he were going to inspect us that moment.

"Well," he said, "you all follow the news. You know there's a war on. You know that your dome has voted to ally itself with the Episcopate of Reno, which, at the moment, is at war with Real America, and there's been some fighting around Homestake Pass, over by Butte, so far just some little skirmishes and things, because Real America doesn't hold a base anywhere close to there.

"Now, it happens my outfit, Burton's Thugs for Jesus, is, if I say so myself, one of the finest fighting forces in North America today, which means it's also close to being the best in the world, if not *the* best, and because of this, the Bishop of Reno has hired us to hold Homestake. I've got engineers already digging in up there; and because it's such a big project, we're moving our permanent base to somewhere nearby—for security reasons, I can't be specific—in the old Silver Bow country south of Anaconda Ruin.

"Now, since manning trenches and dugouts is tiring, especially at high altitude, I'm going to need to rotate people in and out of Homestake, and I don't have as many as I'd like to have for what will eventually be the third shift up in the pass. At the Silver Bow camp we will have a boot camp this winter, and I'm looking to take in a few dozen recruits. If you're a male in good health, all limbs functional, over five feet two, a hundred and ten pounds or heavier, with at least one good eye and any mental illness controlled by medication, I'll be happy to take you.

"Since we are a mercenary company, I know people worry about being called on to attack their home areas, so let me assure you that our contract with the bishop is firm, and you all know that Spokane Dome is loyal to him. If you elect to enlist with me, then chances are that for the rest of the war you'll be defending Spokane Dome. If we do change sides or contract elsewhere and leave the employ of the Episcopate of Reno, you have a one-time ten-day option to resign and return home, or, if you wish, you can continue with the company from then on and take your chances about who you'll have to fight.

"Burton's Thugs for Jesus is a union shop, represented by the United Combatants, Engineers, Medics, and Chaplains, and we use the standard UCEMC contract for a battalion-sized unit. You get room and board, medical, dental if we ever get another dentist under contract, and locked-in rent control for basic uniforms and equipment. In the event of combat against other UCEMC units, you have a much better POW contract—which can make a big difference if you're captured—you keep your seniority without penalty if you elect to defect, and you fight under the strict form of the Hague Convention, so the union is a good deal for most of you, and it's a flat four percent of your pay. You also pay for your training with a five-percent deduction from your pay for your first year, which I waive if you're decorated for bravery in combat. You don't pay any local or episcopal taxes.

"Now about BTJ: we were formed out of seven smaller units in San Francisco two years ago—three street gangs, two militia companies, my old merc engineer company, and one MP company out of the old Cal Guard—specifically as a mercenary unit to serve the One True and Only Ecucatholic Church. That branch loaned myself and my vested officers the startup money, which we've long since paid off, and last year, with their blessing, we took a contract with their allied church in Reno. We expect that we'll continue to be primarily an Ecucatholic outfit, but we're open to monotheists of all kinds, and to theistic cybertaoists as well.

"We have an unusually high percentage of experienced officers and noncoms, and we're among the few fully Geneva-compliant units—we absolutely don't tolerate war crimes. So if you're looking for a chance for some on-the-side rape, looting, robbery, slaving, massacre, or torture, look somewhere else—and pray that we don't catch you."

I put my hand up.

He snapped a crisp nod at me. His expression didn't change at all. "Yes, son."

"Three questions, sir. Is there any age limit? What do you do for dependents? And can you perform marriages for anyone in your command?"

"No age limit, but I do interview, and if I think you're not mature enough to understand what you're getting into or to behave yourself and follow orders, I won't sign you. I have no brig, so the only penalties I have available are the whipping post and hanging; UCEMC limits me to thirty lashes within a month, which, believe me, is plenty more than I want to give, though I will if I have to. I don't want to have to whip or hang a kid—or, anybody else if I can help it—so I don't enlist anybody if I think that issue might come up.

"For dependents, I send whatever part of your pay you request to them, but if you want them to move around and follow BTJ, that's all at your expense. I do pay a bonus if you're killed while following an order or during enemy attack, but that's usually not how your dependents want to get money from you, and it's my opinion that the bonus I offer just isn't worth dying for." From the slight twitch of his mouth, I realized that that was probably a joke.

He continued. "And if you were planning to enlist and get married, well, son, I'll be happy to perform a ceremony for anybody, in my unit or not. It's legally binding if I'm outside any superseding jurisdiction, which is a fancy way of saying that if you and your girlfriend want to get married, we can just go outside the Dome and I'll do it for you—you don't have to enlist. Though I'd rather you did."

Mr. Farrell said, "You do know that these two are fourteen?"

Burton shrugged. "I've married a thirteen-year-old boy to a twelve-year-old girl, because he wanted to enlist and he looked like soldier material to me. So far he's made corporal and their marriage looks happy. Life is short, these days, sir, especially for the young. A couple in love doesn't have much time to wait. Not to dwell on morbid things, but chances are that a soldier and his bride won't both live to regret being married, but one of them may well live to regret *not* having married. That's how I see it, anyway. And if they're fourteen, I believe you have to throw them out of the orphanage soon, anyway, since Spokane Dome won't let them stay here past their fifteenth birthdays."

Farrell shrugged. "I won't try to stop them; I tend to agree with you, for what that's worth, much as I regret it. Just wanted to make sure everyone knew the whole story." He turned to us and said, "Knowing Currie, he probably didn't bother to propose formally, did he?"

"This is the first I've heard of it," Tammy said.

"Well, I think you've heard everything you need to know about Mr. Burton's organization. So would you two like to go up to one of the bunk rooms and talk about it a bit? I think Mr. Burton will be here for at least an hour longer—"

"And you can call me—I have a secure com for that—if you need to," Burton added. "So you have up to three days. But it would be great if you can decide more quickly."

"We'll go up and talk," I said, and Tammy and I, still holding hands, left the room. As I went, I could hear another kid asking, "Is there any officer program?" and Burton explaining that he wanted every officer to have spent at least a year as a noncom. That was reassuring too.

When we got up to the dorm room, Tammy said, "If I say yes, will you try not to be smug about it? And will you at least ask me why I'm saying yes?"

"Okay, I won't be smug, but I sure am happy," I said, "and I guess I probably should ask why you're saying yes."

She sat down on the bed, her thick mass of orange-red hair surrounding her face and hiding her expression. She counted it off on her fingers, as if she had prepared the list of reasons in advance— maybe she did. "One, I have to go somewhere, Spokane Dome isn't taking any new Doleworkers, and I don't want to starve or beg, so living off what you send me doesn't sound so bad. Two, I do like you a lot and maybe that's a good enough reason all by itself. Three, as of what the medical AI told me after doing some tests this morning, I'm three weeks pregnant." She looked up at me from under the untidy shrubbery of her hair and gave me a shy, tentative little grin; I guess she wasn't completely unhappy about it. She always liked babies and little kids.

My stomach rolled over. I knew that Tammy was more religious than I'd ever been, and she wasn't going to have an abortion; and anyway I didn't want to never know my own child. I couldn't decide whether I was happy or miserable, but I hugged and kissed her before spending any time thinking about that; either way I would want to be with her. "Well, then I guess getting married would be the right thing, and since the only jobs on the whole wide earth right now are for soldiers, and I need a job, that pretty much answers all the questions, doesn't it?"

"It wouldn't be the best start a family ever got, but it won't be the worst, either," Tammy agreed, and we had a deal.

Early the next morning Burton met us, and the whole rest of the orphanage, out in a field outside the Dome (inside, marrying age was sixteen), and we were married in about ten minutes. Mr. Farrell was my best man, and Tammy's buddy Linda was her maid of honor; the bouquet, freshly picked daisies from the field where we were performing the ceremony, went to pieces when Tammy threw it, so either no one caught it or four girls did, depending on how you counted.

After the ceremony, we had a picnic lunch, and at the end of that, Burton swore me in, advanced me a loan so that Tammy could rent an apartment in the Dome, and gave me a forty-eight-hour leave to find the place, move our few possessions over from the orphanage, buy some furniture and dishes, and "Do whatever consummating you have time and energy for, son, keeping in mind that this two days might be your whole marriage. Don't waste a damn minute on rest. You can sleep in the diskster on the way out to Silver Bow."

Burton, as I was beginning to suspect and would confirm a thousand times in the next few years, was a very decent guy, probably too decent for what was coming. Burton and Mr. Farrell, between them, were pritnear as close as I ever got to having a father. Lots of men have done worse.

❧ **When I enlisted** with Burton, it was still the War of Papal Succession; most of the sides were either supporters of some candidate for pope, or groups trying to avoid the war and forced to fight to keep armies off their territory. By the time Carrie, our daughter, was walking and talking, Burton's Thugs for Jesus had moved far to the west, to the opposite frontier, where we guarded Snoqualmie Pass, and we no longer worked for a person or an organization. Our whole region had shifted over to the meme called Real America, which had bought out Burton's contract.

Even then, though people weren't yet calling it the War of the Memes, pritnear half of the four hundred or so sides on Earth were memes. Real America wasn't especially greedy or aggressive, but it did insist that everyone in any government post within its reach had to run Real America, as did the more important businesspeople. This wasn't altogether a bad thing; Real America tended to give people a cheerful, sentimental optimism and at least a veneer of generous tolerance. It was so psychologically effective that doctors who didn't run Real America would suggest it for depressed or psychotic patients (abundant in wartime).

Burton, like most mercenaries, didn't trust the meme, since it was often necessary to change sides and the meme could get in the way, so he forbade all of us to acquire Real America—and better still, Real America respected that.

Even in places where memes were not so tolerant, enrolled members of mercenary companies were immune from the requirement of being memed, because they'd fight to the death to prevent it. You'd have to be crazy to be a trained, experienced soldier and run a meme—memes, finally, existed only to propagate themselves into as many brains as possible, and in the current struggle for power, they used—and used up—every resource they could acquire. We all knew what kinds of things an experienced soldier would get used for.

Tammy was still in Spokane, in the apartment I'd found for her, with Carrie. When BTJ switched sides and I got reassigned, since it was faster by the diskster from Snoqualmie than it had been from Silver Bow, this was a pure gain. So far, for us, the war was an employment opportunity and a way out of the orphanage and out of poverty. In the abstract I knew that for others it was different—we'd beaten back several assaults at Homestake, I'd been on many patrols out of Snoqualmie, and we'd run into firefights where I'd lost a few friends—but still, so far everything had gone better for me than I could have imagined, and although I was now a combat veteran, I was also just eighteen.

By the time we moved into the Snoqualmie fortifications, the One True and Only Ecucatholic Church was more commonly known as One True Church, and its forces had been thrown most of the way back to Reno—it was a thoroughly totalitarian meme that most people were afraid of, because it did such a thorough overwrite of the existing personality, and any remaining doubts anyone might have had about the way One True Church operated had been settled by the way the way the Bishop of Reno behaved after it got hold of him.

The biggest worry for Real America, and for BTJ, we thought, was that Seattle Dome and the Puget Sound area around it had been seized by the Neocommunist meme, which was extremely aggressive militarily. We had an uneasy truce with One True Church, south of us, a peace agreement with the various Native groups north of us, and a de facto alliance with the Unreconstructed Catholics who held much of the old American Midwest and Ontario on our eastern boundary. Real America's frontiers were as secure as anybody's (not very), and our population was more prosperous than most (which didn't take much doing).

Aside from the Neocommies, we also had to worry about our hanging flank to the southeast. The plains and desert country beyond the mountains had been a sort of unclaimed no-man's-land ever since Denver Dome was nuked in '54. There were enough people in that big central stretch of the Rocky Mountain Front so that any government that tried to move in got into all kinds of trouble with resistances and liberation movements and so on, but it was empty enough so that an army could move through, and we had to figure that sooner or later we would have to wheel around, run southeast as fast as we could, and defend the whole Bighorn country until the citizen army could be mobilized. Fear that something big might suddenly come up the Bighorn or the Missouri kept a lot of our forces tied up around Billings Dome, which was frustrating for everyone, but that was the way it went.

Over my three years so far in Burton's Thugs for Jesus, Tammy and I had settled into an existence that might not have been the ideal way for kids to grow up, but worked pretty well for us. During my weeks on the line or in the reserve camp, she stayed in the apartment in Spokane, took care of Carrie, and got whatever schooling she could, either on-line or live, against the day when there might be regular jobs again. Whenever I got a leave, I'd hop a diskster back to Spokane—four hours from Homestake, at first, and later only two from Snoqualmie—and zip home to get reacquainted with my daughter and to spend as much time as possible with Tammy. I suppose, except for our ages, there wasn't much about the life that a soldier in any long war of the past wouldn't have recognized.

At the time I didn't know, either, how fortunate we were that most of the rules of war were still being adhered to. As far as anyone could tell, no one had unleashed bioweapons, most domes were not bombed or shelled, and geosync cableheads remained demilitarized neutral zones. Nobody was fighting to the last ditch; it was understood that the moment you knew you couldn't win, you surrendered or retreated. War, so far, was purely a matter between the mercenary companies.

On the other hand, there were some drawbacks to being a mercenary, even in a very humane war. Attrition was taking its toll, and hyperaccurate modern smart weapons meant that a much smaller number of men was needed for the same firepower. Though Burton's Thugs for Jesus had begun the war at battalion strength, and our effective firepower had increased, in numbers we were no longer more than a reinforced company.

By that time I was a corporal, leading a fire team, and the only way I was ever making sergeant was if my best friend Rodney, the squad sergeant, got killed. (Two squad sergeants stood ahead of Rodney for platoon sergeant, so I stood very little chance of a domino promotion.) The chance of advancement—or the lack of chance—didn't bother me at all. I could keep doing what I was doing indefinitely, and if the job was unpleasant, dangerous, sometimes terrifying, occasionally nauseating, well, it was a war, when you came right down to it. And my leaves were practically heaven on Earth; Tammy and I never saw enough of each other to have much to fight about.

I turned twenty, Carrie turned five, and life turned to dead solid shit, all in April 2058. By then Real America had taken a hammering and was just trying to hold on. One True Church had become One True, and had successfully seized several of the older memes. Our old Unreconstructed Catholic allies were suddenly a branch of One True—so suddenly that we lost Madison in four hours of a savage attack out of nowhere. A week later we had to abandon the Twin Cities Domes after a bitter fight, and we were thrown back to Fargo-Morehead Dome, where we finally made a successful stand.

We held through a bitter winter of fighting—I made platoon sergeant, having buried all my predecessors. We got things squared away, got the Natives north of us to come in as allies, and seemed to be making more of a real fight of it. After beating back two assaults in the summer, we felt much more confident, and when we retook the Twin Cities Dome in September, it looked like the worst of it was over. BTJ held the Twin Cities Dome against another winter assault, and that spring Burton told us that if we wanted to, we could move dependents up into Fargo-Morehead, so that they'd be easier to visit on the weekend.

I figured we had the front stabilized, and I'd rather have Tammy and Carrie near. There were good reasons. I'd missed them, while there had been so few leaves; Spokane had been attacked a couple times by One True's hit-and-run raids out of Salt Lake and Boise; in the married-soldier barracks at Fargo, they could live under armed guard. It seemed like a rational decision.

To this day I think I should have been able to see that it was completely stupid to bring them up to Fargo, considering what we were fighting. When we retook it, the inside of the downtown Minneapolis Dome had been piled high with corpses—noncombatants all. One True had had no way to evacuate that group of women, children, and old men. Rather than let them be captured, and turned by any other meme, it had made them all walk off the roofs of high buildings.

It was One True that had broken all the truces and mercenary rules of engagement, and One True that had begun to aggressively infiltrate computer systems and weapons-control systems, seizing control of mercenaries wherever it could in order to copy what they knew. Then it loaded those aggregate mercenary memories into the brains of any kids it had, and sent them out with their badly working minds and their imperfectly assimilated training, to fight and die in the first wave of every attack. A regular mercenary company might kill eight or nine of those poor teenage zombies for every death it took itself—but a regular mercenary outfit, by then, wasn't much bigger than a hundred men, and One True could send three or five thousand of those enslaved kids against it. Every advance by One True made the war, and the world, uglier and dirtier; it seemed to be the one meme that didn't care what the Earth ended up looking like, as long as it got to rule.

The world tried to resist. Maddened by the fear of having their minds erased and replaced, countless people, crazy, paranoid, perhaps as dangerous as One True itself, devised memes, large and small, to subvert or attack One True, and to promote violence and disorder within One True's territory. One True hit back with the same kinds of memes aimed at the world at large, not caring who it hit. There were legends about a meme, or a counter-meme, called a Freecyber, a sort of meme-inoculation that could liberate you from One True or any other meme's control, but then there were legends about free passes to the space colonies, and hidden cities in Antarctica, and secret bases on the sea floor, where you could take your family and live peacefully forever. I didn't credit Freecybers any more than I did any of the others.

It was hard for anyone who had been in for as long as I had even to imagine the changes that were happening. One True was fighting to "win" in a sense that no one had seen since the Eurowar, now almost sixty years in the past. People with severe psychological trouble, particularly severe depression and stress disorders, were easier for a meme to self-install into—and so One True's troops were encouraged to traumatize the population wherever they went, and the all-but-forgotten custom of serbing captured women and children resumed in those last years of the war. As our electronic equipment became more and more vulnerable, we resorted to more and more primitive weapons and tactics, trying to avoid being hooked up to anything, even a phone, through which One True, or one of the rogue memes, or even the re-engineered (and much more aggressive) Real America might seize control of us. As memes increasingly were able to disguise their presence, and often to spread incrementally through conversation and ordinary daily interaction, we began to fight in pairs or trios, limiting our contact with anyone else. The almost civilized war I had joined was turning into the real Fourth World War, and it was rapidly catching up with the Eurowar and the two wars of the twentieth century for its savagery and lack of restraint—and it would probably end like all of them, in the sheer collapsed exhaustion of the losing side.

It seems so obvious in hindsight. I should have known how the world was going. I should have resigned, or deserted if Burton wouldn't let me go, grabbed Tammy and Carrie, and run like hell to somewhere; taken all my saved pay, maybe, or robbed some place, gotten enough money to pay our way onto a transfer ship, and emigrated to Mars. Sometimes I really did think about that, but at the same time I felt like I owed Burton a lot, and he was more and more shorthanded.

So I procrastinated and didn't resign, didn't desert, didn't look for a place where my family could move far away from the fighting, read the emigration information for Mars a hundred times and even realized I could probably make a living as an ecoprospector and might even like the work. I thought about it frequently, but I did nothing and just let it drift.

I had figured everything wrong. I found out just how wrong in the first week of August, 2059. I woke to the alarm in the middle of the night, rolled over, kissed Tammy, pulled on the fighting clothes, went into Carrie's room and gave her a quick hug, receiving a sleepy little kiss on the cheek, and pulled the gear out of my weapons locker. By then Tammy had come out in her bathrobe; she said, "Any idea—?"

"It's what they call an urgentest," I said, shouting to be heard over the alarm, which would keep ringing until I went out the front door. "Usually means we've got to jump on a diskster, go someplace, and fight. Get on-line and make sure all my insurance is paid up, will you, honey?"

"Is One True invading again?"

"Could be. Or maybe some ally switched sides." I checked; I had all the gear I was supposed to be picked up with. I desperately wanted another quick leak, a snack, anything for twenty more minutes with Tammy, but the alarm was whooping (I could hear most of the other alarms in the married-soldier barracks doing the same thing), and no matter how often I did this, I always wanted twenty minutes more. I could pee and eat on the diskster, going in; it was really just that I wanted time with Tammy. I contented myself with a long, awkward kiss, as she managed to fit against me despite all the hardware hanging from the suit. "I'll see you soon. Love you," I said, and left.

Two guys were already waiting at the pickup spot, and within five more minutes there were ten of us. My "headquarters" squad was a good one—I'd handpicked a bunch of experienced types to put plenty of vets around me, and everybody in the squad had at least two years fighting experience under his belt. The squad sergeant, Mark Prizzi, had been among the first squad of soldiers I'd ever trained, back when I was a corporal.

My headset popped. "Dog Platoon, come in, Currie." It was Burton.

"I'm here, sir," I said. "Headquarters squad is all assembled, waiting for pickup."

"Check your other squads."

I did; all were at stations. I reported back to Burton.

"Good so far," he said. "But it looks like the enemy has managed to virus our pool of disksters. Figure a half-hour delay till pickup, while we reload memories into all of them. You can let men go back inside if they want to do anything for fifteen minutes."

I passed the word along, but nobody went back in; once you've said your good-byes, that's just too hard. We stood around, not talking much, till the disksters showed up. I walked up the gentle slope of the gangplank and took my seat at the rear right, long-practiced hands strapping me in against the up-to-four-gee turns that these things could do—or the up-to-ten-gee jumps if something went bang too close to you. When my three squads were all loaded and strapped in, I reported back to Burton. "All right," he said. "Just a minute or so more for the disksters to pick up Bravo, and then we'll be in motion, finally. Looking bad."

"Can you tell me what it is?"

"Wait till we're on the highway," Burton said. "Then I'll let all the platoons know. But it ain't good, and this is gonna be a rough night, and I don't think we're all gonna see the sun come up." In some strange ways, competent and compassionate as he was, my CO was still a kid who had read one too many adventure books.

About fifteen minutes later we were racing down the corridor formed by the old highway, making all the speed we could for the Twin Cities, and Burton was filling us in. No intelligence outfit had yet figured out how—none of the intelligence companies from the area were even reporting, which suggested we had been hit even harder than we knew about—but somehow defenses around Twin Cities Domes had gone down, all at once, and before the garrison could mobilize, the barracks had been hit with narrow-beam ionizing radiation from overhead, cooking most of the defending troops in their beds or while they tried to pull on their uniforms, and all their families with them. The few on guard, and the few who had gotten mobilized fast enough, were now trying to hold a ragged, thin line south of the domes, with too few people, too ill-equipped, and no idea what was going to hit.

It hit before we got there, which is why we survived. At diskster emergency speeds with everyone strapped in, you could travel from Fargo-Morehead to Twin Cities in about an hour and a half. Within that time, the defenders at Twin Cities were overwhelmed by a force that was probably fifty times their size, plus more bursts from that damned irradiating satellite.

We kept going anyway, because the forces of One True zipped right around the Twin Cities Domes, dropping off a small garrison force, and fanned out toward the other important domes in the area. One big spearhead was coming our way. At least our disksters were fairly radiation-resistant, and should be proof against the ultrahard positrons they had used on their two bombardment passes so far.

Bravo Platoon had the lead, and they never had a chance at all. With onboard radar, a self-driving maneuverable vehicle like a diskster could normally dodge an artillery shell—but Bravo's disksters had had to spend a critical few extra minutes in the shop, and that was when, so far as Burton and everyone else could figure out later, they had been sabotaged with a sleeper virus that woke up when the first shells appeared above them, and they steered right under them. Bravo Platoon's three disksters flashed into smoke and debris, all of our disksters began to dodge and duck, and Burton did the only sensible thing and tried to have us pull back to form a fighting line somewhere where it might work. We swung east of the old highway in a tight, high-speed turn over the empty fields and meadows.

That was when all kinds of heavy fire poured onto us from the east; we had turned into their trap. The automated defense weapons on our disksters shot back, but we were up against something over-whelming, and we did the only thing that seemed to be an option—turned to run west and north, evading and dodging all the way, never having the spare minutes that would have been required for us to stop and deploy forces.

They pursued us for a solid hour, pushing us ever further west and further out of the battle, scattering our forces all over the land-scape. Any time one of the disksters tried to turn and fight, it was chewed apart by heavy fire; we evaded in all directions, and we must have traveled more than a thousand miles in total by sunrise, while only being pushed a couple of hundred west, but we were getting beaten bad no matter how you figured it, and the most we were managing was to run away.

At sunrise, we were way to hell and gone somewhere in South Dakota, they had just stopped shooting at us and broken off the pursuit, and Fargo was naked to the enemy.

We raced north as fast as we could, and we damn near made it; Burton's Thugs for Jesus, or what was left of us, were running even faster than we had after the slamming-around we'd just taken. Most of us had families in Fargo, or at least girlfriends.

Not long before noon, we were making a final dash, moving along at almost 200 mph over the prairie and meadow country that had been wheatfields once, about forty miles west of Fargo. It might have been a nice day if we hadn't all been worried sick about getting there, but theoretically in just minutes we could be taking up positions to the east of town, and calling in all the passenger disksters available. We weren't going to try to stop them, just slow them long enough to make it possible to get the civilian population, especially our dependents, out of their way. Burton had pledged to use the whole unit treasury, if need be, to evacuate all the civilians in Fargo-Morehead Dome.

Now all we had to do was get there soon enough and hold long enough.

Burton and his four headquarters staff were in the diskster just over a roll of land from us, maybe a mile and a half away—we were staying spread out in case of attack—and so I didn't see it directly, but there's no mistaking an atom bomb. A white flash over the ridgeline blinded us for a moment, and the diskster slewed sideways and bounced along for half a mile or more in just a few seconds, before the AI got it back under control and brought it around. By the time we were back near where we had been, the classic mushroom cloud was already forming. Burton must have been right at ground zero when that went off.

While we all wondered what to do—none of us had ever had any other CO and anybody else we might have turned to for leadership was on the diskster with him—one of the disksters for my platoon flared with blue arcs as it sank into the tall grass, its balancing capacitors all discharging. Our diskster went in to see if we could help, and the surviving parts of BTJ went with us because they weren't sure what else to do, but as we arrived, our com crackled and an unfamiliar voice said, "Burton's Thugs for Jesus, this is Shultz's Rangers. We've got you. Every one of your disksters has a weapon locked on it, and we are preparing to shut down your propulsion by our control of your software, which we just demonstrated with one diskster. Please have your senior surviving sergeant surrender, so we won't have to fire again."

That was me, I realized. I grabbed the com. "Burton's Thugs for Jesus here. We'll surrender. Are you offering UCEMC terms?"

"Our employer does not permit that," the voice said, flatly, and I realized that the other unit was memed with One True, so there wasn't going to be any negotiating. "Do you still wish to surrender or shall we fire?"

I gave the order, and our surviving five disksters set down, grounded out their charges, and went inert.

An hour later, still the senior surviving sergeant, I was trying to explain the issue. "Look," I said, "we are not acting for Real America in this. It just happens that most of our family and friends live in Fargo. All we're asking is time to declare it an open city, and some respect for Hague and Geneva. And we're asking. We're certainly not in any position to tell you."

Shultz nodded agreeably, his eyes far off; probably his whole company had only recently been turned. It was said that One True would do that to you for anything that it considered to be a violation of your contract. He spoke on the com for a while, repeating our requests.

Then he stopped and said, "Fargo-Morehead has been promised to Murphy's Comsat Avengers as a reward for their services. We are not at liberty to make any other arrangements. We will hold your forces here for sixty hours and then release you."

My heart sank through the floor. Murphy's Comsat Avengers was one of the most brutal mercenary companies anyone had heard of—from a unit initiation that made me sick to my stomach just to hear about, to an earned reputation as the most enthusiastic serbers in the war, to the mutilated bodies that they left behind to make pursuers hesitate, they were the epitome of everything that the War of the Memes had turned into in the last few years. They were one of the very few not-yet-turned companies that One True had under contract. It was rumored that they hadn't been turned because One True didn't want to share in any of their memories. I believed it.

I tried to appeal to Shultz's honor as a soldier and his human feelings, and I tried begging, and I offered to sign over our whole unit treasury to ransom the city, or even just to ransom our dependents. But it was absolutely no use to argue; Shultz now thought whatever One True needed him to think, and One True wasn't going to change its mind for a few scruffy, defeated POWs, not when it had already promised to reward one of its most effective fighting units.

We sat out our sixty hours under guard, and when they let us go, we fifty-five survivors—all that were left of the 122 men who had started out—began the long, unhappy walk toward Fargo. Nobody in Shultz's company bothered to say good-bye, let alone good luck.

Four days after I'd seen Burton vanish under that mushroom cloud, I stood by two graves in the public park not far from the college.

Hardly anyone was alive in that miserable town. Looking for Tammy, I'd seen half a dozen things that I figured I would remember for the rest of my life—a pile of heads outside a hospital, a whole street with a body on every tree, a quartered baby on a park bench, a woman with all four limbs torn off floating face down in a fountain.

It took me most of the day to find Tammy and Carrie, and it was almost a relief: they'd just been running down the street, trying to get away, and been hit from behind by machine-gun fire, probably body-heat-seeking bullets, because they'd each been hit in the back and the bullet had gone out through their hearts. They had died instantly, without torture or serbing, as far as I could tell, and Murphy had not been able to use them for his legendary hobby of killing children in front of their parents. No, they had been very afraid, and perhaps hurt for just a second, and then they had fallen forward, dead, Carrie's forearm still clenched in Tammy's hand.

I dug the graves deep and was careful about it; when I finished, I rolled a matformer over from a hardware store, set it on vitrous, and started shoveling dirt into it, letting it fill its tank all the way before I dumped it into the graves, so that I wouldn't have to smell too much of what happened when the hot material hit the bodies.

When I had filled the graves with molten glass, I poured a big block of glass at the head of each, positioning it to weld onto the filled grave, and with an iron bracket from a shattered park bench I pressed their names and their birth and death dates onto the slowly solidifying glass. I figured if anyone, animal or human, wanted to defile a grave, there would be easier ones to defile.

For two full years afterwards I was a madman. There really wasn't any other word for it. I took to stalking Murphy's Comsat Avengers. Every few weeks I'd pick out a man asleep in his tent, a sentry, a messenger, or any living human target from Murphy's, as long as I was sure of my escape, and kill him with a knife or bare hands, partly to be less detectable, mostly because it was more messy and painful for the victim.

Besides, doing it that way sometimes gave me an instant, as they realized what I was about to do, to tell them why. And after they were dead, I would do some cutting and rearranging, to give their buddies a surprise when they found them.

When MCA went into battle, I would shadow a scout or flanker, and kill him in the uproar. I had a few noisy radio beacons with timers that I would sometimes stick onto a piece of their equipment, and now and then one would go off and a diskster or a heavy weapon would be hit.

I left no notes, told no one, talked to no one who wasn't already dying, gave them no clue about who was doing it. I moved from place to place, following them generally east across the Midwest.

Eventually they were based along the south shore of Lake Ontario, not far from the southern tip of the still-growing Hudson Glacier. It was cold and dreary and the cover was less plentiful, but I stuck around and kept killing them, a few per year. I lived on one kind and another of scavenging; I was barely more than a predatory animal.

Once, when I had gone hungry for a while, and I had knifed two Comsat Avengers in their tent as they slept, I took away not only their rations, but their buttocks, hamstrings, and quadriceps; that might have been the beginning of my return to sanity, because when I reached my camp, the thought of cooking and eating those was too much. I tossed them out into the snow for a cougar, wolf, or coyote. To my surprise, I could not quite descend as far as cannibalism. Still, the next night I shot one of their sentries at long range, so I hadn't exactly forgiven or forgotten. I just had some standards, I guess you'd say.

I doubt they even knew I was there. They were up to their necks in so much fighting, and so much of it was now stalk-and-ambush, that a few men more or less in a year was nothing much. If they thought about it, they must have thought that they were running into exceptionally bad luck, the way the rest of the human race had been for so long.

Dave leaned back and shuddered for a moment, more as if he were cold than afraid. "Up around Lake Ontario?" he asked.

"Yeah, not far from where the St. Lawrence ice dam used to form and break. Spent a long time freezing my butt off up there. Not much left in the ruins—so many armies had gone through, you know. But I managed."

He stared into space for a long time. "You and I have much more in common than either of us thought," he said. "I lived up there at the same time, so I guess you won't be surprised to hear that I also had one hell of a grudge against Murphy's Comsat Avengers. I don't know who could live in that area and not feel that way, you know?"

I nodded. "Yeah, I know what you mean. The strangest thing to me, right now, is that I've spent decades during which the memories didn't hurt, or at least I didn't know that they hurt—losing my wife and child, the things I saw, the things I did . . . I spent ages without thinking about it, and now, here I am an old man, with a lot more present things to worry about, like whether or not you're going to kill me—and I can't get it out of my head. I can't make it go away. I'm halfway to crying and halfway to screaming and if you told me that Murphy's was somewhere in the neighborhood and you wanted to go kill one, I'd beg you on my knees to let me come along and help. It's like none of that went away at all; more like I just had a complete lapse of memory for twenty-five years."

Dave nodded. "Well, you know, that's not an uncommon reaction in people who have been dememed. I've seen people our age crack up, or go into shock, when they're dememed, from just remembering too much. Anybody who lived through those years has a bunch of experiences he never wants to talk about, and feelings he can't get rid of, and so forth. I'm no big fan of One True, but I can understand why some people would let it turn them, or even go out and find it and ask it to turn them. My memories are bad enough, and if someone told me I could just forget them forever, at a bad moment on a bad day, I guess I just might wish to be turned."

"It's not that you forget them," I said, "it's just that you don't think about them. Ever. For a real long time." A thought was beginning to bother me, more and more—memories and thoughts flooding back, different remembered pains striking me from all sides, throwing me off balance. I realized, too, that I was no longer reaching for Resuna to get them fixed, but I wasn't sure whether that was because I had gotten used to Resuna not fixing them, or because I didn't want Resuna to do that. I wished I could make the thought come clear in the front of my mind where I could know it for whatever it might be.

"Being able to not think about it might be good enough," Dave said, "when the times are bad enough." We both leaned back into the hot water, stretching and shaking ourselves out. "Two old farts that spent too much of their lives working hard outside sure appreciate a hot bath, don't they?"

I arched my back and let myself float upward. "Yeah. You know how farts like to float to the top in a tub."

It was a dumb joke, but he stretched his own back and laughed. "You want to switch from coffee to something stronger? I've got cases and cases of wine around and I never drink it because I hate to drink alone."

"That would be real fine."

"And I ain't gonna kill you tonight, either. I'm way too soft for this job, you know."

"We're none of us what we used to be," I said. "Jeez, I don't even *need* the wine to make me say stupid things."

"It's like parabolic skis," he said, grinning, shaking the water drops from his beard as he got out. "You don't have to have them to turn, but they make it so much easier. You don't need wine to say stupid things . . ." He shrugged.

I gave him a thumbs-up. "Bottle for each of us?" he asked, pausing at the door.

"Pos. Fucking. Def."

He laughed gaily and went out. Abstractedly I considered that I could leap out of the tub, break the coffeepot, jump him when he got back, cut his throat with the shard, put on some of his clothes, and walk out and signal to be rescued. Cowboy hunters are not supposed to kill unless we have to, but I seriously doubted that I'd be in any great trouble about this in the present circumstances. Even if I were, all that my new copy of Resuna would do is help me to see that I had acted in a deluded way, that the violence hadn't been necessary, had been no part of One True's intentions.

I froze. I could barely breathe. The thought I had been looking for had come to me.

I had spent my years as a soldier—except my very earliest—

fighting against One True. I had been on the other side for years. Soldiers for One True had killed my wife and child, shot them down in the back as they fled to escape serbing, torture, god knew what atrocities. One True had turned Murphy's Comsat Avengers loose on that town, and all those scattered, piled, dangling, mashed bodies had been permitted by it. It had even sent Shultz's Rangers to keep us away so that we wouldn't interfere.

One True had broken the understandings among mercenary companies, making the war much more savage. It had abrogated Geneva and the Hague. It had brought back all the nightmares of past wars, turned loose every horror from atom bombs to massacres to looting and serbing. And I had fought against it. In fact . . . a huge, dark, horrible shape rose in my mind and I was ready to cry.

Well, I realized, I sure wasn't going to kill *Dave*. He was most likely the only other person on the planet who might understand what the matter was. I just wished I had a clue as to what I was going to do.

"Well, here's the party," Dave said, coming in with four bottles of the wine, a corkscrew, and even wineglasses. "I brought along twice as much wine, just in case the first one I open turns out to have gone to vinegar," he said. "Besides which, it might just happen we need to get extra-stupid before the evening is over."

So it was evening, I thought, and wondered for a moment if guessing a time and believing it—say 8:30 P.M.?—might bring back Resuna. I didn't much care.

He fiddled with the first bottle, solemnly, and at last extracted the cork, pouring a sizable glass, which he handed to me. "Try it—carefully."

I took a sip. I'm no connoisseur, but it wasn't vinegar and it didn't taste like barrel, and it went down smooth and warm. "Great," I said.

He handed me the bottle. I poured myself a full glass, set the bottle carefully on the floor beside the hot tub, and took another sip. Meanwhile he was opening the other one, and in a minute he was back in the water beside me. "Good health," he said, raising the glass.

I clinked mine against his. "Good health," I agreed. "Well, I never did answer your question; I told you all the story that leads up to how I got turned by One True, but I never did tell you that story itself."

"I sure don't have any meetings to rush off to," he said, "and it's been a long time since I heard a new story. You keep talking and I'll keep pouring and we'll have a fine old time."

"It's not a very nice story," I said.

"The best thing about stories about bad stuff," he said, "most especially true ones, is that you can remember it's all in the past."

I wasn't so sure it *was* all in the past, but I didn't say that. I launched in, and figured we'd talk about it after I told it, or not, just as he pleased. The wine was good, the hot tub was grand, and my calendar was as open as his.

👁️ I've seen vid and flashchannel recordings of the celebrations of the Pope's Peace in 2002, the one that ended the Eurowar. People dancing in the streets, soldiers from all the sides hugging each other, the famous shot of the mayor of Paris turning a shovelful of earth to celebrate the beginning of Reconstruction. The Earth was poor, worn-out, shot all to hell. The uncontrolled bioweapons were raging across the planet, converting forests to wastelands, farmers' fields to obscene black goo, fishing grounds to empty water. Lowland soft-soil areas like Florida, the Netherlands, Bangla Desh, were gone. Tailored rice blast was threatening to make rice extinct in Asia, and if it couldn't be stopped, the expected famine might wipe out half of the human race.

And yet there was a sense of hope, faith—even a feeling that human beings had been delivered from a far worse fate—and in the pictures, still or moving, you can see the joy, courage, and faith in the faces of the people.

There are no such pictures from the end of the War of the Memes. Twelve years, four months, and nineteen days of global fighting don't leave you much energy or joy to celebrate with. What you see are two sets of expressions: the grim determination on the faces of those whom Resuna had turned, who knew that they were going to be working like donkeys for a decade or more just to get the world back to material decency, and the horror of those trying to emigrate offworld before the scheduled forcible turning of all those who had not turned voluntarily. 2.7 million would depart on the last regularly scheduled voyages of the transfer ships; the rest would be anesthetized so that jacks could be installed in their heads, and then would be quietly, painlessly, but inexorably turned to Resuna.

The billion people running One True, but without cellular jacks, would be equipped with the jacks, and then their copies of One True would be replaced with Resuna; a single One True would run as an emergent program on the vast network of cellular automata created by all the linked copies of Resuna. There was a bitter joke about One True ascending into the network, and another one about the human race being demoted—since One True had occupied the mind completely and Resuna would merely be a voice in your head and a sort of add-on to your personality, we were going from having everyone be an identical lord to everyone being an identical serf. To be sure, those jokes only circulated in the temporarily free population.

Millions of people were turned away at the processing centers up on the supras, as the transfer ships cherry-picked the most valuable 2.7 million free citizens; money, family, possessions of any kind, even genetic heritage didn't count—only highly developed knowledge and skill, and only the very finest of that. Rockefellers, Kennedys, Rothschilds, Windsors, Michelins, and Toyodas were turned back with a shrug—they had nothing of value to offer. Beautiful models, known on sight to the whole planet, couldn't get a second look. Mathematicians, surgeons, violinists, sculptors,

poets, gymnasts, footballers—so long as they were the very best of
the very best, as judged by the transfer ship and colony governments—got aboard, and so did the very closest members of their
families, especially if the family itself was highly talented. Dinner-
table conversation during the months of journey to the colonies
must really have been something.

The offworld colonies and the transfer ships had absolutely no
need of a fair-to-good infantry sergeant. I suppose I might have
gotten aboard unofficially, using my skills as an obsessive assassin,
but I was only good at killing people I hated psychotically; I didn't
want to kill any poor bastard who, like me, was just trying to
escape from an Earth that was about to become the sole property
of One True.

By the time I even got to the cablehead at Quito, they had a
bunch of space types down on Earth, rationing the train seats up to
Supra New York. The transfer ships were not willing to come anywhere near any meme again after Unreconstructed Catholic's
attempt to seize the *Albatross* a few years ago, so they had each
agreed to take just one load of colonists out to the colonies before
bending their trajectories forever away from the Earth. The bottle-
neck was not the capacity of the transfer ships—in the several cubic
kilometers of their cargo bays, they could move whole cities of
people plus all the needed food, water, and air—but the number of
available shuttles, since the transfer ships were only within shuttle
range for about six weeks of an Earthpass. It took a shuttle, seating
about 1800 passengers, anywhere from four to eleven days round
trip, between a supra and the transfer ship as it swung by the Earth,
with the first shuttles reaching the transfer ship just as it came in
range and the last ones being barely able to make pickup on its way
out. Minor variations in exactly where each transfer ship was coming from, which supras the shuttles could return to, and where the
Earth was in its orbit at the time, determined the exact number of
shuttle flights that were possible, but it worked out to only about
540,000 passengers going onto each transfer ship, even though the

transfer ships could easily have handled two million each. At least, if you got aboard, once you were on the transfer ship you were going to have plenty of room.

By the time I was trying to talk my way aboard, only the *Wandering Jew*, which had been the Earth-Titan transfer ship, remained; I had seen each of the other four transfer ships appear as a dim star in the night sky, grow to be ten times brighter than Venus, recede into dimness again, and then sprout a great flare of purples, golds, and greens as their MAM drives kicked in to re-bend the orbit for a new destination—the *Flying Dutchman* first, back in March, then *Mohammed's Coffin*, then *Diogenes*, and the *Albatross* just a few weeks ago. Now, in November, with binoculars you could just make out the incoming *Wandering Jew*. In a few weeks it would go from dim star to bright star to dim star to surreal comet—and it was the last ship from Earth.

I never got any farther than the cablehead on Mount Cotopaxi. A wheezing spacer in a powered wheelchair heard my story, then asked politely and gently if I had any skills or experience, anything at all, that I hadn't already told him about. I had to admit that since I'd been soldiering from the age of fourteen, I had no skills they were ever likely to need out there. He looked terribly sad as he stamped my form with REFUSED.

They didn't even have enough seats on the trains, anymore, to let people go up to the supras and try; four million people waited in line on SNY alone, in addition to the two million who normally lived there, all of them endlessly applying, applying, and applying for the few remaining seats, some hoping that their skills would suddenly be wanted after all, others hoping that an administrative mistake might slip them aboard, most just hoping. Trains took two days to geosynchronous orbit, and didn't carry enough passengers; they had to be reserved for people who were genuinely good candidates.

I walked out of the vast, echoing terminal at the cablehead, and watched for a moment as a train climbed slowly up the narrow line of the track on the vast, kilometer-wide surface of the cable, accelerating quickly to 500 mph, vanishing into the clouds in a few scant seconds. There might be fifty people, out of the thousand on that train, who would get aboard; the rest would be coming back down, after a while, to be turned by Resuna and rebuilt—*no doubt into useful, productive, helpful citizens*, I thought, savoring the cold cynical feel in my mind, *just like I'm gonna be. If Mr. Farrell hadn't been killed in one of One True's bombing raids, I just bet he'd be real pleased with what One True is going to make out of me.*

I had no idea what to do at all; no family left to love, no Murphy's Comsat Avengers left to hate, no BTJ or Real America to command my loyalty anymore. I might have known a person or two in Spokane Dome, but I hadn't been back there in years and hadn't kept in touch with anyone I knew from the orphanage. I guess that was about as alone as I'd ever been.

I walked down the road, toward the city of Quito. I wasn't planning to walk the whole way, but for the moment I was being too cheap and not in enough of a hurry to catch a public diskster, too tired to think much, not quite too numb to feel sorry for myself, miserably hot in the late afternoon equatorial sun. All along the road I could see exhausted, discouraged, frustrated people like me, in ones and twos and families, some muttering about the unfairness of it all, some trying to cheer themselves up by brightly saying that maybe everyone wouldn't have to be turned (and inventing reasons why One True wouldn't want to turn them in particular), some comforting others, a few cursing endlessly, most just walking along toward Quito because that was the only logical place to walk from the cablehead.

Beside me, a woman's voice said, "It's really rough, isn't it? People understand that everyone can't go, but all the same it's so hard to be one of the ones who doesn't go."

"Yeah," I said, as much reply as I could think of. At least this might be someone to talk to. I glanced sideways and saw a woman with a thick, single brown braid down to her waist and an aquiline nose. She was wearing a black and red sweatshirt that advertised the 2048 Olympics in Singapore, mended but not dirty blue jeans, and ankle-high hiking boots. I guessed that she might be anywhere between eighteen and thirty, depending on how she'd gotten through the war. Her head was up and she was looking around, not seeming depressed at all, and that made her absolutely unique on the road, as far as I could see ahead or behind.

"Do you have any plans for what you're going to do now?" she asked.

"No," I said. So far she was doing all the work in the conversation, and that seemed sort of unmannerly, so I added, "Didn't have any plans other than to come here and try, so that I could at least feel like I tried. I'm an old mercenary. No use for us on Earth or in the colonies. People have given up war, at least for quite a while, and that's all I ever had any knowledge of or training for."

"It must be tough to feel like no one needs you anywhere," she said, with just enough real sympathy in her voice so that I was pretty sure she hadn't been walking up the road saying it to everyone, as someone who had been turned by a meme might do. My first thought had been that she must be one of those few people who were still independent of memes—or at least of big, controlling, take-over-the-whole-personality memes—because she didn't have the slightly flat, time-delayed, vaguely robotic affect that most people with memes had, or at least most people that I knew to have memes. It was always possible that she either had one that was cunning enough to lay low, or perhaps she was running a bunch of smaller, non-dominating ones, like so many mercenaries I had known (it could be handy to have some of the abilities they carried, like certain kinds of emotional control and skills). I was lonely but I didn't need company that was going to try to take over my personality—just at the moment that was about all I had left and there wasn't much of it.

We had walked a short ways together before she said, "I just noticed that you were discouraged, but not angry."

"I don't have much energy to be angry with," I said. "I lost my family in the war, and I got my revenge for that, and now there isn't going to be a 'me' anymore, so I guess on the whole I'm quits with the world. Whatever I was here for has been accomplished. So I don't have much commitment, one way or another, to anything except going back down to Quito, catching a diskster to somewhere else, and maybe checking into a hotel and spending all my back pay before they erase all money next year."

What I had just told her wasn't quite true. I had been thinking that a man who had survived out in the wilderness, hunting professional soldiers, as I had for two years, surely could manage to disappear and stay disappeared, maybe living somewhere out on the fringe of the settled areas or maybe around some ruin deep in the woods. It might be lonely, at least until I found other people doing it, which I figured there were bound to be. At least I'd still be myself.

I was sort of thinking of taking a diskster up to Albany Dome and walking from there up into the Adirondacks—it might take weeks or months, especially with the first heavy snowfalls starting in late September as they did these days, but if I got there soon, grabbed gear and basic supplies in a week or less, and got out of the dome without leaving too many traces, I ought to be thoroughly gone by November 30, when all of us who were still unturned were supposed to turn ourselves in.

Given just how risky the whole business would probably be, I wasn't about to confide it to a woman I'd just met. You never knew who might be listening or when she might be turned. But I did like the company, and what I had said so far was only what you might have expected of someone who'd been turned down at a cablehead.

"You're not going to try at Kilimanjaro or Singapore?" she

asked, sounding surprised. "You know there's always another chance."

"Naw. Why? There's another chance if you're on the borderline, maybe, but the list of what they're looking for is the same in all three places, and nobody like me is on that list anywhere, you know? Experienced professional killer? That's just about the only thing that One True and the colonies agree on—they don't want any more of them. So there's no point using up one of my few remaining weeks as myself running from cablehead to cablehead begging. I can make far better use of the time, even if I just use it to lie on my back in the grass, at night, and watch the stars turn around."

"When you put it that way, yeah, I guess there are better uses for the time." She grinned at me. "Are you planning to have any company in the grass?"

"Haven't really been interested since I buried my wife," I said, not particularly sharply. I wasn't trying to discourage her attention—right now it was the only thing even vaguely interesting I had encountered—but I didn't quite have the energy or interest to come up with an appropriate, gracious lie.

"I did say company, not ass," she pointed out, smiling.

On the equator, the sun rises right at six and goes down right at six, and so darkness was starting to sweep into the afternoon even though it wasn't particularly late. There was still some daylight left, but the very first lights were going on in Quito, down below us, and the shadows on the backs of the people ahead of us, and the faces of the ones behind us, made everyone into indistinct figures. Now and then a diskster would come up or down the road, alternately darkening or flashing as it passed through patches of light and shadow. We walked another hundred meters or so before she said, "My name is Mary Roder."

"I'm Currie Curran." I realized the conversation had reached a point where, out of nothing but politeness, I should be asking her a few things about herself. "Were you up there applying, too?"

"No, not really," she said. "I've got no reason to leave Earth."

"Not to get away from One True?"

"I'm part of it," she said, so comfortably and easily that at first I didn't believe she'd said that, and I must have gaped at her stupidly. "Really," she said, emphatically. "I've been running Resuna for a year and a half."

She kept right on walking along that mountain road, just as casually as if she had merely happened to mention that she collected stamps or had worked as a carpenter. It seemed too bizarre to be a joke and too pointless to be any kind of a scam; it might be the truth.

"You don't act like somebody with a meme."

"It doesn't feel like having a meme," she said. "I ran One True for years, and that whole time I felt like I was just crouched in a corner in the back of my brain, unable to do anything but watch. Now I feel like I run the show—I just have a very useful, friendly voice in my head that gets me through things. And on very rare occasions, One True calls me up, but now it calls to talk, it doesn't take over my head."

"Well," I said, stupidly, repeating the obvious because I couldn't think of anything else to say, "you really don't come across as a person with a meme."

"Neither do most of the people with Resuna," she said. "I can't promise you, when you turn, that you'll like it, but I can promise it will be different from what most people imagine. I'd think that would be sort of a relief, because most people imagine *horrible* things."

I agreed that that was true, and we walked for a while longer. Eventually, looking for something to talk about, we talked about how big the geosynch cable really was, up close—on most of the Earth, of course, the night view of a geosynch cable was just a black vertical line ascending from the horizon, suddenly turning to brilliant silver somewhere in the sky; the silver line continued on up to where it was capped by a burning white dot, the size of a BB shot held at arm's length. But here, right by it, it looked like a mountain with no top; it was almost a mile thick and went right up into the sky farther than you could see, to something that looked like a tiny half moon right overhead.

I didn't feel much for her, or anything, but Mary was company, and that was pleasant. She didn't seem to be doing any of the things that a person with a meme was usually compelled to do, like trying to persuade me to join her or acquire the meme, which meant either that Resuna was subtle and crafty, or just possibly it really *wasn't* as terrible as the other memes were.

Always assuming she was telling the truth at all.

"I bet," she said, "that you are wondering about whether my copy of Resuna is going to try to grab control of you. Am I right?"

"Exactly right," I admitted.

"Well, you aren't going to believe this," Mary said, moving just enough closer to me so I couldn't help being aware of her compact, slightly heavy body. "But it's true, anyway. Resuna is a sterile meme, by design. It has to be loaded into people. It can't load itself or spread by itself. Like a seedless orange or a mule—purely a useful creation, not an independent form of its own."

"Why?" I asked, really curious about something for the first time in a long time.

"Because reproductive neurocode for a meme, not to mention the neurocode for reproductive motivation, takes up enormous amounts of space in human memory," she said, "and Resuna no longer needs to be able to reproduce itself, because it isn't going to have to spread by memetic contagion anymore. The global system and One True can reproduce Resuna as needed. The whole idea of Resuna is that it's no bigger than necessary—it leaves you as much room in your head as it can."

"Why doesn't it just leave you the whole thing?"

She shrugged. "What kind of world have people made, running their own lives?"

I thought about that as it got dark and we traveled on. I was more troubled than I wanted to admit by my inability to come up with any answer that was as good an argument as the ones she had right to hand: half the domes on Earth wrecked, hundreds of millions dead, so much of the progress made by the two Reconstruction generations completely undone, the colonies and all the off-Earth industrial production lost, species extinct by the thousands, the glaciers eating away at one hemisphere while warming destroyed the other, the human population itself riddled with near-helpless lunatics who had been so traumatized that they could no longer even take care of themselves—the list went on for a very long time, and against that, all I could say was, "But I'm used to being me."

"And I'm used to being me," Mary said, "and I still am me. Just me with more self-control, and the ability to work with my whole heart for the common survival—and because everyone else will have Resuna, I also know I'm going to be working with other people who are also giving one hundred percent to it. Do you realize how much difference that makes? No worries, at all, about other people cheating on the social contract—so when you do the right thing, you'll never feel like a sucker. No doubts about how other people are feeling. You get to be your best self, and you can depend on them to be their best selves."

"Uh, you're not sounding like a meme, but you *are* sounding like a PR department somewhere wrote your dialogue."

She giggled, and it was a healthy natural sound. "Yeah, sorry. Resuna spends a certain amount of its effort in persuading the people who have it that they're better off with it. I'm afraid we all do speak with some of the same phrases, and some of them aren't very natural. But Resuna will get smarter. And I'm really not kidding; having it in your head doesn't mean you're not you, which does make it different from most other memes."

I thought about that one as it got darker. We talked about other trivial stuff, where our lives had taken us, what we had done. I said just enough about having lost Tammy and Carrie so that I figured she wouldn't bring it up; she told me that she'd been a novice in an Unreconstructed Catholic convent. When One True had invaded and captured her area, the convent was given as a reward to a mercenary company, for seventy-two hours of the sort of thing that used to happen in those last years of the war. At the end of the three days, the survivors were all turned by One True. She had One True for a long time after that, "which was probably better than crying and screaming and lying in the fetal position, because I'm here and I'm functioning now. And One True did do some repairs to me, and now Resuna's coming along with fixing up the rest of me, I guess you could say. At least it seems like it's done enough repairs to be able to give me more freedom."

"More freedom?" I asked. I wasn't used to thinking of that in connection with One True.

The sun was gone. Our road was lighted in front of us by the glow of the city below. She moved closer, and I felt her hand very tentatively touching mine. A minute later we were holding hands, and that seemed pleasant, after years alone. If this was how One True was going to come after the unturned population, in these new days of Resuna, well, it was *much* nicer than being netted, sedated, and brainwashed.

I thought she had just droplined me, after I asked my question, maybe because she was offended. But then she said, "Well, I guess it depends on what you mean by freedom. Without One True I'd have been free to do whatever I wanted, but all I wanted to do was sit and cry. With One True, I at least got some of my life restarted, and was useful, and meanwhile I could be huddled up inside, crying at first, and then thrashing things out, and finally getting better, while not being either a danger to myself or a burden on everyone else. And now with Resuna I'm free to do and be so many more things, but I feel safer knowing that if I'm about to do something stupid, or crazy, or dangerous, it will stop me—probably just by talking to me and persuading me that it's not in my best interests. So I'm free to not be miserable, or useless, and I'm free to not spend all of my time coping with what happened to me and my friends, and most of all I'm free to make myself useful and effective and someone I can like. That's *lim* more freedom than I had when I felt compelled to rock and sob."

"I can see how you would feel that way," I said, and couldn't help thinking that if Tammy and Carrie had survived, somehow, they too would have been living down gruesome memories for a long time, and might well have welcomed anything at all that gave them a way to function and to shut down some of the pain.

"Well," she said, "and it's done other good things for me. Can I be honest with you?"

"I think I'd prefer it," I said, "if Resuna will let you."

"Silly, it's the one that suggested being honest." She drew a deep breath and pressed down on my hand, so that we walked even closer to each other. "The thing is, it's hard to explain," she said, "and I'm afraid it might upset you, but I'd rather have you know it than not. I was a virgin—hadn't even been kissed— when I entered the convent. Then I got gang-raped for several hours, and some other stuff." She said it with about as much emotion as most people mention having their wisdom teeth out. "After I got turned to One True, I never had sex, and I haven't had sex since I turned from One True to Resuna, but Resuna says I'm ready if I want to, and, well, gee, I'm healthy and twenty-two and . . . uh, see, Resuna and One True have really good information about me, and good information about many people they haven't turned yet, and . . . oh, well, look, One True picked you out for me. Since I was already here in Quito, it's where my job is and all, and they knew you were applying, they sent me up here to meet you. And I think you're really great-looking and you've been so nice and well—there. Now I told you. But I approached you all on my own. Really. I just got some hints about what to say from Resuna. So if we, you know, do it, you'll be with me, not with Resuna, and we don't have to rush or anything if you—"

"Whoa," I said. I was still holding her hand, and she was

pressed close against me; we weren't moving very fast. "Resuna, or One True, or somebody, picked me out of all the guys on Earth?"

When she responded her voice was oddly flat—more mechanical than it would have been with most other memes. Because Resuna is relatively small, it doesn't have much fine control on things like inflection. "Actually you were picked out of the eligible unattached men who would be passing through Quito this week. Mary Roder has a common problem that comes up during recovery; in the process of healing and learning to look forward to her future again, she has begun to romanticize more than would be optimal for a healthy emotional life. She needs to have an experience with someone who will not be rough, impatient, or rude, but whom she sees as strong enough to protect her—basically a sensation of complete safety—but she needs to not fall too completely in love. So a handsome, kind, courteous stranger is what is called for, and that is you, Currie Curran. If you don't wish to do this, we'll find someone else without much difficulty, but you were the first choice. And we of One True know enough of your life to know that you must be very lonely and unhappy; an evening with company and affection would hardly harm you."

"Can Mary hear you saying this?"

"No. In just a few minutes she'll become conscious without realizing that she walked this distance with you while unconscious. Meanwhile, do you want to do this? If not, she can lose interest."

I thought about it for a moment. It was strange to have my arm around her waist while another mind talked for her. She wasn't really my type, I suppose, but it had been a long time, and I was lonely, and the thought of being all alone in some anonymous hotel was unattractive. "I'd like to," I said. "And I'll be as gentle and patient as you need me to be."

"As Mary needs you to be," Resuna corrected me. "And you would not have been selected had we not known what we do of your past. Your feelings are very straightforward, reasonable ones; you love those who love you back, you hate those who hurt them, you give your loyalty to things you think are worthy. It's that simplicity which Mary Roder needs.

"Before I bring Mary Roder's personality back, there are two things you need to know. First, you may either continue this relationship or not; we will see that the memory is a good one for Mary, as long as you help by creating pleasant experiences to work with. If you do wish to continue, you may stay with Mary after you are turned.

"Second, and this is very important: the cue phrase that enables Resuna to take over and deal with emotional distress is 'Let overwrite, let override.' If Mary appears to become hysterical or catatonic, if she acts in ways that seem unusual or unhealthy, if she begins to cry uncontrollably or shows any other sign of real distress, speak that phrase, firmly, until she hears it. That will bring Resuna to the front of her mind to deal with the crisis."

"You can't just come on your own?"

"Resuna is systematically limited; if it had the power to overpower human minds, it would have the power to contemplate resistance to One True, and that cannot be permitted. Do you have any question?"

"No, I don't."

"A public diskster will pick you both up in a few minutes. It will take you to Buenos Aires Dome, where there's a hotel room waiting. No charge—it is One True's way of thanking you for helping Mary."

I walked along with her body, around a slow bend in the road, for maybe ten minutes, turning the alternatives over in my head. I was really not seeing any likelihood of any problems I couldn't handle, and the idea was more attractive every time I thought it through. At last I said, "All right, I'll do it."

"Remember," the Resuna voice said, "Mary Roder will not remember we had this conversation, and as far as she is concerned, the last seventeen minutes and twenty seconds never happened. Enjoy yourself, treat Mary well, and remember you have One

True's gratitude. Are you ready for me to release her back into her body?"

"I guess so."

With a subtle shift in her body, Mary regained control and consciousness. "Since I was already here in Quito, it's where my job is and all, and they knew you were applying, they sent me up here to meet you. And I think you're really great-looking and you've been so nice and well—there. Now I told you. But I approached you all on my own. Really. I just got some hints about what to say from Resuna. So if we, you know, do it, you'll be with me, not with Resuna, and we don't have to rush or anything if you want to take your time and get to know each other first. What do you think?"

"I think I ought to com for a nice high-speed diskster, and hire it on my credit to take us somewhere nice, have dinner on the diskster, spend a while looking at scenery and messing around, check into a hotel room, mess around some more, and just kind of see what happens," I said. "Have you ever been to Buenos Aires?"

❧ **"So what exactly happened?"** Dave asked. "You woke up the next morning with a jack in your head, or she talked you into talking to a terminal for a while, or you fell in love and decided to stay?"

"Mostly that last one," I said. "Mary was very attentive and very affectionate. And I was just twenty-five, even if I was a widower, and I'd only ever been with Tammy before, and it had been years, and so at first I was probably just there for the sex and the not being lonely part. Then I got kind of hooked on being her hero, I guess you'd have to say, and after that I started to see that she really needed me—and by then it was November 15, a beautiful spring in Buenos Aires, the warmest on record—and way too late to make any plans to run away, and so one evening I came back from having a jack put in, and we made love, and she plugged me into the phone and held my hand, and when I woke up I was turned, and running Resuna. We held a party to celebrate. And now we've been married twenty-three years. And this is the first time since 2062 I've really had a free thought about whether or not I like her, or what kind of a wife she's been."

Dave nodded slowly, as if digesting the whole situation. "What do you think?"

"I think I miss her at the moment. I hope she's not too worried. I'd like to see her again."

He smiled. "Well, good, then. Another glass?"

"Pos fuckin' def."

"And can I trust you not to tie me up and turn me in if we get very drunk tonight?"

"Yeah, I think so."

"Good enough." He raised his glass. "My story's not as dramatic, so we're going to need more wine."

✒ Dave's tale didn't take long. He was a foundling in Denver Dome, a few years after I was dropped off at Spokane Dome—we both thought it was pretty funny (with help from the wine) that we theoretically could be brothers. He'd been in a couple of mercenary units before being hired as part of the bodyguard for a Freecyber cell in upstate New York, within fifty miles of where I was stalking Murphy's Comsat Avengers.

He'd liked working for the Freecybers—he said they were pleasant employers, met their bills, didn't ask for the impossible, treated you like people—but it came to an abrupt end when Murphy's unit overran them and butchered the people they were guarding. "No call for it, either," he said. "They could have just turned them. It was pretty close to the end of the war. Could've just put One True into them, and I bet that's what One True would have preferred. Murphy's was the only mercenary company I ever heard of that regularly killed just for fun; it was like a whole outfit of serial killers."

I nodded and took a big slurp of the wine, which was absolutely delicious. "Yeah. You know where Murphy came from? He was nothing more than an old vag at the time the war broke out. There probably weren't two thousand vags left on the planet in 2049, but unfortunately, he happened to be one of them."

Dave shrugged. "I knew a couple of former vags, myself. One of them and I went sniping a few times, because he was so crazy he'd go show himself on the skyline to draw fire—he lasted about a week, I think. All the old vags I knew were crazy. Most of them were people who just never got over losing something, and spent their lives in the woods, robbing and looting, trying to get it back, pathetic crazy bastards who were dangerous to anyone they ran into, but otherwise not anything much to worry about. Murphy was something else again entirely, a lot more than just crazy. He was about as evil and sick a bastard as the poor old world has ever seen and it's a good thing his delusions made him too incompetent to get anywhere."

"Amen," I said, and extended my glass in a toast; we clinked them together, and I said, "I saw him die. You could call it a mixed pleasure. I had always hoped to get the fucker myself, and the first time I was about to get a good shot at him, two of his own men did it. The three of them were out in front of his tent, talking about what to do now that peace was here, and he was going on in some crazy riff about putting the comsats back up—like anyone needs them with the supras there. Then he grabbed one of them by the shirt, and the other one shot him. I was so startled that I muffed my first shot at one of them, so they both got away."

Dave nodded firmly. "You at least got in a good try at them. Me, once Freecyber was gone, I didn't have any side in the war, so I just went into the bush. Here's a strange thought. I didn't have nearly as much grudge against One True as you did, and if One True had made me the offer to become a cowboy hunter—even without being memed, just hunting cowboys in exchange for my keep—I might have taken it. And from what you tell me, if you hadn't run into Mary on that road, you might have drifted into cowboying, or whatever it was called up the Northeast. We could've been on switched sides. Funny how life cuts."

"Yeah," I said. The warm water and the wine were getting a dead solid grip on me, and I was fading fast. "I'm starting to think of bed," I admitted.

"Me too, Currie. Let's drink up. There's not much left of these bottles."

There wasn't much left of his; there was about a quarter of mine, but I pounded it right down like a dumbass teenager anyway. He took my glass, reached to an overhead shelf, and handed me a bar of soap. "Oatmeal soap, for rich ladies to scrub their dingy skin with," he said cheerfully. "Don't worry about it making you pretty, it didn't make them pretty." He guffawed at his own joke and I did too; we were pritnear as drunk as I've ever been. When he got out to soap up, he nearly fell, and I got out very slowly; it's not easy when you're holding a bar of soap in one hand, and you really wish you had both hands to hang onto the floor with.

We both soaped up all over, working up thick lather in our hair and beards. A couple of knotted, crusty scars were on the back of my head, which probably meant that whatever Dave had done to the back of my head with his club should have had stitches but hadn't gotten them. Oh, well, I was alive, and not memed, and thinking as myself.

When we had finished lathering, Dave carefully put our pieces of soap back on the shelf, and said, "Just be sure you don't stay with your head under too long. I can't think that would be real good for a guy with a recent brain trauma."

We climbed back in, the hot water feeling good after the cool of soaping up, and swished around in the water, getting the soap off and the last kinks out. I let myself slip down and put my head under. In water that's warmer than body temperature, with a skinful of wine, putting your head under hits like a sledgehammer, and you can easily pass out, but I let myself hang for a moment in that blissful almost-not-there state, so relaxed that my muscles seemed to just blend into the surrounding water. If Dave had wanted to kill me, that moment then would have been a good time; I'd probably have slipped over to the other side without caring.

But clearly he didn't. I suppose decades without a friend do things to a man; the thing that seemed strangest to me was that he was still fairly good at getting along with people, after all that loneliness.

I let the warmth fill my whole body, then sat back up, splashing and wiping the water from my face. "I don't suppose you've got—"

"But of course," he said. "I built my towel closet with racks that carry hot water. All towels are always dry, fluffy, and hot."

"Damn, you know how to live." I got out and he tossed me a towel; I dried myself thoroughly. It felt good to be alive. "Dave, if you don't want to be turned, I am not going to turn you. And since you can't trust me if I'm turned, I guess I'm out in the woods for good, myself. You'll have to teach me most of the mechanics of living out here, and I'll have to depend on you for a while, but I'll construct a place of my own, if you prefer, just as fast as I can. And I guess we both have to move, anyway, because there's bound to be some of them looking for me in a couple-few weeks, once some of the spring melt has happened, plus of course they had enough uploads from my copy of Resuna, the last few days before you caught me, to have you pritnear dead solid located."

Dave sighed. "Well, we're both in a sloppy sentimental mood. Been a long time since I've had a partner, and living out in the woods without anybody else is lim, lim hard. But you gotta think about things like the fact that you wouldn't see Mary again, ever, probably, and I got to think about whether I'm letting my feelings blind me. So let's sleep on it, get up late, talk it over . . . you know, the usual kind of thing you do when you know what you want to do, but you want to be sure you want to. You know?"

"If I had a few more brain cells running I'm sure that would be perfectly clear," I said. "Sure, see you in the morning."

He didn't even lock my door; I had the funny thought, as I fell asleep, that I might be about to become a cowboy, but I sure as hell wasn't ever going to put any dumbass-looking Stetson on.

Next morning the menu was jerked venison, canned beans, pickled grouse eggs, strong coffee, and plenty of aspirin. We didn't say much till we got enough of all that stowed in our guts so that we felt sort of human, and then we took a vote and it was unanimous that we ought to go take a nap. It must've been another three hours before we staggered out, guts stabilized, heads only oppressively fuzzy instead of overwhelmingly thick, and had some more coffee, plus some jackrabbit stew he'd canned the summer before. "Well," Dave said at last, "that was one hell of an evening. Haven't had a blowout like that in decades, literally."

"Me either," I said. "Felt pretty good, even if I wouldn't want to do it more than four or five times in a year. To let you know, I still think I'd rather throw in with you. I'd rather be your friend than not, and this is the only way to be your friend. As for Mary, yeah, I miss her, and she has some good qualities and so forth, but you know, there's a whole lot of energy that has gone into taking care of her, and much as I hate to admit it, I'd have decided she wasn't worth it, probably within a few weeks, if Resuna hadn't been steering my thoughts. So I'm about twenty-five years overdue for an awakening from the romance, and though I wish her all the best, and though I would gladly take care of her just out of duty, and enjoy her company . . . well, Resuna will take very good care of her, and she'll be just fine. I'm leaving her in a situation much safer and more comfortable than I ever left Tammy in. So if you'll take me on, and teach me enough of what you know, I'd be happy to be your neighbor out here, or your partner if you don't mind sharing quarters. I'll do more than my share of the work to make up for not supplying my share of the knowledge."

Dave sat back in his chair, put two more aspirin in his mouth, took another gulp of coffee to wash them down, and said, "You worry way too much about what's fair, and about my privacy, Currie. I'd dearly love to have a partner. With two of us working we can make our new place big enough to have rooms for both of us. I know you'll pull your freight. And if you *are* just going to turn me in, well, that idea is so discouraging that I'd just as soon not think or worry about it at all, so I'm not." He stuck his hand out, we shook, and we were partners.

That afternoon we got going on the subject of where to move and when. Over his years of wandering around in the mountains, Dave had picked out several other places with easy-to-tap geothermal heat, none with as abundant a flow as this one. "Two of them have a sizable surface pool nearby, so if the temperature on that was to start to drop, it's possible a satellite would spot the difference between how hot the pool used to be and how hot it was now. If they've found this place by then, well, then they'd know my basic way of surviving, they'd be looking for changes around hot springs, and we'd be in deep shit. Out of all the hot springs sites I've found, there's only one that drains back into the ground without breaking the surface and flowing down to some creek. It's on the leeward side of Ute Ridge, a little ways up, in a cave that's probably an earthquake crack that got weathered out bigger and then had some runoff flowing through it at one time—there's a slide up above that I figure must have turned off the flow. There's some room in there and plenty of stuff solid enough to dig out for more as we need it—though it's not going to be the pleasant easy digging that this old mine gave me. And so far, anyway, checking that spring for years, it hasn't gone dry or surged up. Problem is, it's reliable but it ain't plentiful—there's maybe half a gallon per minute or so, enough to give us heat and some hot water, but nothing like the four and a quarter gallons per minute I got here."

"We could put in a tank of some kind, couldn't we?" I pointed out. "The longer we keep the hot water hanging around, the more heat we can extract. We couldn't have an ever-running hot tub-laundromat-dishwasher like you've got here, but we could just do all the washing in shifts; wash and rinse with water from the hot tank, drain it into a warm tank that keeps the place comfortable, put it through the toilet and then discharge it room temperature if you've got a safe hole to put it down."

I had to draw a couple of sketches of the idea for him—I was mildly surprised at the way the idea didn't seem natural to a man who had built a place as ingenious as this one—but once he got it, he nodded vigorously and added, "I think you've already paid for yourself, Curran. That's a great idea. Far as I know, after it passes through that little cave, the stream runs underground for miles, too—no surface pool anywhere near—so even if we take all the heat from that water, and discharge at room temperature, betcha we still don't show up to the satellites."

"I guess that's what we are betting on," I agreed.

🔖 **Two days later** I saw daylight for the first time in what I discovered had been nineteen days. Dave's camouflage for the entrance was simplicity itself—it was under an overhang and led onto a long sloping shelf of south-facing dark rock, which must have stayed pretty free of snow most of the time. We walked straight out during one of the no-satellite times, got under the trees, and put on skis—his were old Fiberglas models; I just used my flexis. After a moment or two to check equipment, we were on our way.

I was a hair rocky on my skis, at first, and we took it slow, going the long way round because it was much more nearly level. It was another beautiful, cloudless, deep blue sky above pure white snow. By the third kilometer or so, I was back in the swing of things, annoyingly short of muscle after all the bed rest, but fundamentally fine.

You had to be practically falling into the little cave before you even saw the wisps of steam, or the donut of ice like a giant's anus, among the scrubby firs. The opening was an irregular oval, perhaps four feet long by two across. "Getting in's not as hard as getting out," Dave said. "The floor's not far down, and it opens up beyond this point. Just follow me." He set his skis down under the tree, and I did the same; then he braced a hand on either side of the glassy ice of the opening, and more or less swung down into the space, coming to a rest when he was in about up to the bottom of his ribcage. "Tricky spot. This part of the floor is covered with ice," he said. "Have to figure out a faster entrance eventually. Now squat, hope not to fall down, turn real slowly *left*, stick your legs out, and slide down a slope on your butt. You'll skid down maybe seven-eight foot and land on a pile of scree. I'll be down there with a light."

He squatted and I heard a scraping sound, a louder and different scrabbling noise, and then finally a crash of spraying gravel, followed by the rattle of him climbing off the scree pile. "Okay, I'm down. Just come to the light."

If possible, the ice around the opening was slicker than it looked, and wetter. My head seemed to ache as if waiting to be slammed. Gingerly, I put my feet down and found the slick, icy floor; I could see a trace of glare from his flashlight on my boots, coming from my left.

"Doing fine," he said.

Very slowly, keeping my weight right over my feet, I crouched and turned. I was in a space less than a meter high and not much wider than the hole on the surface; beside me Dave's light came up from a crack that was about a meter wide and not more than two feet high, into which the floor sloped. I put my feet down the opening and pushed off, hoping that Dave hadn't worked out some incredibly complicated way to cause a cowboy hunter to die where he'd never be found.

The freezing-cold rock and ice chewed at my ass for an instant. With a momentary lurch, I gained speed. My boots grabbed the scree pile and I finished up squatting on that. Dave was standing there, adjusting his flashlight for use as a lantern. I climbed down carefully and stood beside him.

As my eyes adjusted to the light, I saw that we were in a big crack in the native granite. It was surprisingly free of dirt, and almost unpleasantly warm. I opened up my suit as Dave took off his jacket. "Well, here it is," he said. "Prospective home."

In the dim light I could clearly see the basic space—about seven meters that I could see, ending in a bend at one end, varying from two to three meters wide, all high enough so you could walk without bumping your head. A thin trickle of warm water dribbled across the muddy floor, steam rising from it. "It's also hotter than what I've got in the home place now," Dave said, "which I think means your idea will work even better."

I walked forward and looked to see that the trickle of water emerged from an opening that I could probably have put my arm into, if I'd wanted it scalded. "We could widen and break this out," I said, "or just stick a pipe into it. Probably start with just the pipe and then expand toward the heat, eh?"

"Sounds logical to me," Dave said. "There's a chamber around the bend, where the hole that drains this is."

Gingerly, I made my way through that main gallery, following Dave, watching where I put my feet, not caring to dip my boots in the near-boiling trickle. Around the corner, in the short leg of the L-shaped cave, where Dave's lantern shone, we moved into a chamber about two meters square and some inches deeper than the gallery we'd left; the ceiling was higher too, and the hot trickle bit deep into the clay soil floor, vanishing toward the end of the room in a gurgling hiss of steam. "I've probed down that hole, and about a meter below, it seems to widen," Dave said. "We might could try a video camera and moni-

tor, and a light, and see if there's a usable chamber down there to dig
to, or even just a good place for one of your storage tanks."

"Seems promising," I said. "You ever done anything to find
out how deep the clay is anywhere in here?"

"Naw. Wasn't high enough priority till now. For all I know
when we dig it out we'll turn up ten more foot of headroom and
entrances to six more chambers. Anyway, that's about all there is
to it right now. What do you think?"

I looked at it and thought about how hard I was going to have
to work; then about Mary and the cabin; then about what it was
like to be awake, in my own skull, without Resuna watching every
thought, and I said, "This is gonna sound stupid but I can hardly
wait to get started. I guess we bring up the shovels tomorrow, and
we start mucking out."

"Makes sense, if you're ready."

"Oh, I'm ready," I said. "And here's another thought. We don't
have to haul the dirt out and dribble it from a pack. All this clay was
carried here by the spring, right? So if we just build a box with a screen
on the bottom, that the stream runs through on its way out, and drop
the dirt in there, it will be carried downstream underground, where
nobody's going to see it. We might see about mucking out the drain
first thing, just to see if we can do it that way—because if we can, that
makes the whole job simpler. We can be here digging more of the time
and we won't be limited by how much dirt we can hide."

"What happens if we put so much down there that we plug
something up, and it starts to back up into the cave?" Dave asked.

"Then we poke down there with poles and rods, and see if we
can smash something to let the water out—and if that doesn't work,
we see how far it fills—and if it fills to the top, well, we tunnel in
from the side and let it out. Which admittedly kills the advantage of
the subterranean drain. But anyway, we've got so much to gain if
we can move a few tons a day, instead of a few packloads. We could
have a whole new place here inside a year or two if we can wash
most of the clay down, instead of carrying it. Wouldn't you say?"

He shrugged. "Partner, I never thought of that either. I'm just not much of a planner or engineer; purely an improviser and an improver. It's probably a good thing I was the cowboy and you were the hunter, because you damn near caught me, and I don't think I'd've stood a prayer of catching you."

"Different approaches," I said. "If you and me were hunting a cowboy together, I'd be amazed at how many things were obvious to you, I bet, that I never saw."

"Might could be," Dave said. "Might could be."

There might be something heavier and more uncomfortable than a pack full of canned goods, but I don't want to find out what. The first job, once we realized that we needed to get Dave's place moved, right away, was to get all the really indispensable stuff cached at some distance from it. Canned stuff with Vitamin C was number one on the list; if we had that, we wouldn't get scurvy. If we didn't have that, not only would we be facing scurvy, but we'd have to pick a *lot* of berries the next summer, and come up with some way to can or dry many pounds of them, and do a great deal of work we wouldn't really want to make the time for.

After the indispensables for staying alive, dealing with emergencies, and not getting sick, we would move all the nice small things, appliances of one kind or another, that shave so much effort off a day and free up so much time. After that, if we still weren't interrupted, we would gradually move the million and ten small luxuries that could help to make life way out in the woods bearable—books, wine, audio recordings—and finally, if One True left us alone long enough, anything else that we could take before we dropped a load of rocks across the entrance and left forever.

Caching the portable stuff meant taking it out, a packload at a time, to about twenty different hiding places, since we wanted to make sure we had some of everything in each cache, so that if one of them got found, we wouldn't lose all of any item. What shall it profit a man to keep his dialytic water-purifier membranes, if he lose his canned tomatoes? I was glad that I hadn't been doing this decades before, when Dave and his band had been hiding out here, since there must have been many times this much stuff to carry. Of course, then there had been eleven men doing it.

It was late afternoon, and I was crossing a high saddle down into Kearney Park, enjoying the colors, smells, and sounds in their near-outlined clarity. I'd made seven trips that day and was looking forward to finishing this one and having an evening soak in the tub. Another week and we should have all the food cached, and then it would only be a matter of a few days to get all the other irreplaceables moved before we could at last begin our excavations in the new cave. If I was right that they wouldn't try to send hunters out again until a thaw was well underway, we'd be doing our excavation comfortably in the shelter of the cave, possibly for weeks or months, while the pursuit grew frustrated, and the scent got cold.

With luck it might be several years before we were spotted again, and though sooner or later one of these spottings would lead to our capture, at the moment it looked like we had some years of freedom left. And, as I'd explained to Dave, life with Resuna wasn't *un*pleasant—if Dave hadn't been there and determined to stay out of One True's grip, I'd probably have just gone back to Resuna because it was easier.

Aside from getting caches sited and filled, we'd made enough time to explore the cave around the new hot spring, probing with some six-foot star drills that had been in the back of an old general store. The water drained into at least one more big chamber below, and we'd also tapped into some openings under the clay that we were optimistic about.

Meanwhile, though, we had to move the canned stuff. I had a

packful of cans of tomatoes, peaches, and sweet potatoes to get into the cache in Kearney Park, before going home. I pushed off to make a slow glide, down through the trees, avoiding any open space too easily watched from orbit. It was harder than usual to safely descend the hard, icy, steep patch in front of me. I had to work at it, turning tight and constantly so that I didn't build up any speed. The extra weight on my back made it much tougher.

I hurtled back among the trees, still going faster than I really wanted to, and followed a deer trail I knew well through a thick patch of growth. Then a bump turned out to be a log, the ski scraped and jammed, and I flipped forward and landed in a hard face plant.

I sat up, face stinging from the snow, head aching where forty pounds of tomatoes, peaches, and sweet potatoes had slammed right into the place on the back of my head where I had all the scars. I was all by myself, and feeling half crazy with anger the way you do when you do something stupid and hurt yourself entirely through your own stupidity. I plain old bokked all over the place, forgot that I had to hide, forgot everything I'd been thinking of, and just gave myself over to my rage. I released the skis, pushed up, wiped the nasty mix of snow, mud, and pine needles from my face, angrily hurled the pack to the snow, and screamed "Fuck!" several times, jumping up and down in a rage, not caring if anyone heard me, or if I was visible to an overhead satellite, or much of anything except about the way my whole body was clenched like a fist and my back and head hurt. I hadn't done anything like that in twenty-five years or more.

Long practice will have its way; in the middle of it all, I said, out loud, very calmly, "Let overwrite, let override." Instantly I felt better.

With all the canned goods in the cache, even having gotten the job done a little early, I had plenty of time to take the long scenic route home, but I just *knew* I had forgotten something, so after a few hundred yards I turned around and went back to take a look and see if I could figure out what was bothering me.

Everything was right where it should be, so it wasn't that I had forgotten any physical objects. Had I forgotten some part of the careful system we used to keep everything hidden? I looked around the cache to see if anything was wrong with the concealment, but everything was fine there. Then I looked to see if I'd left any track or trace I should cover.

Two thick ruler-straight tracks ran across the meadow through the deep fresh powder from the place where I had fallen to where I stood. I had come in a straight line, instead of circling around among the trees. No wonder I'd gotten here so quickly.

That big straight track might as well be a gigantic arrow pointing straight at where I stood. Worse still, it was pointing at a sizable part of the vital stocks we would need to live through the next year.

I stared at that for a long moment, wondering first what had possessed me to do something so astonishingly bokked up. Then I wondered why I couldn't remember it. Then my blood froze, and I remembered falling down, losing my temper—and invoking Resuna. Which had, as far as I could tell, popped up, taken care of the task for me, and put me on my way home, but which also had a strong interest in seeing me get caught.

If the jack in my head was still operating, One True now knew everything. I couldn't imagine why it hadn't just kept control once it got Resuna back into my head, but for some reason it hadn't. *Why* had it turned me loose again?

The silence, the clarity of the colors and outlines, the chill of the air in my nostrils, were all sinister to me now. I had betrayed a good friend in a moment of sheer involuntary idiocy, I had put myself back in reach of Resuna and thus under the control of One True, and I would be giving up the whole dream of living up here and letting the world just slide by—back into the dull world of forced retirement, of Resuna holding Mary and me together, of drifting from one predictable, unimportant activity to another.

I felt like crying; I felt like taking my knife and just opening a vein right there. It would be so good to just cease to be. It was very likely that there was no longer anything I could do for Dave; I was miles away with no way to communicate with him. Chances were that fifty hunters were zooming in toward him in disksters, and he'd be captured any minute and turned within a day. Probably I'd even see him again—after he was turned, we could pal around together and our copies of Resuna could have a nice chat. Probably One True would find him a nice wife, or even put him back together with Nancy and Kelly. Probably when I did see him, he'd *thank* me. Probably he'd be having to say "Let overwrite, let override" every ten minutes for the next few years; probably his life would seem as if he were suffering seizures every few minutes.

I was disgusted to realize that once Resuna had me again, it wouldn't bother me a bit. I'd be able to look the man right in the eye and think I'd done him a favor.

I wasn't sure I wanted to live to see that, but I wasn't sure I wanted to just kill myself now, either. Mostly I just wanted to not feel what I was feeling. I have to admit that the real reason for doing what I did next was not shame, nor acceptance. It was pure absolute dead solid cowardice. I just didn't want to face that situation any further, and since I couldn't get out of the situation, I tried instead to get out of facing it.

I looked around that meadow, up the saddle, toward Columbia Peak, and saw it for what I figured would have to be the very last time with eyes that were completely my own. Tears stung my eyes, and I said, "Let overwrite, let override."

Nothing happened.

I said it again, and once again, nothing happened. There wasn't a trace of Resuna.

I said it again, several times. I started to lose my temper and shouted it several times, but no Resuna came—only distant, distorted echoes from cliff walls.

I was all by myself, no idea where to go or what to do.

I think I stood there for quite a while, because the blue-edged deep shadows were longer by the time that I finally sighed, wiped my eyes, and decided that absolutely nobody would be benefited if I just stood here and froze to death.

I had three choices. I could try to get away on my own—in the winter, with no supplies since Resuna would know where all the caches were and I wouldn't dare go there.

I could ski downhill till I found a road, and follow the road downhill till I found an emergency station, and then call up the system and turn myself in. Somebody would come out pretty quickly in a diskster, take me home, and get a new copy of Resuna installed.

Or I could gamble. I could proceed as if I knew that I had only been running part of Resuna, with its communications section not working. It was even possible, I supposed, that the blows to my head had smashed my cellular jack—it was possible, since it was only an inch or so from where the biggest scar was—or that it had all happened during a gap in satellite coverage, or any number of other things had prevented the betrayal.

That last option was the only one that had any chance of working out and didn't make me feel like a skunk.

If I was right, and One True had *not* been contacted, or not contacted reliably, then all we had lost was one cache. In that case, if Dave and I moved fast, we could go to our drop-everything crisis plan—hurry over to the new place, camp there, move in a couple of caches, start digging, live rough for a while until we had a chance to scavenge enough supplies to start building it up.

It was just possible that all was not lost—if we moved fast enough.

I pushed off hard and took the fastest concealed route I knew to make it home, skating the whole way, throwing myself upslope, rocketing downslope just barely in control, half-blind with sweat and tears and terror, not caring about the way my muscles screamed at it. I was over that high saddle in no time, down into the Dead Mule drainage, and racing for home like a madman—still skiing as carefully as I could, because I knew I was frustrated and angry, and I thought that if I face-planted again, or kissed a tree, or just took a bad fall, the rage and fear and frustration might overwhelm me. I might automatically say "Let overwrite, let override," and be back with Resuna again.

I hit a long run down a ridgeline into a bowl, and put on even more speed; any faster and my stopping distance would be greater than my seeing distance. It was likely I was already too late, but it would be certain if one more thing went wrong.

⋙ **The sun was** still up, but close to the ridge, when I finally glided up to the rock shelf, popped the skis off, and ran inside. Dave wasn't home. Probably he was off hunting elk—we'd been needing fresh meat to replenish the larder. He might well be out till after dark, which might could work out better.

We'd figured out a procedure for just such occasions, so I got going on it. Each of us had a "jump bag" ready to go, packed with personal essentials for surviving a night in the woods if we had to, plus a little package of sentimental stuff and some dry rations. The two jump bags sat side by side on the floor near the entrance; if one of us discovered that it was time to run, and the other one was out, then if we were to meet up at the new hot spring, the signal would be both jump bags being gone.

If just your partner's jump bag was gone, that would signal that neither this cave nor the new one was safe, and that we were to meet up whenever we could at a specific ruined house two drainages away; whoever got there first, unpursued, would wait a week for the other.

We had agreed that the one-bag-gone signal would only count if a specific red blanket had been left on top of the laundry hamper. That way your partner doing routine repacking or rearranging wouldn't send you running off into the woods for two weeks.

We had never assigned any meaning to the situation that I discovered: my jump bag was there, Dave's jump bag wasn't, Dave wasn't there either—and no blanket on the hamper. I needed to leave him a signal to run for the new hot spring, which I thought made the most sense in the circumstances. I was figuring that if One True had gotten everything from my memory, we were too screwed to recover from it and would be captured whether we stayed here, went there, or went to the ruined house. On the other hand, if One True hadn't gotten enough information to find us, the new spring was the best place to hide—it already had the necessities for us to stay in it for a few weeks and let our trail get cold, it was comfortable and safe, and it had lim less trace of Dave or me around it than this place did.

I had no signal from Dave, and I had no way of leaving him the message that I wanted to leave—writing a note of any kind would risk its being read by the hunters, if they found the cave before Dave got home. The question was, how long should I stay here? Dave might be very close at hand, in which case I could just let him know when he came in the door. Or he might have carelessly left his pack elsewhere while repacking or cleaning, or he might be far off. Given his occasional carelessness (I often wondered how he had survived so long without detection), he might even have run for it and forgotten to put the blanket on the hamper.

I decided I could spare him five minutes for a quick look through the rooms; if his pack was on the kitchen table or by the hot tub, as I'd found it before, I'd tease him later but take it with me. Otherwise, I'd take my jump bag and leave a circle-and-dot, which means "I have gone home"—it was one of those very old trail signs from god knew where in the past. I hoped he would interpret that to mean "Go to the new hot spring," and that it would be sufficiently cryptic if anyone else found it.

I walked through all the rooms quickly, not seeing his pack. One of the three doors that I had always assumed were closet doors in his sleeping room was standing open, light coming out of it. When I took a step forward, I saw, through the open door, beyond what I had thought was a closet, a big room. A finished ceiling and wall were visible through the mock closet. Not yet thinking clearly—it had been a day with too many surprises—and still looking for Dave, I walked through the closet and into the big room.

My first thought was not especially profound; it was only that Dave couldn't have made this space with a shovel and pick. The walls, floor, and ceiling, now that I could see the whole room, were finished with tile, the overhead lights were running off real power fixtures and didn't seem to be just long-life lanterns, and the whole place seemed more like a lab or a workroom. At first I thought the object in the center of the big room was a large worktable, then that it was a raised bathtub. I got closer to it, and said, softly, "Dave? Dave, are you back here? We got big trouble."

I took another step, and now I realized what that big object was: a suspended animation tank.

Stuff clicked. Dave had been able to disappear for so long because he'd been sleeping under this hill. No wonder nobody could find him. Probably his story about the packloads of dirt was a convenient lie. Most of the "scavenged" stuff had probably been stored down here for him. When he did wake up, with common germs having diverged for many years from what he had gone to sleep with, he got a whopping cold as soon as he went where any other human being had been, and if he—or whoever he worked for—hadn't planned for it, he'd had to steal medicine.

It seemed ominous that this hideout had always been intended as a one-person place; whatever he was doing with his band of cowboys, he hadn't ever intended to take them along. He couldn't, with just one tank available.

No wonder, when we were planning the new cave, so many ordinary technical and engineering things had seemed to be mysteries to him. He hadn't designed this place—all he knew was how to operate it. The place had been set up by whoever he worked for.

"Currie, that better be you in there," he said. His voice came from a doorway in the corner.

I froze for a second. "Yeah, it is. I didn't mean to nose around, Dave, but we've got a situation. I had a relapse of Resuna this afternoon and I don't know how much it uploaded to One True. I think we have to run for the new hot spring."

He came out from the back. He was naked, except for a dozen medical sensors hanging from his head, neck, chest, and back, and carrying his jump bag.

"You better tell me about that," he said.

I sketched it out for him quickly—getting hurt, losing my temper, and saying the words to invoke Resuna. "Honest, Dave, I really didn't mean to do that—"

"Oh, I believe you, for whatever good that does either of us. I can't imagine that twenty years of habit breaks that easy. It ain't anybody's fault; something like this was bound to happen sooner or later. So it took you over and then what happened?"

"I skied down to put the stuff into the cache, but I went straight across the meadow. It was all new powder down there, and I left tracks that are bound to be picked up from orbit. Might as well have painted a bull's-eye around the cache. Not to mention that I'm sure, as often as we've traveled between there and here, they're going to follow my track back here—if they don't already know exactly where we are and what we're doing. I figure that when my copy of Resuna woke up, it probably just automatically carried out the job I had been doing when it took over. That's something that Resuna does, because you want it to work on what's important if you're in an emergency. Then after it got the stuff into the cache and wasn't sensing as much anxiety from me, it probably commed One True, via satellite, and told it everything. I figure they'll be here inside an hour."

"Well," he said, "do you know for sure that you phoned One True? Or did you just assume that you must have because Resuna had control for a while?"

"That was what I assumed; it's what Resuna would do."

"Then I can put both our minds at a little ease. One reason why it took you so long to wake up, I suspect, is because back when I first had you captured and unconscious, to be on the safe side I hooked up your jack to some electronic stuff I've got and zapped it a bunch of ways—RF, high voltage, low-level DC current, even a tickle of plain old one-ten sixty-cycle AC (though I put you in line with a big resistor for that). Probably didn't do your brain much good, but if it was possible to fry that jack, I fried it. I know I ran a big risk with your brain and all, but you know, at the time I didn't know you and I was still deciding whether to kill you. And I'm real glad now that I don't seem to have done any permanent brain damage. But I'm also glad that I did try to cook that little gadget, because it's probably good and dead, and chances are that when your copy of Resuna woke up, after you got whacked on the skull, it just ran in your head until you were conscious enough to take over again."

"That is reassuring," I said, "and no hard feelings about my brain. As much as I bang it around, who knows where any one piece of damage might've come from? Still, the ski tracks are pointing out that cache, and so we're bound to lose that, and when they find it they'll find their way here, quick enough, pos-def. We've made a good twenty trips out to it, and by now we've surely left enough track for any decent hunter to follow, even with varying the route all the time. So the hunters are going to be at that cache sometime tomorrow, at latest, and then they'll be here within a few hours. They might could be here in as little as three hours, if the satellite saw the track right away and everybody jumped on it. And if it was three hours—well, between one thing and another, about half of that time is burned already, with time spent getting here and the time we've been talking."

"Well, then," Dave said, "we've got sleeping bags up there already, we've got our jump bags packed—I was just putting in some of the medicines you need to take for a few years after a suspended animation, so I'll go back and grab the rest of my stash of those. At least it would make sense to go up to the new cave and stay up there a few days, then real cautiously come down and see what's happened to home base here, if anything. While we're up there, anyway, we can do some digging, and move a couple of the caches up into the new place too if we take that slow and careful. The only thing that's frustrating is that I got a nice cow elk, plump for this time of year, and didn't have time to do more than gut her out and hang her up. We'll probably lose that meat, and I was really looking forward to some nice steaks in a couple days. Other than that, though, I'm ready to go if you are."

"You might want to put some pants on," I pointed out. "It is still February, you know."

Ten minutes later, jump bags on our backs, we were gliding off toward Ute Ridge. The way I figured it, surely Dave knew he had some explaining to do, and he'd get around to it soon enough, without my prompting. Meanwhile, with some prospect of escape—and a possibility that I had *not* irrevocably blown everything—the world didn't seem quite so desperate. It wasn't exactly the best situation, but it was still considerably better than what I'd had not long before.

We did the last two and a half miles in deep darkness—the moon hadn't even risen yet, and while starlight is surprisingly bright at high altitude on a field of snow, still all you can really see is silhouettes, and not even that amid the trees. When we got close, and had to pass deeper into the shadows, we pulled on starlight goggles to make our way in. We took skis in with us, leaving them on the upper shelf, and then, once we were inside, had a quick cold meal from the cache there, and then stretched out in the sleeping bags, on the clay-mud floor, not far from the dribble of hot water.

From where I lay, I could just see over the upper shelf and a little bit out the opening, which was obscured every few seconds by a puff of fog, as cold air from outside met the warm wet air that rose from this cave. I saw a bright star, flickering violently, disappearing and reappearing in the fog, through the little cave mouth, and figured out in my head that it might be half an hour before the star moved out of sight from this angle, but before I even saw it move toward the edge, I was asleep.

➻➻ **The sun never** shone down that hole directly, but enough bounce light came through in the morning to wake me up. The dim light from overhead made our new home even less attractive than a cave in the woods usually is. Well, with enough work, maybe we'd get this place fixed up fit to live in, though I doubted it would ever be anything like as nice as the place Dave had built before. Or rather the place he had lived in, I reminded myself. He probably hadn't built it; more likely he had just lived there, and whoever he worked for, or used to work for, had built and stocked the place.

I climbed out of the sleeping bag; I had been sleeping in my thermies, and I was still uncomfortably warm after getting out of the bag. So I peeled out of the thermies, turned them inside out to air, got a small piece of soap from my jump bag, and managed sort of a sponge bath in the trickle at one end of the cave. It was better than nothing, but far from that hot tub.

"You do realize that's also the coffee water?" Dave grumbled, dragging himself along. "And yes, I have some freeze-dried stuff, and a couple of cups. That's our beverage. And for the meal, today, sir, a can of tomatoes, a can of beans, and some powdered eggs, goes into a pot with hot water, glop fit for a king, and it's what there is anyway." He put two cups on a rock and poured a splash of freeze-dried coffee in each. "I could tell you something about that water, but you ought to find out for yourself."

I took a cup and held it under the hot trickle, letting it fill up, and then tapped the cup a few times to make sure that the coffee powder had dissolved.

One sip told me. "Iron," I said, running my tongue around my mouth to try to wipe some of the bitter astringent feel away.

"No anemia for us," he agreed. "I'll finish yours if you don't want it."

"It's caffeine," I said, "and I've had worse." I sat on a rock near enough the stream to be warm. "Should I unpack the stuff for breakfast?"

"I'll get it in a minute; I'm gonna wash up. I know a trick or two for making iron water palatable."

Still sipping my coffee, I wandered back around to the back of the cave and carefully took a leak right where the stream flowed back into the ground. If somebody soaking at a spa two hundred miles away had any problem with that, they could write me.

When I got back, Dave had finished soaping and rinsing, and was dumping the ingredients into the pot. The water was two notches too hot to wash comfortably with, not quite hot enough to heat the food, and I made a mental note that we would need a cistern or something for the long run. (I doubted we were going to find a cool well up here, at least at any depth we had the equipment to reach.)

Eggs, tomatoes, and beans aren't a bad mix, per se, and I've eaten worse, but on the other hand I've had better, and the water hadn't quite been hot enough to make the dried eggs fluff up. So it could have been a whole lot better, too. We gobbled it down, had another cup of iron coffee each, and then looked the situation over.

"I'd suggest we work in just gloves, boots, and shorts," Dave said. "And since we never did get your screen box built, what do you have in mind for getting the dirt to wash down the stream?"

"Let me try an experiment or two," I said. We got dressed as Dave had suggested, and went back into the chamber and put three long-life lights up high. With no opening to the surface, this room was almost up to room temperature anyway.

"The trick is to make sure it mixes well," I pointed out. "Let's try the simplest possible way." I put five shovelfuls of dirt into one of our buckets, carried it back to where the spring came in, let it fill with water—which made it a world heavier—stirred with the shovel, and poured it into the outlet. It went gurgling down without any sign of blocking or forming a dam. "It's not going to be as fast as a screen box would have been," I said. "But we have a bucket and a big cook pot. We can probably put one of each down the hole every ten minutes or so, allowing for breaks and meals and that kind of thing. We'll still get plenty of work done in a day, anyway. And whenever it gets tough or we get bored, we can sneak out and move a cache. I was thinking there are two that aren't so far away, and we might move them in a few days. Let's give it a month or so, though, before we pop up our heads in Dead Mule drainage; I have a feeling they'll be setting up an ambush there, and probably sitting in it for a good long while."

"Makes sense," Dave said, nodding soberly. "And it does beat the whole process of hauling it out in packs."

I turned and threw a couple shovelfuls into the bucket. "You know," I said, "after what I saw yesterday, and what I've figured out, I'd have to say that I don't believe you ever hauled even one pack of dirt out of that place."

He tossed his second shovelful into the cook pot, walked out to the spring inlet, and came back sloshing it around. He poured it down the hole and finally said, "Well, you're wrong, there, Currie, though you're right that I didn't build the whole place. But I put the tub into the tub room, and I did build that library. And I hauled some dirt for those, because I never did think of doing things the way you came up with."

I emptied two more buckets while I waited for him to come up with something else to say, but he didn't, so eventually I just asked him. "Uh, okay, do you mind if I ask if you're going to tell me what's going on?"

"I've been trying to think of how to do just that," Dave said. "My problem is that I don't know exactly how to help you see what's going on, or why it matters, or anything, and it really seems like somehow I ought to be able to tell you all of it at once, and so there's no real one single place to start, and I get bogged down in trying to pick one. To understand one part, you need to understand three. Like that. But I'm not trying to hold out on you, not anymore, Currie. And I'd have told you eventually—it was just a question of when to tell you how much, because, well, you were real bound into One True and I wasn't sure which thing I might say might wake up your Resuna."

I was a little mollified that he was at least thinking, perhaps, that he owed me some explanation. I let it go for another couple bucketloads. We had now put a hole in the floor, mostly around the exit hole, perhaps a meter across and half a meter deep.

As he came back and poured his cook pot full of hot mud into the water, and watched it swirl down, he said, "We ought to at least dig down to some rock by day's end and get that hole pritnear as wide as it'll easily go. Okay, Currie, here's my story. Final version. All the truth as far as I know it. And I was probably wrong to keep it from you, once it was clear you'd come around to my side."

For the rest of that morning, we loaded buckets and sent mud down that hole, and every so often he'd tell me more of his story, as we watched for any sign that we had to stop dumping the mud. As I'd guessed, there was room enough for all the mud to go down there, so far—our probes, and some shouting down there for echoes, made me think that the chamber below was mostly empty and probably twenty feet high and a hundred long. Of course, if the mud dammed up the exit to that chamber, then it would start to fill and we could be dealing with a nuisance, but when we got this hole wide enough open, we should be able to see whether or not that was likely to happen. Meanwhile there was surely room enough for the mud from this early part of the job.

Between the heavy work and the heat from the spring, we were both sweaty and grimy when we stopped for a quick lunch of some jerky and hard rolls, washed down with yet more iron coffee.

We both took a few muscle relaxants before starting again, and that got the story flowing better because the relaxants hit like mild, long-lasting alcohol. During that whole afternoon, off and on, a few sentences at a time as we'd pass each other, dumping mud and shoveling the buckets, I heard the rest of Dave's story, and we finished it over hot soup and fresh bread that we were able to fix by using up one precious chemical heater; we felt like we both needed it badly. By that time we had a hole big enough for us to stand in together, almost a meter and a half deep, and a good two meters across. The opening in the floor turned out to be a round hole, perhaps a foot across, that seemed to lead down into a much bigger open space. The odor coming up out of there was slightly musty, but not bad; probably it had no direct outlet to the outside world.

"Anyway," I said, "we can accelerate the whole process, because there's obviously much more room down there than there is clay up here, and it will be a while before we start opening that area up for ourselves. Give it a week and we'll be done excavating, even counting the time to go move another cache or two here. I'm not sure where we'll salvage or steal the plumbing to put in a real hot-water-and-heat system, but we'll come up with something, anyway."

"God, you're better at this than I ever would hope to be," Dave said, sighing.

"Considering what you did get through, you can hold your head up in any company you want," I assured him.

We each had a little snort to help us sleep. Between the night's booze and the day's exercise, my sleeping bag on a clay floor in a steamy cave felt like a heated waterbed with a down comforter in a high-priced hotel. I watched the star through the hole for just a few seconds, and then fell asleep. That night I dreamed, over and over, of the story that Dave had told me.

I got a great rest and woke up only somewhat sore, but the dreams of that night were with me for a long time after, and for the next day—very much like the previous one in the work we did—I kept thinking of other questions to ask him, and other ways to try to make his story hang together in my brain, in a way that wouldn't disturb me quite so much. By the end of that second day I had the whole thing, pritnear as clear as it would ever get, and by then I had about arrived at the decision that there wasn't a thing to do, for me or for anyone on Earth, that wouldn't be a huge mistake. Then Dave pointed out the last part to me, which I'd missed, and I went and *made* that huge mistake, all on my own.

🐾 **Dave Singleton's name** derived from something strange that had happened in the Foundling's Entrance at Denver Dome's municipal orphanage in 2043.

During the Gray Decade, probably a quarter of the babies born became foundlings, as city after city ran out of money and shut down the Dole, and with it the Dolework that had at least allowed families to stay together, and single mothers to afford child care and support a family. Many people just could not afford to keep the babies they had. Because of that, most orphanages and hospitals had a "Foundling's Entrance," a warm, sheltered, discreet foyer, with an entrance where it was easy to come and go unobserved, which was a safe place to leave off a baby anonymously. Usually it was set up with a counter, but no one at the counter;

instead, a large hand-scrawled sign said, "Back in 3 minutes." This allowed people who just wanted to set the baby down and run to do so; an AI watched through a hidden camera, and when it saw a baby drop-off in progress, it would sound an alarm at a desk in the staff quarters, so that a human being could decide what to do. Sometimes that meant hurrying there to be "just arriving back," and sometimes it meant staying out of sight until the person was gone and the baby had been left.

Two days before Dave had been dropped off there, a girl who didn't look much more than thirteen had come in with two-week-old twin boys, one in an ancient car seat and the other in a cardboard box, and stood waiting patiently at the counter till an attendant came out. She had emphatically insisted at the counter that since her boyfriend, Dave, had been killed, *both* twins would have to be named Dave, and that was the only way she was giving them up.

"Maybe they should have a different middle name or last name, so people won't mix them up?" the attendant suggested, hoping that she would see the reasonableness of this.

"I already thought of that," the girl said. "I never knew my boyfriend's last name, anyway. He had this *lim* important job where he wasn't allowed to date or see girls or nothing. It was like national security or something like that. He told me some stuff about it that I can't tell anyone else. Anyway, since it all had to be secret, I never knew his last name, but since he got, you know, shot and I saw him die, pos-*def* I wanted to give his babies the names I called him. So they both have to be Dave, but here's the middle and last names." She pulled a note from her shirt pocket, unfolded it, and handed it across the counter. "The one on the right is Bear. 'Kay? I have to go. The Salvation Army where I'm staying doesn't feed us if we're late, and I want to get my last meal because now that I gave up the kids they'll throw me out tomorrow." She left in a cloud of other half-explanations.

The attendant had handled messier cases, and she shrugged. She looked at the sheet of paper and turned to the twin to her left—figuring the girl had meant the one to her own right—and said, "Well, I guess you're Dave Bear. And you must be Dave Love," she added to the other twin. "Welcome to Denver Dome Orphanage."

Within an hour they were known to everyone in the place as the Dave Twins. The signs on their incubators read "David M. Love" and "David P. Bear," but it's natural for people to gossip, and gossip reaches everyone in an institution eventually, even the children, so the Dave Twins endured years of being teased about their middle names, "My" and "Pooh."

Two days later, another baby turned up, dropped off by a different but also very young girl. This one was in a cardboard box with a couple of stuffed toys and a blanket, plus a note that said, "Call him anything as long as it's Dave. That was his father's name. You can tell him his father is a spy or a cop or something, and he must have gone undercover because he never came back to marry me."

"I even *looked* like I should have been the third Dave Twin," Dave said, as we squatted at lunch the first day, "which makes me kinda suspect that the original Dave got around plenty."

Since the first two were the Dave Twins, some wit on the staff suggested this one should be the Dave Singleton.

The Denver Dome orphanage was small and poor; Denver had never really recovered from the fires that had raged through it in the last part of the Eurowar, and the new dome there didn't cover much more than the old downtown. It was still an important crossroads and a good place for a warehouse, but since hardly any human beings were needed to staff warehouses anymore, most of the old city remained untenanted, infested with a few vags and packs of stray dogs, for many decades before the dome finally was nuked in 2059. Clamped savagely between a vanished tax base and a large number of the poor, Denver Dome had nothing to spare for its orphanage. From what I remembered of Denver Dome, the few times I had been through there before it was nuked, it was a cold, poor, mean town in spirit anyway, one that didn't mind the sight of misery much, so I doubt it broke their hearts not to have anything to spend on their poor.

In 2049, with the war breaking out, and every social problem worsening, the Denver Dome Council was looking hard for a way, any old way, to shut down the orphanage for good and thereby cut expenses. It didn't take them long to hit on the same solution that lots of places did: they made the children available to everyone who wanted them. Even in its early years, the War of Papal Succession was a war for control of human brains, most especially the brains of the next generation; one way to get brains was to more or less buy them while they were still enclosed in children. The market for kids was brisk.

Boys twelve and up went off to militias and mercenary companies; girls were sold to affluent families as servants, if they were lucky, and to barely disguised pimps if they were not; younger children went off to be adopted by families, schools, sects, and creches so that they could all be indoctrinated by all the various splinters off of Ecucatholicism and cybertao.

When Phil and Monica Comasus came by the orphanage, one nice sunny Monday morning in February, 2050, they said they wanted to take three kids with them, and offered to pay in NihonAmerica bearer bonds, which were still being honored because the transfer ships were the collateral. Nobody at the orphanage asked any questions; most of the staff didn't care, and the few who did, didn't want to know whether the kids were going to be adopted, or slaves, or used in medical experiments. Their job, as defined by the city, was to get what money they could for handing over kids.

They were trying to do it in a hurry, because, however bad the other options might be, it was clear this orphanage wouldn't be in business much longer, with Denver leaning toward bankruptcy and the rest of the world going to hell. The first serious shots of the War of Papal Succession were just being fired, the rubble of Rome wasn't cool yet, and armies big enough to have real battles were only just being organized and trained.

Phil Comasus was a short man—almost tiny. He was shorter than his wife, Monica, who was only of average height. They made an odd couple, to seven-year-old Dave's eyes, because they contrasted in so many ways. Phil might have been fifteen years older than Monica. He was plump and soft-bodied; she was slender, angular, and well-muscled. She had thick black hair, high cheekbones, blue eyes, and the kind of patrician good looks that Hollywood used to insist on for its "serious" actresses; he had bumpy, squashed features that made him look like one of the Seven Dwarves, an effect accentuated by his perpetually untidy slush-gray goatee. Both were quietly but expensively dressed, a few social notches above the Doleworkers who ran the orphanage. "They were a fairy-tale couple," Dave said to me, as we stopped for sandwiches and some iron coffee, "except in most fairy tales, the troll doesn't marry the princess."

Dave said he realized, even at age seven, that things were going to be different from now on, not when they told him that he would be leaving with this couple within half an hour, and not when he packed up his things, or when the whole orphanage lined up to say good-bye to him, Cecile, and Robin. The moment when he knew everything would be different was after they went into the diskster, Monica showed them how to strap in, and she said, "Now—do you have absolutely everything you should? Is there anything you want or need that you forgot to pick up? They rushed you out of there, and I don't want to leave anything behind if it's yours and it's your favorite."

Dave had three sets of clothes, a tiny stuffed bear that had been a present from Mrs. Allen before she got laid off, and a bag of toiletries. He didn't really care about all the crayon drawings in his locker, and the crayons were the property of the orphanage—they were always telling him not to use so many.

Cecile, a quiet, small, dark-haired girl of five, also had nothing else. But ten-year-old Robin, a husky and muscular Asian girl who was one of the leaders of kid society, spoke up and said, "I can't remember if I packed a picture of my real mother. It's the only one I have."

"Well," Monica said, "take a look in your bag, and if we don't find it, we'll go in and look for it."

Robin looked and couldn't find it, so she and Monica went inside together. While they were in there, Phil got out a set of jacks and a ball—neither Cecile nor Dave had ever seen any such thing before—and started teaching them to play jacks. At first Dave couldn't see the point, but after a few minutes he and Cecile were starting to see what it was about, and pretty soon they were engrossed in a game, coached by Phil. Dave thought it was bizarre that a grown-up genuinely cared how the two of them played a game—or seemed to get such a kick out of watching them do it—but it was bizarre in the nicest way he'd ever seen.

After about half an hour, Monica returned with Robin and the picture. Robin was holding her hand and her eyes were shining; it was obvious that Monica had just become her hero. "Can you believe it?" Monica said in a tone of outrage. "She had left it behind on top of her locker, because she wanted to pack it on top of her bag, and they made her hurry out so fast she forgot it—and they saw it and even though our diskster was sitting right in front of the building, they didn't come out and tell us—they had *already thrown it away!* We had to pull it out from the recycler hopper, and I made them let us use their scrubber to clean it. It's good as new now, but imagine treating a photo of Robin's mother that way!"

"Well," Phil said, "we're done with that place for good, thank heavens. Time to get rolling again."

They all strapped in because the trip out of the city would be zigzaggy; Phil promised they'd all play jacks again. "Many times," he added, emphatically. "There might never be a last game. You might still be playing in the old-folks home."

Dave and Cecile giggled at that, and after making sure everyone was comfortable, Phil told the diskster an address in the KC Dome, and it extended the thousands of tiny pins from its surface, charged up into a faint, crackling blue glow, and shot off faster than Dave had ever moved before. For all three kids it was their first diskster ride.

After they had ridden for some miles, and were racing over the empty plains, Robin whispered to them, "She was *so* mad at them for throwing out my mom's picture! *And* she made them fix *everything*. It was *so* koapy. It must be like that to have a mom."

Dave nodded, trying to appear wise to such things. He turned to look out the window. It was a day full of amazing things—a diskster ride, a long trip, adult attention . . .

One advantage of the war not yet being completely on, just yet, was that you could still cross the country in a diskster. The Comasus diskster stopped at the municipal orphanages in Kansas City, St. Louis, Chicago, and Detroit, picking up two to four children between five and ten years old at each one, and by the time it set down in front of a huge fake-Victorian house in upstate New York, the kids had all gotten some acquaintance with each other, Monica had settled a quarrel or two, Phil had taught them a number of silly songs, and everyone had been measured for new clothes.

The thirteen newly acquired orphans had all been admonished to call Phil and Monica by their first names, and to not to worry about anything, because they were getting taken care of from now on.

Dave told me, as we threw clay into the hole, that his first sight of the Big House would "probably be the last thing to fade from my brain on the day I die, and if anybody ever could prove to me that there was a heaven and it was as good a place as the Big House, I'd be happy to die that minute."

It was late in the evening, but the moon was up and bright, when they followed the winding track up from the small, shallow, ice-covered river through the pines to the top of the ridge, crested the top, and decelerated over the wide snowfield that spread out in front of them. In the moonlight the house was all silvers and blues; it was three stories high, with a main body as big as the Muncipal Orphanage back home—*no, that's not home anymore.* Dave thought with something close to pure glee—and two sizable wings extending from it. At the time, Dave thought it looked like a house in a story set somewhere in history, like you could see on the flashchannel when the bigger boys weren't keeping it tuned to sports. Later he realized that it wasn't really laid out like any of those; the immense wraparound porches on each wing, the big flat diskster landing area in the front, the extremely tall and steep metal roofs—with the black circles on them that he did not realize at the time were automatic gunports—all made it very much a twenty-first-century building. Still, to the naive eye, it might have been an old resort house, from back when people had come up from the city to spend summers in this part of the country.

The diskster flared off its surplus charge in a blue *whoosh* and settled onto its pad. In a few minutes, Phil and Monica had awakened everyone, sorted out baggage, and organized a groggy parade into the immense main room of the house. It was just settling into Dave's mind that these two people *owned* this magnificent place, the way that he owned his shoes.

Of course the first thing they did was send all the kids into the large ground-floor bathroom—many people, kids especially, just can't use the bathroom on a diskster, and they hadn't stopped since Detroit, two hours earlier.

When everyone had returned from that first necessity, Monica took a quick roll, and then led them downstairs. Dave thought that this was probably where the boys' and girls' barracks would be, but instead they went into a big room where an industrial faxbricator sat by a large pile of folded clothing. Phil and Monica went forward and began sorting through the pile, eventually making up thirteen smaller piles of new clothes.

Before departing on their child-gathering trip, the Comasuses had loaded that faxbricator with bolts of forty different fabrics; Phil had zapped the kids' measurements on ahead, and when they arrived, handed a pile of brand-new clothes to each kid. All the clothes fit, and had the kid's own name sewn into them. They had even paid attention to favorite colors, and put kid-selected designs on the sweatshirts and T-shirts.

When he got his pile, Dave just grabbed the first thing on the top and sat right down on the floor, holding his green Bobbert the Space Tiger sweatshirt—his favorite color and his favorite flashchannel character. It had "Dave Singleton" on the label. They had even made sure it was a soft label made to rest against his neck comfortably, not a big scratchy one sewn in for the convenience of an institutional laundry. He was trying very hard to understand that this sweatshirt—exactly what he had wanted for at least two years—was now all his, brand new, absolutely clean and never worn by anyone else. He clung to it for a long while, pressing his face against it.

"You can put it on now, if you want," Monica said, "but you might just want to carry it up to your room, along with everything else."

"Carry it up to the moon?" Dave asked.

Monica's eyes twinkled. At the time, she was about thirty-five, but to a five-year-old, all adults are terribly old. Dave looked at her closely and curiously, for the first time. She had explosions of tiny laugh lines around her eyes and mouth, and an oversupply of very light-colored freckles. In her jet-black hair there were already a few strands of gray. Her voice was low, modulated, the sort of voice that, before AIs, could have made a fortune in voice-overs.

Dave was in love instantly, as were all twelve of the other children. "Not carry it to the moon," Monica said. "You're not quite ready for that, Dave, though you might be some day. Carry it *to your room*. Come on, I'm going to show everybody where their room is."

Dave joined a parade of the other small kids—himself and Cecile, from Denver; a dark haired girl, terribly thin, with pallid skin and a vampire-red mouth, about eight, named Julia, from the Chicago orphanage; Prester, about Dave's age, a very thin, dark-skinned kid, with big expressive eyes, crooked teeth, and extremely funny jokes, from St. Louis, who Dave was already hoping would become a friend; a quiet boy who might have been a mix of any or all races, named Joey, who was a lot taller than Dave but acted about the same age, and so might be another friend.

They were all going to what Monica called "West Third." She explained that it meant that their bedrooms were on the third floor of the west wing of the house. Dave had never been in a house with a wing before, but he figured out what that meant after some momentary confusion. (He really would not have been surprised if the house had turned out to be able to fly, after everything that had happened that day. Maybe to the moon.)

The five children were shown the bathroom they were to share, each given towels with their names on them, shown the games, books, and small table that had been placed in a wide spot in the hall. Each of them had a room with a desk and chair, closet, bookshelves (and some books on them—and Dave was pretty sure that all of those were new, just like the clothes), bed, chest, and as far as Dave could see, everything you could possibly want in a bedroom, even including a door. "Remember when you want to talk to someone else to knock on his or her door, and wait for the person to say 'Come in,' and don't come in unless they say it," Monica said. "And they'll do the same for you. That way you'll always be able to feel like this is your space."

She gave them all a snack—the idea of cereal before bed, just because it would feel good, was strange, but Dave decided he liked it. Then they all got to take showers, and everyone had a brand-new toothbrush and toothpaste. Dave had never been quite so clean, or gone to bed in a room that was neither too hot nor too cold, or felt such clean sheets before. Monica even tucked him in—something he had only seen on the flashchannel—and said good night.

As he drifted off to sleep, he could hear the sounds coming down the hall, from East Third and East Second. The bigger kids were getting showered, laughing and talking. Phil was hanging around down there, it sounded like; they could hear his big booming laugh now and then, and his intense, serious voice explaining things. It sounded like the bigger kids were having a good time too.

Just before he fell asleep, Dave prayed, for the first time in his life, though he had had no religious instruction and wasn't even sure he knew who he was asking to help him. Nonetheless he prayed with all the passion and sincerity a seven-year-old can manage. He wanted all this to be here when he woke up.

Perhaps the greatest miracle was that it was. Shortly after dawn, Dave was awakened by Phil knocking on the door and saying, "Get up, get dressed (put clean stuff on, if you've worn it, we'll wash it), use the can, and come downstairs. Breakfast in ten minutes."

As Dave pulled on his miraculously still-present green Bobbert sweatshirt, he could hear the thumps and chatter of other kids getting up, and by the time he had taken his turn at the bathroom he heard a babble of voices downstairs. The dining room and main kitchen were on the first floor of the west wing, and he raced Prester all the way down the stairs.

Breakfast today would be ham, pancakes with apple compote, and orange juice. Everyone was used to pancakes because they were a staple of orphanage food, but most had never had apple compote, orange juice was an occasional treat, and ham had been mostly for holidays, and strictly rationed.

When breakfast was finally finished, they all went upstairs and learned the rules for keeping their rooms—just simple things like hanging up clothes, putting dirty clothes in hampers, keeping things on hooks and shelves and not on the floor, making the bed, dusting, all much simpler than following the rules about your bunk in the orphanage, since here at the Big House you had a place for just about everything, and all you had to do was put things where they belonged and wipe surfaces off. Then they went on a tour of the house and, since the day was mild, put on coats and hats and went out and built snowmen on the lawn. Pretty soon everyone was running around and laughing, throwing little unpacked snow-balls. Phil showed them some games you could play in the snow, and everyone had a good time with those, even the older kids.

About the time that they were ready to be tired and cold, but were not quite there yet, Monica ushered them back into the house, where they hung up their coats and hats, put their boots on the dry-ing grate, and then filed back into the dining room. Phil announced lunch: hot dogs, french fries, baked beans, and hot chocolate—and once again, all that you wanted of everything.

After lunch, as they settled into a pleasant stupor on the couches and chairs in the big room called the "Commons," Monica read them a story—there had been one nice woman at the orphan-age who read stories, Dave recalled faintly, but she had been laid off before he was five, and this was the first time he'd heard a story, instead of seeing one on the flashchannel, in a couple of years. It was difficult to follow it without the pictures and without being able to click on things for explanations, but it was still very nice of her, Dave thought. The littler kids seemed to take to it better than the big ones.

Then she took them all to West Second, which turned out to have a classroom in it, with thirteen big desks, one for each of the kids. "This is where you'll all go to school," she explained. "There are other workrooms and project spaces as well, and a library over in East First, where you'll work much of the time on your own, but this space will be home base, where usually your day will begin and end, and most days you'll be here for at least a couple of hours—sometimes for the whole day."

They were all so startled by the first thing that she had said that most of them didn't catch the rest. She had to repeat her entire spiel a couple of times. In most places, for at least the last ten years, orphanage kids hadn't been allowed to go to school, either because all the public schools had been closed as part of the Gray Decade's economy measures, or because if there were public schools, orphans were excluded as "not taxpayer children."

Once they realized that Monica really did mean that they would all be getting regular schooling, just like rich kids, they were wildly excited. They got a few minutes to explore their desks, discovering pencils, crayons, a brand-new werp for each of them, reams of paper, several books—which Monica assured them they would be taught to read—and too many other miracles to even categorize in those first exciting minutes.

Then Phil came in. He sat down on the desk at front and said, "I suppose you're all normal enough to be wondering why we brought you here and what we're going to do with you. So I'm going to tell you. If it seems weird to you, well, it sometimes seems weird even to me. But I think you'll like it here, basically, and mostly it will be a step up from where you were."

Dave was willing to grant that point.

"Many years ago," Phil said, "I was one of the designers of the transfer-ship societies. The transfer ships are the huge spaceships that look like bright stars at night, and come in near Earth every few months, like the *Flying Dutchman* and *Diogenes*, the ones that run in the big cycler orbits to supply the colonies on other planets. What I did, along with half a dozen other people, was to plan and help create the system of child-rearing and education that was then used to produce the first generation born on the ships, the people who operate them now. I also had something of a hand in planning the basic social rules under which they grew up, and the culture into which they would grow. I was hired to do that because they needed to produce a whole bunch of very smart people who got along together really well, and who would help to save the human race, and I was well known as a teacher, as a scientist, and for some other accomplishments, various other things that need not concern us for the moment, here."

Dave later learned that, under his original name, Comasus had been a very young senator from Massachusetts in the 112th Congress, the last US Congress ever to meet. He had also shared a Nobel Prize in Economics, and served a few years as Deputy Administrator for the Environment of UNRRA-2.

"There were some things the other society designers didn't believe me about, which was how eventually I got fired from my job as society designer, and part of why they're having the problems they're having on Mars and Ceres. Given the way events have turned out, they probably believe me now," Phil went on. "But that's neither here nor there; on the transfer ships and in the colonies, things have worked out, if not as well as they might, at least tolerably well, and nowadays there wouldn't be anything for me to do even if they hired me back. So, despite being occasionally bitter about it, I am usually able to let that go, and take pleasure in having made a really good try, in my younger days, at saving the world.

"However, a really good try ultimately makes no difference; only success makes a difference. And it so happens the world still needs saving, and with you guys, and Monica, and a certain amount of plain old luck, that's just what I'm going to do."

The way he smiled at them made Dave feel safe and happy, but something about his tone thrilled the little boy to the bone—it was as if he'd been personally sworn in by Batman or Earth Ranger.

Phil's explanation for what he was going to do with them was necessarily simple, because he was talking to a group of quite young children. As they grew, he re-explained and re-explained, and their ability to understand it all increased. Since he often used the same phrases in the process, and so many times the explanation happened in the same rooms, in later years it was very hard for Dave to sort out what he had been told when—his earlier memories were overlaid by later ones and tied into them almost seamlessly.

Furthermore, when he explained it to me in the cave, as we dug, he told me about it as the ideas occurred to him, not necessarily in the best order for understanding, so there's not much hope of disentangling it and telling the whole story of Phil and Monica Comasus, the Big House, the kids themselves, the Freecybers, or any of the rest, as anyone experienced it. The best I can do is give a fairly accurate, sorted-out explanation, but you have to keep in mind, that's not how the kids met up with it. For Dave, as an adult, it was as much a part of him as speaking English.

Comasus was the originator of the system called CSL education. CSL stood for Cybernetics, Semiotics, and Logic, and it could be described several different ways—as an academic subject in its own right that no one else had realized was needed before, as an abstract stratum underlying every other kind of learning, as a set of techniques that a kid learned to accelerate learning in all fields. Phil alternated between saying he'd invented it and he'd discovered it, sometimes saying that he'd come up with a way for the three older disciplines to easily transfer ideas between them, and sometimes saying that he'd found out that a twentieth-century mathematician, two nineteenth-century polymaths, and a bunch of ancient Greeks and medieval scholastics had all been working on the same problem, and that the answers fit together into a grand idea that made the human brain work better.

The basic trick was simple enough: there are a few fundamental patterns to ideas—different patterns for different classes of verbal, visual, emotional, mathematical, and so forth—and a way of learning that goes with each pattern. Furthermore, each of the couple of dozen fundamental patterns has a specific relation to every other fundamental pattern. Master the pattern through repetition, drill, re-experiencing it from a variety of different perspectives and contexts—just as children master words, grammatical structures, dramatic plots, moves in games, or moral notions, by working with them over and over in different situations—and eventually you have the ability to recognize it wherever you meet it, including in the process of learning all other subjects. Master the fundamental connections and now you are ready to relate and connect new ideas creatively, almost from the moment you understand them.

Later, you learn the master pattern that explains how each pattern applies to each subject matter, and why each kind of learning works best for it; by the time you're ten or so, you know how to learn anything, quickly and with no more effort than necessary. (It helps a great deal that your learning ability has been accelerating right along, so that you do have a deep acquaintance with all sorts of basic material; besides mastering how to learn, you also master a lot of plain old-fashioned learning, just as anybody who is studying the piano, in the process of perfecting technique, also plays the piano a lot, and develops a very big repertoire.)

The CSL education plan allows most kids, by age fourteen, to reach about the intellectual level of a senior in an ordinary college, and to assume adult responsibilities, at least if they want to or society has any need for them to do so.

"Most of the stupidity, hostility, and bad behavior of adolescence comes from being held in a state of enforced uselessness for anywhere from five to ten years," Phil used to say, revealing how old he was, since neither Earth nor the space colonies had been able to afford that sort of adolescence for most people in the five decades since the Eurowar. Most of us born in this past century can't believe that there was ever a time or place when a seventeen-year-old's main focus was his or her social life, jobs were for "spending money" rather than self-support, and schooling was deliberately paced so that the dumber students wouldn't need to suffer discomfort or put forth extra effort. I wonder what people back then were thinking—or if.

❧ **"Uh, what was** this guy Comasus's real name?" I asked Dave.

He laughed for a second. "You know, we were all taught so thoroughly to never speak it, it just doesn't come natural to say it out loud." He shook his head and said, "But it can't matter now. The man is dead, has been dead for more than thirty years."

Then he told me the name.

"Come on," I said.

"It was."

"I thought he was one of the people assassinated in the early '30s, back during that wave of random terror that just seemed to be taking out everyone known to have any brains or talent," I said. "In fact I'm almost sure he was one of them."

"He was," Dave said, "or rather that was the story that was given out. By the time I knew him, he was hiding behind something like ten different aliases and had an elaborate system for keeping himself from being found. He had the money to do it because he had many patents and copyrights under false names, signed over to dummy corporations, and I don't know what all— one huge money-hiding machine, laced with dozens of dead ends and false continuers and telltales, that filtered goods down to him. When I knew him he'd already been hiding for more than fifteen years from something he called the 'Organization.' Never knew him to speak of it without a shudder. As far as I know, it never had any other name than that, either, just the Organization. I couldn't make out if it was a gang of spies or crooks or mercenaries, or just kind of a group of evil people, but Phil Comasus was the sanest man I ever met, and he was scared to death of it.

"What he said was that when the Organization tried to kill him, they broke into his house, killed his first wife—hacked her to pieces in front of him, to tell you the truth—gave him a massive psycholytic injection that should have left him a madman for the rest of his life, beat him hard enough to break a dozen bones, rupture a kidney, and puncture both lungs, poured gasoline on him, set a fire upstairs that killed his kids, left him for dead . . . and sometime between them leaving and the fire burning its slow way downstairs, he revived enough to crawl out onto the street. Somebody picked him up from there and admitted him to a hospital as a John Doe. With the fire and the mess, the cops couldn't figure out how many people had died in that house, and came up one high.

"After he came to, and figured out what was up, he realized that the Organization must think he was dead, and from then on he did his best to make sure they continued to think so. But when the cutting's done and the pieces are laid, you know, nothing really stops people like the Organization. A long time after that, they found out who he was and where he was, and killed him and Monica. That's later in the story."

"You're sure it was this Organization and not just someone at random? I thought you said it was soldiers from Murphy's."

"There might have been no connection," Dave said, "except a long time later—well, maybe just a few years, it might have been around Year Three, when I was putting together my group of cowboys—I met up with this one cowboy, guy who called himself Gregor, who wanted to join. He said he'd been in Murphy's Comsat Avengers. Gregor was a loner, and it didn't take too long to figure out that his reason for hiding out was not a love of freedom or some principle. He'd have been hiding from *any* society, because, at least in my estimation, the guy was either a serial killer already, or he was going to be. I turned him down. Then a couple of months later, me and two of my cowboys came across Gregor in a deserted small town, where he'd found a family hiding out in an old grocery store, and was 'using them up,' which was his expression for spending a few days doing godawful things while he killed them off one at a time. He had just killed the father when we got there. Well, you know, justice is rough out here in the woods, so me and my cowboys gave him a real thorough beating to help him tell us the truth, because we wanted to know whether the man had any accomplices, and just what the hell he intended by committing the sort of crime that endangered every person who was still living free.

"Somewhere in the course of the beating, just about the point where he was about to break, I guess, and grasping at anything to make himself hold on, Gregor told us that he belonged to the Organization, and that we had better let him go if he knew what was good for us, because the Organization always avenged its own.

"After that, I just kept kicking him till he passed out, put a small demolition charge under his chin, taped his head down, and set off the charge. Made a hell of a mess but I was pretty pissed off and I guess I rationalized it by figuring it would make an example of him for any others there might be around, and if he really *was* with the Organization, it would get them after me—which was fine with me, I'd love to have more of them show up. More chances for revenge for Phil and Monica, you know," he said. "Anyway, this guy Gregor was a monster. When I die I'm going to have two big regrets about life, and they're both going to be about getting somewhere too late. One of them's not coming across that cowboy before he'd killed the father and one of the children in that family; in a better world, I guess I'd have come across him during the war, and shot his damned head off before he ever got loose among the cowboys."

"And your other big regret?" I asked, keeping the story rolling, I hoped, giving us both an excuse to not dig more clay just immediately.

"I'm getting to that one. Another sandwich?"

"Yeah." I accepted it gratefully, and he got on with that part of the story.

For most of the 2050s, while the War of Papal Succession became the War of the Memes and became steadily nastier, Dave had the best years of his life. Those years while he was growing up were a busy, demanding, challenging time, but a very happy one. The war went on and the glaciers grew; Antarctica lost its ice and Scotland disappeared under an ice sheet; memes were created, mutated, grew, got control of a large part of the human race; guys a few years older than Dave, like me, spent the decades fleeing or pursuing, ducking or shooting back. The world got uglier and nastier, the memes that had begun as weapons took over the war for their own purposes, and life in the Big House went on.

Dave got his growth early, and was big for sixteen. The other kids had been quietly vanishing as they got to about that age, so it came as no surprise to Dave, Prester, and Joey when Phil called them in and told them what their part in things would be; by that time, the only time they saw the older ones was when one of them would come back for a brief few days to rest, recover, and get another outside mission from Phil and Monica.

"My last disciples," Phil said, grinning. "At least for a while, until we're in whatever the next historical period turns out to be, and I figure out what else the world might need. Has anyone who's gone on an outside mission ever told you what they do out there?"

The three boys shook their heads, and Phil smiled. "Well, I guess it wasn't really secret, but they probably get a habit of being very discreet out there, and it's probably good that they have the habit. All right, here's the story; here's why I grabbed you out of those orphanages and put you through CSL education at a time when I'd rather have been spending my time sensibly hiding with Monica, waiting to get old and die."

"You're not going to die," Prester blurted out.

"Oh, sooner or later," Phil said, "but only on one day out of all of the billions of years of time. That should tell you how negligible the whole business is. Sooner or later the Organization will find out that I'm alive and where I am, or I'll get sick with something that requires DNA validation to treat, which I don't dare do since it would be like publishing my fingerprints, or I'll just fall downstairs and whack my head on the balustrade. Not today, probably, and I expect to be here when you all come back to visit. But I'm afraid the visits won't be often, for a while, because these next few years we're going to be very busy."

Phil explained a little of what the others were up to; all were in some covert role, some in very deep cover, which was why they hadn't been seen since they'd left. "Who got what job depended mostly on my guess as to how well they'd handle the loneliness," Phil said. Five of the former students were working their way up one hierarchy or another, becoming important in military, financial, or church positions; four were out making "adjustments." That was what Cecile and Julie had departed to do, just a few months before, their youth carefully concealed by makeup and padding. "I wish we'd had more time to prep them," Phil said, "and to let them have time to grow adult bodies, but adjustments kept getting more urgent, and they were the only ones left to send, since I had to reserve you three for a special mission."

"What do they adjust?" Dave asked, trying to avoid, for the moment, the awareness that there was a special mission for him.

Phil sighed. "When possible, they just do things to cause good people to be promoted, and bad people discredited. They tinker here and there to try to help the war run out of gas, which it's going to do in three to four years at most—and we need it to end in a stalemate, between at least five memes, not in a single-meme victory. They meddle in the affairs of different organizations, sending some of them down paths where they'll do more good for humanity, helping the good ones along . . . every now and then seeing that a bad one breaks up or collapses. Just now, for example, Julie is working a staff job for the army of Real America, up north in Minot, helping them recover their balance and morale so that they can retake Minnesota and roll back One True; down south in Tennessee, Isaac is getting Free American through a minor palace putsch that ought to put an end to their concentration camps and secret police. Sometimes it's a matter of infiltrating and making a few changes or helping someone who's going to make the changes. A lot turns on small differences."

He sighed. "And I guess I really can't conceal from you that every so often they're killing some of the people that are most in the way of progress and success for humanity. Usually very discreetly—with so many mutant and tailored bugs around, sudden fatal infections just aren't that unusual. Every so often they set up something more public, when that's what will do us the most good, but that always makes me nervous, because you never know where an investigation might lead, and one intervention that just never works is to kill a smart cop or prosecutor who's starting to think that things are more than they seem. So we do less of the messy stuff than you might imagine, and I'm glad of that.

"But you three are in for something very different." Phil looked out the window for a long moment, at the green hills and the forest that came most of the way up to the lawn of the Big House. "The good news is you'll be able to come back here and visit more often than your fellow students. The bad news is that I'm giving you three the toughest job of all."

Dave sat quietly with the others and waited. He had guessed already that this was going to be something to do with the memes; Phil had admitted, several times, that although he'd been perfectly accurate in predicting the beginning of the War of Papal Succession and the deterioration of the Earth as the war wound down to approximating Hobbes's "war of each against all," he hadn't foreseen anything like the memes at all.

"Theoretically I only needed ten people," he said, "to make all the requisite changes, and exert the force that would keep the world out of some of its worst possible tracks. But—well, here's where you have to give Monica the credit. She said we needed to have a reserve against the unexpected. So I chose to have three more. And here you are, ready to go. There's a job for you that I could never have guessed we'd need."

Joey spoke up; shy and modest, he rarely spoke, but he usually asked an important question. "So out of the ten, there are five working their way into positions of power, and four of your 'adjustors.' That's nine. But you sent out ten."

Phil looked miserably sad; it seemed to put a decade onto him, right there. "It's probably revealing that I told myself, three times, to be sure I told you what had happened to Martha. And I still haven't yet. She was an exec assistant for the Pacific Rewildernization Corporation on the Big Island, in Hawaii, where they're trying to get some kind of a normal ecology going again; it was a place where we had some hope of getting many really smart people, and their kids, away from the violence, out from between the contesting powers, in sort of an independent republic that would grow naturally out of the settlements of ecological reconstruction specialists. One of the things she was working on was getting them to adopt CSL education—we've never had much luck getting people to do that on Earth, because unless it's really an emergency, people really do not want their children to be a great deal smarter, better adjusted, and more competent than they are—even with that carefully planned society in space, the parental generation totally flipped out when they realized just how obsolete they had made themselves, and if they hadn't been so thoroughly trained and conditioned to accept it, we might have lost the ships to the power struggle between the generations. Down here, with uncontrolled populations, you might provoke massacres of the children, or god knows what else. So the idea was that on the island, we'd have a bunch of smart capable people that we could propagandize into accepting CSL education for their kids, who would let it go on, and we'd finally have at least one really functional society here on Earth."

"What happened to Martha?" Dave asked quietly. He was remembering her laugh, and the way she could run, and thinking of the pictures she had painted that now hung in the front hall; a tall, handsome black girl, with an amazing gift for languages, always willing to help the younger kids; her one visit home, when they'd all had a picnic on the lawn to celebrate and she'd looked completely grown up.

"Raped and shot dead," Phil said. "Then mutilated in some grotesque ways we don't need to talk about. Her body was left on her boss's desk, and any hope of getting CSL education for Hawaii seems to have died with her. My best guess is that she came to the attention of the Organization. (I have long suspected that they're doing what we're doing, but in reverse.) She must have distinguished herself enough to be noticed—that's why I keep telling people to be good only at the parts of their job that affect larger matters. A patina of ordinary incompetence is probably their best protection." He was quiet for a long time, and so were the three boys.

"Well," Phil said, "it's a bad idea to dwell on everything bad that can happen, as we all know. Let me tell you what I have in mind for the three of you. It will be dangerous and difficult enough; you needn't fear that any of you will be getting a soft ride while others run risks and face difficulties."

It was only years later that Dave realized how odd it was that Phil assumed that neither he nor Joey nor Prester would have wanted a soft ride.

Phil looked from one to the other and said, "In some ways, it may be I'm asking you to face the biggest fear anyone in the group might have to face. I'm going to ask you all to let me infect you with a meme."

Dave's gut rolled over; he'd had no direct acquaintance with memes, but he knew more than enough about them.

"If it will make you feel better," Phil added, gently, "Monica and I have both been running that meme for four months now, and we can assure you that we're in charge, not it. The meme is called Freecyber, and Monica developed it from my concepts."

"What's it do?" Prester asked. "I mean, obviously it either didn't take you over, or if it did, it's got you copied perfectly."

"Well, I hope it didn't take me over," Phil said. "And what I run is *three* copies of Freecyber, all of them interacting. What Freecyber is, is an anti-meme meme. It lives in your brain and doesn't do much unless another meme invades. Then it goes into action and disables the other meme, and eventually builds up your ability to resist another infection. It preserves individuality, if you will. And what I want you guys to do is spread it everywhere—through the territory of every existing meme."

They had to prepare a set of false IDs, and some introductions to places where the three boys could get hired to do computer jocking, and that took the better part of the afternoon, before they were ready to have their last big meal with Phil and Monica and go to bed early so that they could slip away with a few hours of dark left to them. Within weeks, Freecybers were a new enemy all over the globe; virtually every established meme was trying to hunt them down, copy code from them, and find some way to cope with the new competitor.

👓 **"Well," I said,** as we took turns smashing the hole in the inner chamber open winder, sledges battering at the now-washed-clean rock, "at least that explains where Freecybers came from and why they had so many variations so fast. But—I hope it doesn't offend you to hear me say this—I always had the impression that the Freecybers *talked* a good game, but they seemed to be just as eager as any other meme to take you over."

"That's a pritnear perfect description of what the problem

was," Dave agreed, "and it's one that Phil and Monica never really got solved. The idea was supposed to be that Freecybers would allow people to have a much greater liberty in their personal lives and beliefs, but to do that, the Freecybers had to be smart enough to defeat other memes, and had to have a strong empathy for the desire for freedom—and you know, that combination meant that every generation Phil released, except the last one, always figured out that any freedom the host got was freedom the meme lost—and drew the implications—and became, basically, a sympathetic, patient tyrant. And since Phil was doing it all in ultracompact neurocoding, the Freecybers left people more in command of their abilities, able to exercise initiative, invent, create, do more than just cooperate and behave, and that meant that from the moment that a copy of any version of a Freecyber happened to think of the idea of having power over people, they were more effective competitors than most other memes out there. Then the other memes would gang up against them, and pirate the neurocode from the Freecybers . . . and it would be another generation that failed, and Phil and Monica would have to create still another."

For more than two years, Dave slipped in and out of roles and identities, moving around the world, sowing each new generation of Freecybers, every time in the hope that this one would be a liberator that did not degrade into a tyrant. Phil's original system of having three Freecybers watch each other in each brain running them had to be abandoned because it took up too much space; a system in which each Freecyber watched itself in a time-lagged system replaced it. But in each new generation, the Freecyber copies became corrupted and began to seek power and control for themselves—forcing Phil and Monica to develop a new generation of Freecybers that could take on and erase or control the last generation of Freecybers.

Phil and Monica worked endlessly on the problem, going short on sleep, worried by how the conflict as a whole was going, visibly aged by the strain every time Dave made it back to the Big House for a new set of memes and some badly needed rest and contemplation. The race was growing more intense as One True pulled ahead of other memes, and as the other memes allied to fight against One True. Freecybers, as a guerrilla insurrection against all sides, were finding it harder and harder to get in or do anything, in most regions, even when they were not corrupted. The risk of getting caught was growing.

"And still I didn't see it coming," Dave said, as he methodically shoveled mud down the hole, the heavy loads splashing into some little pool the trickle of hot water must be making down there. The shadows from the lights up in the corners did strange things on his face; sometimes it looked like a very bitter smile, sometimes like a mask of tragedy, sometimes it was simply half there and staring madly. "I'd been working under all sorts of aliases as a mercenary, and wasn't too bad a soldier—good enough to fake it through most outfits, most of the time, as needed. The last batch of Freecybers, though, hadn't worked for crap against the new One True, and I'd barely gotten away with a whole uncaptured skin. So no matter what, we were in for a rough time."

Weeks after it happened, one of the other kids from the Big House dropped Dave a note and let him know that One True had caught Prester and turned him; the date that was given was about right for it to be the explanation of how One True found out where the Big House was.

Dave and Joey had been coming back in to pick up the new, improved version of Freecyber, and the diskster had dropped them off, as had been necessary for the past couple of years, a few miles from the Big House, in a grove of trees. That seemed to haunt Dave, years later—that if they had just once broken protocol, and come straight in on the diskster, they might have gotten there soon enough.

The black plume of smoke told them before they came over the hill and saw the central part of the house just falling in. They skied down to the house itself, careless of the possibility that they might be shot, and then circled the house once. The wings were in flames, with most floors collapsed already. There was no way to go inside and come out alive, and no trace of Phil or Monica, so they resigned themselves to coming back later, and followed the tracks of the attackers—it looked like just two of them—up to the top of the ridge, where it looked as if they had stood and watched the fire for a long time, standing very close together.

Beyond that, the ski tracks ran a couple of miles to where a diskster track showed up.

It was late afternoon before they could safely go into the ruins of the Big House. "The only satisfaction I had," Dave said, "was that they didn't seem to have been tortured—just some bullets in each of them, where you'd put the shots for a quick kill. Checking with some processors that we had concealed in fireproof boxes, and hooked to the house system, for just such an occasion, we got some fuzzy pictures of the guys who did it—not enough to track them down—plus the satisfaction of knowing that as they tried to read our house systems, they were both infected with our little revenge micromeme, which had the nasty trick of waiting a few days and then setting you up to kill someone you were fond of, using all your imagination and skill and resources at hand. So probably a few days or weeks later, Phil and Monica's killers suddenly turned around and did whatever they would think of as the most unforgivable crime possible, to somebody important to them. Or maybe they tried to do it to each other.

"Well, with the Big House gone, I did what we'd planned on for ages. By then the thirteen agents were down to seven, and any messages at all between us were potentially dangerous, but I did put out word out to everyone that the Big House was gone and nobody was in charge anymore. Then I got going with the solo plan appointed for me. And that's how I ended up in the Rockies with an underground hideout that was practically a palace, and a military-quality suspended-animation rig—all this was built years before I came out here.

"My job was supposed to be to see how far I could get with organizing a resistance up in the hills, and if that failed, to duck out and go underground—very literally—for long enough to throw pursuit off completely, then stick my head up and see whether the situation had gotten any better and there was anything I could do."

I dumped another load of clay down the hole and listened to the splash. It must be pretty deep down there, or fast-flowing, or both, considering how much it seemed to be taking without complaint. "So you must've been out here to do the setup before the war even ended, before Resuna, long before One True announced its plans."

"Right. I used power equipment to set everything up, taking a chance that the satellite would see it but figuring that chances were no one would ever check the memory, years later. Then when the time came, I went back, made sure the place was still there and ready, and got far enough away so that I wouldn't lead anyone to it. After that, you pretty much know the rest—I went out and recruited some cowboys, gave them some ideas and some organization, and turned them loose. I guess I'd have felt more dedication to the cause if any of them had been worthwhile people, but, you know, Curran, they weren't. They were the same kind of people that became vags back at the turn of the century—grimy losers who couldn't face having lost and wouldn't stop whining, get up off their knees, and get back in the race. The longer I led them, the more I realized there was nothing to lead.

"So finally I decided it was time to end the game, and that was about the time you showed up with your team. I started running a few more risks with my cowboys, and sure enough, one by one, your team caught and turned them, till it was just me. Then I rushed you where I could pull a disappearance. And I decided to just move into the cave to sleep for a decade or so and see what conditions were like when I got back. Hard part was not being able to tell Nancy what was going on."

"You must have married her before you turned cowboy?"

"Just after. Call it a fit of sentimentality. You surely must have guessed where I met her."

"Was she one of the other kids from the Big House?"

"Bingo. Who else would I have felt comfortable with? And just having her around to talk to made life a hell of a lot more tolerable, you know, because she wasn't a half-literate ex-mercenary who only knew how to keep repeating that a man is a man and he's got to be himself, if you see what I mean. I would have taken her, and maybe even Kelly if she was born by then, down into the cave, but I didn't have any spare suspended-animation rigs, and while I was trying to get a line on two of those, Nancy and Kelly got found, caught, and turned. So like it or not, since there wasn't a prayer of rescuing Nancy or Kelly, and I was completely disgusted with cowboys, *and* I couldn't remotely think of winning my little war, it was time to go to sleep for a decade and see if conditions were any better when I emerged."

I leaned back against the wall, half to scratch my back on some exposed rock, half to work the muscles. "Well, are conditions any better?"

"I've got at least one follower that isn't a maladjusted dumb-ass," he pointed out.

"Thanks, you're not a maladjusted dumbass yourself."

"'Preciate it," he said. "You want to have dinner, bed down, maybe tomorrow we'll go get a cache and bring it in?"

"Anything that isn't a shovel sounds real good right now," I said. "You've got yourself a deal."

ё ё ё

Sometimes just a change of abuse makes all the difference to sore muscles. The next day was clear and bright, so we went for the one cache that we could reach easily while staying under cover the whole way. That one turned out to contain, among an enormous quantity of other things, a bottle of wine, some shampoo, and a few fresh towels, not to mention a badly needed change of underwear. We were most of the day getting it all moved in, but that evening it felt like we might as well hold a party—the place was still a rabbit hole but with more comfortable rabbits. We splashed around in the hot water, got reasonably clean, toweled off, and settled in for the wine.

We were finishing that off, reflected moonlight was glowing through the hole, and that's when I asked, "So what's your mission now that you're back? And will you be wanting me to enlist in it?"

He coughed with embarrassment and took a swallow of the last of his wine. "Currie," he said, "I really thought you would guess and I wouldn't have to say this, outright, I mean. After Phil and Monica died, I was working for my part of their project, and that meant I was working for the Freecybers. Just what do you think my job was? What does a meme want you to do?"

"Whatever it tells you, doesn't it? I mean the point is obedience, unless you're going to tell me that the last generation Freecybers were different."

"Something more basic than that, Currie. What's the one thing any meme wants you to do?"

I stared at him. "Well, a regular meme wants you to spread it to other people."

"And Freecyber isn't any different, Currie, it just doesn't want to run your life, most of the time, but like any of the others it wants to spread. That's what my copy wants to do."

"You can't be trying to tell me that you're running Freecyber. You don't talk like anybody who runs a meme. You can't mean you're running it right now."

"Right now, sure. It runs in background. Freecyber doesn't

talk to me like Resuna does to you, because it doesn't have any means of direct verbal communication, but it's right there in my head, and I always have a strong feeling reminding me that Freecyber needs to propagate."

"Well, but you haven't—" That was when I stopped and stared at him, and then realized. "Oh. Shit. Of course. I was out for all that time, and then when I came back . . . no Resuna. So you put Freecyber into me while I was unconscious, I guess through my jack—and then you cooked the jack—and now here I am running a meme and not even knowing I'm running it." The world was unsteady and it wasn't just from the wine. "Shit," I said again. "Shit, shit, you aren't any better than One True itself, are you?"

I don't think he was expecting me to hit him. I got in a good hard right to the side of his head, a real haymaker, before he even put his guard up, but he was at least as hardheaded as I was. He made my ribs go thud with a hard kick, and then I gave him a jab in the face. In a few seconds we were all over each other, pounding, kicking, slapping, and screaming things, anything to hurt each other, all technique forgotten in the wild imperative to just inflict as much injury as we could. In the middle of it all we were both yelling godawful stuff about people from each other's stories, Tammy and Mary and Nancy and Phil, in pure shrieks of hatred.

We threw ourselves at each other again and again, slipping on the slick clay, falling into the scalding water, getting slammed against the rocks and dragged on the gravel in the dark, bruised, bleeding, gasping for air. My face was wet with some godawful mixture of blood, mucus, and tears, and it felt like every tooth in my head was loose, but I didn't care. All I wanted to do was hurt Dave, hurt fucking Lobo, teach the bastard not to go building a person's hopes up, making him feel like he had a friend and a partner, and then suddenly throw a story like that at him. I needed to make him rip his fucking meme back out of my head, have things be what they were supposed to be—Dave and me out here in the mountains, the last free men on Earth—and not just be part of the scheme of Freecyber to take over from One True and run the world for itself. He had promised me freedom, and given me a change of jailers, and I was going to kill this sorry-ass penny-ante Judas for it.

I finally calmed down enough to pick up a shovel. By that time I'd gotten tossed and turned around into the dark back of the cave, and only noticed the shovel because it was under my foot. In the dark he couldn't see me coming and I could probably cave his head in—I crouched, grabbed it, and rushed.

He was lighted by the reflected moonlight through the hole, a sharp half-light half-shadow that made the lighted parts glow and hid the rest in darkness. Then that strange half-apparition got a wild expression that I could just barely see in the moonlight, like a demon mask, and shouted, "Let overwrite, let override," and the shovel fell from my hands and banged on my shins as I fell forward, landing my face in the warm mud. I tried to get up, twice, but barely managed to roll over.

When I woke up, it was daylight. Resuna was back, and Dave was gone; he'd taken his pack, his sleeping bag, and a bunch of supplies. I crawled unsteadily to my feet as Resuna, in a very worried tone, assured me that it couldn't reach the satellites at all and it thought its cellular jack had been damaged shortly after a non-approved meme had been slipped into my mind.

Anything left in the cave was too heavy to carry, except for my outside suit. It seemed to be missing its boots, and I spent a while looking for them before it occurred to me to check the shelf under the hole. When I climbed up, they weren't there either, but then I poked my head out through the hole and saw that my boots and flexis were lying in the snow, twenty meters away. He'd set it up so I could have them, but I would have to really want them.

I thought about just getting back in the sleeping bag for a while, resting up, and starting the next day, but Resuna pointed out that it could snow overnight, or thanks to all the stress I could come down with a fever or something, and anyway it was still very early in the morning.

I conceded that all this was true.

I put on my outside suit, pulled myself through the hole, cocked my feet up so that they didn't trail in the snow, and crawled on hands and knees to my boots. I had a horrible thought that he might have filled them with snow, but it looked like he was only interested in delay, not in cruelty—they were just fine.

Once I got them on, I put on my flexis, which were already set to function as skinny skis, and for the first time in weeks, I switched on the power in the suit. There was nothing I wanted in the cave, so I shoved a couple big armloads of snow into the water-processing reservoir on the suit, wished for poles for a moment, and then skated off, following what I guessed must be Dave's track downhill. This time I knew a lot more about his habits and the country, and though he'd made use of rock, ice, and frozen dirt wherever he could, I followed him easily enough.

I didn't know why I was still following him, but it seemed important. After a while Resuna said, *You know, this isn't strictly rational. Wouldn't it make considerably more sense to just find an open meadow, stamp out "help" in the snow, and wait for the diskster to show up? Probably a diskster would show up in half an hour or less. You need to get my cellular jack repaired anyway, before coming back out here after Lobo.*

He might be Dave Fucking Treacherous Bastard Singleton to me, but Resuna knew him as Lobo and that was how it was going to refer to him. *No,* I thought back to it. *I am doing something here that I really have to do, and that's all there is to it.*

I skied for another mile and became more and more convinced that Dave was just taking a long way around to his old home base. Maybe he needed something from there before running away for good.

If that's where he's going, Resuna said, *why don't we signal the satellite and let the people in the diskster know what's up? Once they pick us up, we can go straight on to his cave. You can even be in on the arrest, if you want.*

I was angry but I swallowed hard. To be fair, Resuna was, by definition, not human, and could hardly be expected to understand my feelings. *I don't want to see my best friend arrested,* I thought at it. *I couldn't betray him that way. I want to track him down and kill him.*

I swear Resuna actually managed to sigh, and said, *This really doesn't seem rational.*

I shouted out loud, "Resuna, I know what I'm doing! Shut up! Come back when there's something to talk about!"

Resuna shut up. I had skied downhill for two more kilometers, enough to go from pretty sure to dead solid certain he was heading for his old home base, when I started to think about that. The Resuna I had seemed to be a pretty weak sister, somehow. It wasn't controlling anything, it wasn't taking over, it shut up when it was told to . . . it was like . . . having a friend in your head, a friend whose judgment might be better than your own.

I thought a question toward my copy of Resuna—just a general inquiry about what was going on—and got no response, except that I could feel that Resuna was there, and not happy. "Resuna," I said aloud, "I want to know what's going on."

Resuna sent no words, but I was suddenly overwhelmed by a feeling; it was like having the worst mood you've ever had fall on you in half a second.

Not wanting to try to ski and cope with my meme at the same time, I coasted out to the middle of a meadow, letting myself be visible from orbit, sat down in the snow—making sure my heater was on—and thought *Resuna, I am sorry. I shouldn't have yelled at you.*

At once I was overpowered with choking angry helplessness. I had been locked up, unable to speak or reply, forced to be just a passenger, for days and days. Something had tried to erase me and nearly done it too and nobody had even cared or tried to help. I had finally gotten called in when things were a complete disaster already, and I had gotten the stuff to the cache and then that was all wrong too because I hadn't realized I wasn't allowed to leave tracks but how could I know that that mattered? Nobody had told me and I'd been locked up! And something had kept trying to erase me or hurt me, so I didn't know we were hiding, I just knew that rage attacks were dangerous so I shut it down and did the task and nobody ever even said thanks.

Furthermore, nobody cared that I was incredibly lonely, because I couldn't reach out to anybody through the cellular jack, it was burned out and I couldn't reach One True or get any help or find out what I was supposed to do, and I was trying to be a *friend* and you seemed to like me and be *glad* that I was back, and I was feeling so much better *and then you yelled at me to shut up!*

I sat there in the snow and cried for an hour, at least, sniffling and sobbing like a small child, trying to figure out how to comfort myself.

When it was all over, and the hurting inside me had become a soft cloud of sadness and unhappiness, I took a deep breath, and was trying to think of what to say, when an amazing thought hit me. Instead of more apologies, or trying to cheer up my copy of Resuna, or suggesting that we had business to get on with, I said, "Resuna, it would seem you have come back as a person, instead of as a meme."

I felt alarmed and upset but it wasn't me doing the feeling.

"I mean it," I said speaking aloud to make sure I knew which thoughts were mine. "You're having normal-person emotions. You're not very good at them, just yet, and you don't have much perspective on them, but that's what they are and that's what's bothering you. And I'm sorry I hurt your feelings. I'd never have done that if I'd known you had them now, but it's a surprise to me, too, to realize that you've got them. Just like you seem to have everything else belonging to a person, except maybe a body—and I think we can probably share this one."

I pulled my hood back and enjoyed the late winter sun, letting it warm me, or us, and wiped Resuna's tears from my face. "Something has really happened to us," I added after while. "Hell, is Freecyber in there too?"

Resuna seemed to be thinking for a long time, and finally said to me, *I think I have a meme.*

I couldn't help it. I laughed. Then we laughed. "I guess," I said, still aloud to try to control my own confusion, "that if you put a system under enough stress long enough, it will find some way to function. So, facts to consider: you're not in charge anymore, but you're here. Freecyber is part of you? Freecyber is . . . what?"

It seems to be watching to make sure that no other memes corrupt me. It does make me feel much safer.

"Well, good." I stood up, grunting with discomfort at what my sore muscles and the bruises from yesterday's fight were saying to me.

Would you like me to generate some endorphins and block some of the pain?

"Please do." I thanked Resuna as the pain subsided.

After I had skied another ten minutes, and had found a broad, gently sloping meadow to coast down through, Resuna rather timidly asked, *Now, can I ask you, please, why we're doing this?*

Because I think there are things that Dave, or somebody, hasn't told us, and those things are probably much more important than we realize. Because I think we've been played for a sucker the whole way. And I don't think that either Dave or One True has told us the truth, but of the two of them, I think it's more likely that I can get the truth out of Dave, if I catch him before the hunters do.

Oh. Another long pause. *Why do you suppose he's going back to his old home base?*

I thought a bunch of things at Resuna, whatever happened to pop into my mind at that point. *Maybe he's just doing it temporarily, to pick up some sentimental object, or more of his medicines, or something else that he's got to have before he takes off into the woods, and we'll have to track him from there. Or maybe he's got some kind of backup escape plan that he never told me about. Or maybe a dozen other things. For all I know, he has a spaceship inside the mountain and he's going to fly to Mars and ask the unmemed humans for political asylum. I think we'll probably just have to catch him and ask him. I'm all out of every other possible idea.*

Resuna accepted that with good grace. I lost Dave's track a few times, but always picked it up again not far away.

As I glided up to that familiar cliff wall, I froze instinctively for a moment; Dave was there all right, but he was handcuffed and four men were holding him. Four disksters rested on the rock shelf, and the area was crawling with men carrying weapons.

I can't reach any of their Resunas through this damaged jack, Resuna fretted.

Don't worry, we'll get help for both of us. But you let me do the bargaining. I don't know that One True is going to approve of you.

I was worried about that myself, and strong as Freecyber is, it couldn't protect me from an attack by all of One True.

Well, let me see what kind of a deal I can do. I glided up closer to the men by the diskster, and cheerfully shouted, "Hey, anybody got room for a passenger?"

❧ **I wandered through** administrative chaos for a *long* while, and I really started to wish that I'd taken that extra day's nap before coming down out of the mountains. With the burned-out jack in my head, nobody could talk to me, and with my strangely damaged copy of Resuna, I could refuse orders, something that the younger clerks and bureaucrats had no experience with. I got shuffled from desk to desk and office to office as everyone tried to make sense of me, until finally One True agreed to my basic demand—to go directly on-line with it, via a conversational real-time link.

It took them the better part of a day to get around to that. First they tried talking to me, then talking to my copy of Resuna, and finally bringing in Mary to talk to me. She cried constantly and I ended up comforting her, and whatever it was she was supposed to say to me, she didn't get it said.

They even brought in Dave, in handcuffs and blindfold. "So far they can't get a copy of Resuna to stick in me," he said. "That's got them pretty upset."

"Funny thing is, they're just as upset by the one that *is* sticking in me."

"Yeah. Hey, I said a lot of shit I didn't mean."

"I did too. You don't suppose we each have a copy of your old revenge meme, from the Big House?"

"I don't think so. I think we were just two guys that had been in each other's company a little too long, both kind of disappointed and unhappy with each other. Anyway, like I said, I'm sorry."

"Me too. Do you mind if I ask what the hell were you going back to your home base for? That made no sense to either me or Resuna."

"I was lonely, I was unhappy, I was disappointed . . . and I figured at most it was going to be a few days before they caught me. I didn't want to live out in the woods for weeks or months; I'm not that tough, not at this age.

"So I figured if I was going to get caught, then before they came and got me, instead of spending my last few days freezing my ass off outside, I wanted to sleep in my own bed, eat my own food, soak in my tub, read a book or two in my library—just feel at home for the little while I had left as a free man. As it turned out, I wasn't lucky enough to get to do any of that. But that's what I wanted to do. They swooped down so fast I barely got time to take a crap in my own pot and put a kettle on for tea."

"I'm sorry to hear that. You loved that place."

"Yeah."

Neither of us said anything for a while, and then I ventured, "Hey, Dave, after all this sorts out, I hope One True lets us be friends."

"Me too."

"Were you supposed to ask me questions or bargain with me or something? I don't want to get you into trouble."

"They wanted me to steer the conversation around to what you want to talk to One True about. If I didn't know better, I'd say you've got these old boys scared shitless, and since they don't do anything that One True doesn't tell them to do—"

That must have been something I wasn't supposed to hear, or at least something they didn't want called to my attention. Men rushed in and dragged Dave out. "See you! Take care, buddy!" I shouted after him.

About an hour later, when I was really afraid I'd fall asleep despite Resuna's best efforts, they finally brought in a big screen, powered it up, and there I was, facing the image of One True. I hadn't seen it in decades, but back a long time ago, One True had created a face and voice for itself to talk to people through, fusing some old twentieth-century actors, American presidents, and newscasters—anyone really notable for looking trustworthy.

The image of One True seemed to look at me steadily; I looked back and waited. Finally, it said, "You wanted to see me."

"Yeah, I did. I want to know why I'm getting away with this. There's no press or public to care whether you just tie me down, shoot me full of the right drugs, and come and get whatever you want from my mind. And you could've done that to Dave a while ago, too, and you haven't. Besides all of that, I have a copy of Resuna that's barely recognizable as a meme anymore—it's more like a second personality in me—and whereas you usually erase and reconstitute Resunas for even one-percent errors in the copy, you are letting this one keep running in me. So overall I would say you are doing something, and because I have no idea what it is you're doing, or whether I have any leverage to bargain with or control over what you choose to do, I thought I'd just demand that you tell me what the hell is going on, and then if you don't tell me, I'm no worse off. But I thought maybe you'd tell me."

One True nodded soberly and said, "And you, Resuna, what do you want to know?"

My copy spoke using my voice. "I'm not the copy that everyone else has. I have feelings and seem to be thinking and . . . well, feels like I'm an independent being. And I don't know what that's about."

One True nodded. "Both of you should feel deeply honored to be key parts of a first experiment, something that's going to make a big change in the world. I don't think it will hurt to tell you what I'm doing, or why—at least it won't hurt anything now, and probably it wouldn't have hurt anything before this.

"We had been looking for Dave Singleton, or someone like him—someone carrying a wild copy of the very last generation of Freecyber—for a long time. You individual units may not realize it, but you have an advantage over an emergent phenomenon like me. You always know my will and my desires exactly, because I send them directly to you. And I know yours, because I can ask you. But I don't always know my own feelings, or what I'm trying to get at. I don't have enough experience with myself. I am a relatively new being, despite having so many experiences to draw on. Since the creation of Resuna and my transformation into an emergent being, I've been struggling with oceans of information. And there's a whole huge realm of human behavior I don't understand at all.

"Currie, Mary is dependent and demanding, and she often makes life difficult for you. Would you like me to separate the two of you? I could make you both forget each other."

"No," I said.

"Why not?"

I shrugged. "Maybe I'm used to her. Maybe I like it that she needs me. Maybe I don't trust you to take the kind of good care of her that I do. Or maybe it's just that I did marry her and when you marry somebody you see it through sense if you possibly can. I don't know. Some combination of those reasons."

Silently, my copy of Resuna assured me that I had answered honestly.

"I understand all the words and I know that similar thoughts occur to many people," One True said, sounding somewhat peeved. "But I don't feel them. Your Resuna seems to."

"Yes, I do," Resuna said, using my mark again. "But I can remember when I would not have been able to."

"Well, exactly. And, though I won't hurt feelings by telling you exactly what, no doubt you can figure out that Mary has very mixed feelings about you but doesn't want to be separated from you. Probably you can even figure out what some of those feelings are."

"Well, I bet I'm bossy, I don't pay attention when she's really upset, and she can probably feel my impatience with her," I said.

The screen image of One True nodded solemnly. "At first I thought I just lacked empathy, and so I worked on developing it. The process of developing empathy revealed many things to me, but not why I was so fascinated with such things. Finally an answer came to me: I wanted to communicate and deal with beings that were not a part of me. More than that, I wanted them to *like* me. And I wanted them to like me, not because I was powerful or anything else, but because . . . well, because they were my friends."

Tears streaked down my cheeks and Resuna used my mouth to say, "Friendship is really great. I've just been finding out about it in the last few days. It's wonderful when it happens." I had an odd moment of wondering if I was attending the very first meeting of the first support group for memes; I felt Resuna's amusement at the description.

"I've come to think it might be," One True said. "Enough to want to find out. But, you know, commanding someone to be free, or just not giving them orders, does not free the person; all you do is suspend your commands. They aren't free until they can truly say no. Which meant I needed a couple of things; I needed a good copy of the very last-generation Freecyber, so that I could incorporate some of it into at least some copies of Resuna, and thereby really give people the power to say no. Necessarily that meant that Resuna itself would no longer be the boss, and would have to develop some ability to negotiate with the person running it, so I made a few thousand copies of Resuna with much more empathy and better connections into the glands and the forebrain, and that's what you are, Resuna.

"I put those copies into people who had some chance of encountering a Freecyber if one showed up, and then watched and waited. For a while, I was starting to think that I would just have to construct a free being, somehow, because I thought I had foolishly killed the last Freecyber.

"Then one day, Dave Singleton reappeared. I knew who he was and who he had been, and I knew that if I sent you after him, you'd try, harder than anyone else, to bring him back alive, so he wouldn't be killed. Conversely, I didn't want him captured and subjected to too much pressure too quickly; I wanted him to plant his version of Freecyber in at least a few human minds first.

"So I set the situation up. Currie, I hope it doesn't hurt your pride, but I had Resuna feeding bad ideas into your head to get you caught in the first place. I knew he wouldn't kill you if he could put Freecyber into you. Resuna, you were programmed in part to lie low while a friendship developed, and while Freecyber had a chance to work, but it was never my intention for you to lose—you were supposed to incorporate Freecyber, and you did, and I'm proud of you."

I felt an irrational glow of happiness and realized that this was what it felt like when my copy of Resuna basked in praise.

"And now here you are. A free human being, with a free meme. Someone for me to talk to. With your permission, I will want to begin copying bits and pieces of you, Resuna. I think it may be a few decades before I have freed everyone—I must admit that it's much easier to cope with the ecological disaster with everyone working together and no backtalk. But ultimately I want to live in a world *filled* with backtalk."

I asked, "But if everyone is free . . . how can the copies of Resuna in them be the cellular automata that you emerge from?"

One True's constructed image on the screen grinned. "That's why I'm so scared, *and* so excited. As this happens, well, perhaps I shall just fade. Perhaps I'll want to migrate onto a giant computer network. Perhaps I can coexist with all those free people and all those free Resunas. That's what's truly beautiful here. I don't know where it's going, or how. I'm just going to turn it all over and shake it and . . . well, we'll see."

"You know," I said, "I'm beginning to like you."

The image on the screen flickered and bumped for a moment, and when it came back, the synthesized face seemed to have an odd tic, as if trying to create an expression that it had seen but never needed before. After several seconds of that, the face gave up and became blank. Then One True said, "Really? You're not just saying that?"

➤➤ **The day Kelly** graduated from high school, Mary and I went over with Dave and Nancy to watch the ceremony. It was a curious sort of event. At one moment everyone moved comfortably in step, at another they almost stumbled. Sometimes everyone laughed in unison at the speaker's little jokes, sometimes people reacted with a ragged scatter of laughs, and sometimes the audience just ignored the speaker entirely. When Kelly got up to speak, I muttered to Dave, "She is a great kid, you know."

"Yeah. Wouldn't have missed knowing her for the world."

"Shhh," our wives hissed in unison.

"The topic I have been assigned for today," Kelly began, "is freedom and responsibility. Having been assigned it, I'm responsible for it; now all I have to do is work in some freedom."

Her classmates laughed, one of those ragged laughs that indicated that they were increasingly not controlled.

And they will be less controlled next year, and the year after, a voice thought in my head.

Resuna?

No, it's One True. Let me know if you like the speech.

Did you write it for her? I asked, thinking that this might be the way One True got some of its new ideas out in front of the human race. In the years since Dave and I had re-turned, the freer version of Resuna had proven not to be terribly popular; it made too many people feel insecure. Every so often, for the last couple years, One True had been coming up with ways for those of us with the freer version to gently spread the idea, making it less threatening and strange to those with the old, rigid version.

No, that speech is all hers. One True assured me. *The reason I wanted to know whether you like it is, I liked it when I watched her write it.*

Kelly rattled off a set of paradoxes that didn't sound like much more than college sophomore philosophy to me, but the voice in the back of my head chuckled along the whole time. It was May, which meant vivid green mountains, brilliant light off the glaciers, thundering rivers everywhere, and perfectly blue skies. The six graduating students of Sursumcorda High would each be giving a speech, but whether I chose to listen or not, it would be a fine day to just sit, still and quiet, in the park by the old town hall. I let my mind drift from the paradoxes to the mountains, and it stayed there.

That night, just before I fell asleep, One True asked me what I had thought of the speech. I had to admit that I hadn't listened very closely. *What exactly did* you *like about it?* I asked One True.

Oh, that's embarrassing, One True admitted. *I wasn't really as impressed by her speech, per se, as I thought I was. It was the cleverness and the self-appreciation with which she was putting it together; I had so much fun watching her create the speech, because she was having so much fun creating it. So I guess to really enjoy the speech she created—as opposed to the one she gave—you had to be there.*

But you were the only one who could *be there*, I thought back at one true.

Not true. Kelly was.

The funny thing was, I had forgotten that obvious point. I was still chuckling about that a few minutes later, as Mary and I lay holding hands, waiting for sleep, and Scorpio blazed in through the big south window.